"I woke up here with you."

Her attention sharpened. She'd been maintaining watch on the approaches via the hallway door and the exit out via the lanai, only sparing brief moments to look at him throughout their conversation. Now she honed in on him specifically and the sheer intensity of her focus brought the world around him to a standstill.

"The people you were looking for. Where are they?"

Cold washed through him. "I was assuming you and your team extracted them already and came across me in the process. You didn't find them yet?"

PRAISE FOR THE NOVELS OF PIPER J. DRAKE

"[S]izzles with suspense and danger."
—**Publishers Weekly** on *Total Bravery*

"The premise is well-paced, intriguing and thrilling; the characters are colorful and energetic; the romance is captivating and sensual."
—**TheReadingCafe.com** on *Total Bravery*

"Piper J. Drake's knowledge of her subject matter, attention to detail and excellent character building brought the beauty of Hawaii and Mali and Raul's romance to life. A really enjoyable novel overall."
—**RedHotBooks.com** on *Total Bravery*

"4 Stars! With an action-filled plot riddled with suspense and tension, Drake's latest in her True Heroes series is the best one yet. Steady pacing, engaging storytelling and genuine, vulnerable characters (coupled with the endearing heroic dogs that protect and love them) make this romance shine."
—*RT Book Reviews* on *Absolute Trust*

"The central romance was very strong, and I definitely count *Absolute Trust* in the win column."
—**DearAuthor.com**

"This whole series is a great concept. If you're an animal lover and want a hero story, this book is for you."
—**WritingPearls.com** on *Absolute Trust*

FIERCE JUSTICE

ALSO BY PIPER J. DRAKE

Extreme Honor
Ultimate Courage
Absolute Trust
Total Bravery

FIERCE
JUSTICE

PIPER J. DRAKE

FOREVER

NEW YORK   BOSTON

Copyright ©2019 by Piper J. Drake
Excerpt from *Total Bravery* copyright © 2018 by Piper J. Drake
Cover design by Elizabeth Turner Stokes. Cover illustration by Michael Heath.
Cover copyright © 2019 by Hachette Book Group, Inc.

Forever
Hachette Book Group
1290 Avenue of the Americas, New York, NY 10104
read-forever.com
twitter.com/readforeverpub

First Mass Market Edition: February 2019

Forever is an imprint of Grand Central Publishing. The Forever name and logo are trademarks of Hachette Book Group, Inc.

The publisher is not responsible for websites (or their content) that are not owned by the publisher.

The Hachette Speakers Bureau provides a wide range of authors for speaking events. To find out more, go to www.hachettespeakersbureau.com or call (866) 376-6591.

ISBNs: 978-1-5387-5957-8 (mass market), 978-1-5387-5958-5 (ebook)

Printed in the United States of America

OPM

10 9 8 7 6 5 4 3 2 1

To all the lovers of onigiri and ramen, and especially the people who take the time to turn hot dogs into cute octopi.

Acknowledgments

Thank you to Madeleine Colavita for your amazing patience and your thoughtful feedback. It's always a challenge, learning to work together and understand each other. Ultimately, Arin and Jason's story is that much better with your help.

Thank you to Courtney Miller-Callihan for reminding me to be kind to myself.

Thank you to Christopher Baity, Executive Director of Semper K9 Assistance Dogs, for your insight into working dogs. Any exaggerations or errors are my own—because sometimes we writers need to stretch a few truths to make things work—but hopefully the story is plausible thanks to you.

Thank you to Katee Robert and Åsa Maria Bradley for calming me down in those moments of panic when imposter syndrome swallowed me whole. I'd be lost without you. Also, thank you to Christiana Ellis for the perfect phrase in a moment when my brain was completely frozen.

This book was written when my heart was far away, with

Matthew. We started long distance and being long distance again this year was hard. Thank you for providing insight on all things action and military-related. Here, too, any exaggerations or errors are my own. And thank you for reaching out across the many miles and answering my calls when I randomly needed to say, "Hi." Daisuke.

And finally, thanks to my readers. The True Heroes series is continuing because of you, and I hope you'll enjoy.

FIERCE JUSTICE

CHAPTER ONE

T his is…not exactly who we are looking for." Arin Siri paused, cautiously approaching her German Shepherd Dog's find.

King currently sat to one side, happily chewing on a tennis ball as his reward for the find. The unconscious man at her feet definitely had to have something to do with the people they were looking for—for one boy in particular—because her canine partner wouldn't have signaled a find unless he smelled the target scent. But no one else was in sight and there was no immediate reason she could discern for why this man was here. He was too well-fed to be a worker on the farm they were searching, and he wasn't dressed like a supervisor either. There were too many questions, and this man was not awake to answer them.

She took a few steps, cautiously circling to get a good look. He might need medical attention and she firmly believed it was worth the effort to save a life. There'd been plenty of times in her past career when she'd had to argue her stance with others on her team. Those were times best left to fade the hell out of her memory.

She studied the unconscious man, trying to make as quick an assessment as possible while keeping an eye out for nasty surprises. There was no sign of grenades or other party favors. Good.

The man lay belly down, unmoving. His face was turned away. She couldn't see if he was breathing so she crouched close, her weapon ready in case he moved suddenly. With her left fingertips, she touched his neck for a pulse.

Lucky man; he was still among the living.

There were no bullet holes or obvious injuries on his back or limbs. To be honest, whoever he was, he was in excellent physical condition. He had very nice musculature showing even in his relaxed, unconscious, state. There was something vaguely familiar about him.

He was dressed in a thin T-shirt and the kind of light-weight pants hikers wore to protect their legs in dense brush and heat. He blended into the greenery and thick foliage along the edge of the nearby taro farm, so he was lucky she and King were on search in the area. Depending on what the hell was wrong with him, he could've lain here undiscovered until he really did die.

Speaking of which, she pulled out her smartphone and checked for a signal. Amazingly, she had just enough to send a text message requesting medical evacuation. She'd follow up with the satellite phone once she had more information.

She rose and made her way around to his other side, hoping to get a look at his face. Until she knew what injuries he had, she wasn't about to flip him over.

King remained where he was, a few feet away, jaw dropped in a canine grin as he panted, tennis ball sitting between his paws. It wasn't as hot as it could be. Hawaii's Big

Island was cooler in the valley at this time of day, but the humidity made the air thick and heavy. The big GSD was well acclimated to tropical climates at this point, but he still had to dissipate body heat however he could. That meant panting.

For her part, Arin was sweating. Everywhere. Her protective vest trapped sweat against her torso, even with the help of the light moisture-wicking shirt she wore underneath it. The heat and discomfort could be blamed for her irritability. Or maybe she needed a good cup of coffee to start her morning instead of the bitter muck they'd passed out earlier before deploying search teams for this mission.

There were two other search teams besides her and King, on a mission to find where victims of human trafficking were being housed and forced to work on this taro farm against their will. Once the search teams had the workers safely located and protected, they could take down the farm itself. At the same time, Arin had made a promise to look for a specific boy named Huy. There was a lot to accomplish and the longer she took here, the more worried she was about achieving the best possible outcome.

From her new position on the man's other side, she studied his face and decided no amount of air-conditioning or coffee was going to improve her mood. She'd met him before, a little over six months ago.

She didn't know his name, but she'd been curious about him ever since they'd faced off back on the island of Oahu. It'd been a different mission, different plantation, but the same human trafficking ring behind it all. He and his team had been privately contracted security on the perimeter, not aware of exactly what they were providing security for. He and she had come to an...understanding of sorts, and gone their separate ways.

His eyes, closed now, were burned into her memory. They'd been so dark a brown they were almost black, and the intensity in his gaze had left her breathless. He'd also been aiming a gun at her, with purpose. She'd had her rifle pointed at him in kind, so it'd been a fair situation, however tense.

She extended her left hand cautiously, sliding her fingertips into his dark hair. It was slightly longer on top, cut neatly short on the sides, and...soft. Almost silky. She pushed aside that tactile observation and continued to explore with her fingertips until she encountered the answer to his current state of unconsciousness. The man had a bump the size of a goose egg on the back of his head.

Well, then.

He probably wasn't going to die, but he needed to be checked for a concussion. It was a nasty bump.

She pulled several zip ties from a cargo pocket on her pants. After binding him at the wrists and ankles, she stepped back a prudent distance. Her initial meeting with him had been decidedly confrontational. There may have been a tiny bit of violence involved. They'd both walked away from the encounter, but only by mutual accord. It wasn't clear which one of them would've survived otherwise.

He was secured for the time being. As worrisome as it was to have found him out here, she had a promise to keep and a boy to find. She'd get this man medical attention, then move forward from there. It was the right thing to do and it was best to make it happen as quickly as possible. He was a private contractor, like she was, and if he was on contract to protect the farm they were searching, he could pose a serious threat to her current mission. It'd be best to get him away from here, someplace where he could be questioned about his involvement.

Even if this man remained unconscious, she had the feeling he was still going to be a serious pain in the ass. It was better to make him someone else's problem.

She looked at King. Her partner had been watching her all this time, regarding her with a warm, alert gaze. He, more than any other living being in this world, was attuned to her. She retrieved the tennis ball and smiled. No need to call his name to get his attention. "*Bewaken.*"

King would watch their captive while she made her report. Next up, conversation with another actual human being. It was only a couple of hours past sunrise and that horrible cup of coffee. It was still too damned early in the morning for talking to people.

She cleared her throat and pulled out the satellite phone, enunciating clearly without raising her volume above a quiet conversational level. "Bravo, this is Charlie."

"Copy." On the other end of the line, Raul Sá's voice sounded relaxed, but years of working with him let her pick out the hint of worry. "Received your text. Medical team en route to your position. Is one of the targets injured?"

Of the people she worked with on a regular basis, Raul was one of the few she could be reasonably nice to before noon. Well, at least she didn't snap or snarl at him. Most of the time. He was a good friend, maybe her best, and they'd worked together back when they'd both been active military before going private. He'd joined the Search and Protect Corporation on Arin's recommendation and she didn't regret his addition to the team. He had a greater capacity for keeping the bigger picture in mind, where Arin tended to focus on a singular objective. Plus, he was just a better human being than Arin, as far as she was concerned.

"Negative. I didn't find any of the targets yet." She

considered the unexpected situation. "We have a potential hostile in custody."

There was a moment of pause.

"Charlie, this is Alpha." Her team lead, Azubuike Anyanwu, or Zu when they weren't on a mission, had one of those deep voices that could resonate in your sternum.

"Copy." Oh, he was going to give an order she wasn't going to like. He always gave those personally, rather than have someone else relay bad news for him.

This mission had been initiated by a task force sponsored by the Hawaiian government, but it was the Search and Protect team spearheading the actual search for the victims. An instance of government task force leveraging private contract resources, sure, but it meant she was coordinating with Raul, who was a liaison and advisor to that task force, and taking orders from her team lead, Zu, when she and King needed to get back to work. Her best came out when she was on her own, with only herself and King to consider. Coordination and taking orders didn't come as naturally.

"Medical team is too far ahead to send in local law enforcement." Zu sounded irritated. It wasn't likely aimed at her so much as the unexpected situation, so she didn't take it personally. "You'll need to provide escort back out of the valley."

Ah hell.

"I'm only half-finished with my sector." It was important to conduct the search in the same timeframe as the other search teams. Otherwise, the people they were searching for might move into one of the other sectors and be missed. These people were afraid, far from any kind of known safety, and probably even frightened of the canine partners doing the majority of the search. She didn't normally question a directive, but this wasn't the military and she did see a need to voice the consideration.

"Bravo team and I will expand our search sectors to cover the remaining ground." Zu remained resolute.

Bravo. Raul had enough to do coordinating the search effort as the liaison to the task force. He'd have to stretch to finish searching her sector with his canine partner, Taz. The solution wasn't ideal. She didn't continue to question Zu's decision, though. If Raul couldn't handle it, it was on him to raise the issue. They were all big boys and girls, well past the need to needlessly push themselves past their limits.

"Copy."

Her mission had changed. Now, she needed to know what this man had been doing out here and determine whether he was going to pose a threat to getting any captives they found to safety. At minimum, he could be a distraction. At worst, he could actively be a danger to anyone they managed to rescue, and her team.

But there was a possibility he also had useful information on the human trafficking organization, which the authorities could use to further disable it.

She glared at the man, still out cold on the forest floor. "You had better be worth it. There are people out here who need us."

CHAPTER TWO

As hospital rooms went, waking up in this one was one of the better experiences Jason Landon had had to date. The ceiling lights were off, thankfully, and the soft light filling the room was natural. It had a homey feel to it, as opposed to the sterile look of other places or the desperate wear and tear of more beleaguered facilities. He turned his head, cautiously, and found not a window but an actual lanai door on the wall to his right.

Caution amped up to full awareness.

This room was on the ground floor. Not good. He needed to get to a more defensible position. He started to roll off the side of the hospital bed.

"Stay."

The woman's voice was pitched low but held every bit as much authority as any commanding officer or drill sergeant's. He whipped his head around to find her seated in a chair against the opposite wall, within arm's reach of him but as far away from the open door to the hallway as possible. He instantly regretted moving his head too fast as the rest of the room seemed to catch up in his vision and settle around her along with the onset of a steady pounding to the back of his skull.

"*Tch*." She didn't sound happy.

He stared at her, willing his vision to clear. Dark hair was easiest to see, tied back in a ponytail. Her face, fuzzy at first, was a light shade of golden brown. High cheekbones and soft lips registered in his brain as her face gained definition. Lips were a favorite feature to him, and he focused to pull his brain back online. Her top lip was delicately curved, and her lower lip was full and plump. Amazingly kissable. Her facial features came together in a sweet countenance completely at odds with the irritated tone of her voice.

Once his vision cleared, he reached for some memory of why she looked familiar to him and what the hell he'd been doing before he'd ended up here in the first place.

In reference to her, there'd been an encounter, someplace else, outdoors and...on top of a roof somewhere. Same fierce scowl, but it'd been partially hidden behind the scope of a rifle. The ache in his skull eased a fraction as he matched his recollection with the severe expression she was wearing now. Dire, but not menacing, she wasn't an immediate threat.

She was striking. Not simply beautiful, and she most definitely was with that face and those curves, but vibrant with the kind of energy that would've made her stand out even in a crowd. Alone with her in a small room, she filled the space with a readiness for action that demanded he do the same.

Okay, yeah. Now he remembered her. Relief washed through him in a cool wave as he did. He hadn't been sure he'd ever meet her again, thought he'd have to search for her, and here she was.

He'd been leading a team on a private security contract, protecting the outer perimeter of a plantation on Oahu. She and her people had successfully broken through all layers of security and infiltrated the main building complex. That had been a blow to his pride, and he'd been working to up his strategic planning skills ever since to make sure it didn't happen again. Not that he was currently in a position to apply his improved skill set.

Despite his still aching head, he grinned ruefully at the memory, because that day had tossed his world upside down. He'd been angry as hell with his failure. Her team had been good, all of them, and they'd distracted him with an actual explosion out in the far fields where he'd thought the valuable crops were. But when he noticed none of his client's personal security rushing to put out the fires, he'd checked back at the main building complex to find several of those resources neutralized and her on the roof with a sniper rifle.

Petite, dark beauty combined with deadly competence. He'd been captivated by her.

He'd confronted her until he saw the captives, the slaves, fleeing. He'd been completely ignorant of what the true property of value was on that plantation. Seeing those abused people had stopped him cold.

Now he had no idea what she was doing in a hospital room with him—months later and on a completely different island—seated as far as possible from both exits but with a clear line of sight out either of them.

"How many nurses have you scared?" At least his voice was working. His throat was raw and he could kill for a beer right about now. Hell, he'd settle for water.

His lady companion sighed and if anything, managed to look even more disgruntled just by drawing her brows together. "One was in here a full five minutes checking your records and fussing with your sheets before she looked around the room. The way she gasped and clutched her chest, I wasn't sure if we'd need to hit the call button for her cardiac distress."

He barked out a laugh despite the strain to his aching

throat. "I have a few burning questions for you, but we need to get out of here."

She raised one of those gently arched eyebrows, and her expression brightened. "Yeah? You have a concussion. You need to be under observation."

Maybe, but it wasn't a good idea to stick around here. Memories were coming back now, catching up as his brain engaged. Conversation helped. He remembered how long it'd been since he'd seen her, what he'd been up to in the meantime, and why he'd come to Big Island in the first place. Maybe he'd even explain it all to her, later.

"We're on the ground floor. We both need to not be dead." He scowled as he reached for his IV and realized the same arm was handcuffed to the hospital bed railing at the wrist. Maybe she wasn't a companion so much as a keeper. "This is not a good start."

"There's only one level to this hospital, so ground floor was the only option." She came to her feet, though, the motion fluid and graceful. He wondered if she danced. As she moved closer, there was an odd scraping noise and a large black and tan dog came into view, too. He must've been lying on the floor, almost under the bed. She glanced down the hallway first, then out the lanai. "This is an interior room, though. The lanai opens into an enclosed garden."

"Copy that." He glared at the handcuffs. "Look, I get the reason for these. I'm actually surprised there aren't police officers in here. But I'm also somewhat surprised to be alive and would like to stay that way."

"We have teams outside the room." Now that she was standing, he saw the rifle and scope leaning next to her recently vacated chair. She also wore a shoulder harness with a handgun. "However, if you're ready to start explaining what you were doing and what we might be expecting, chances of remaining secure in this location would be greatly increased."

He forced himself to pause and think through the massive headache. It might be good to leave in the IV for a few seconds longer. Hydration wasn't going to cure a concussion or the accompanying headache, but it could keep it all from getting worse. "You're last line of defense."

She didn't respond.

Security wasn't a simple thing. It was always set up in layers within layers, starting with some sort of outer perimeter and progressing inward. Sure, the hospital had its own alarm and surveillance systems for everyday safety, but she was here because she was watching him. If she and her team were protecting him, she was the final thing standing between potential attackers and their objective. He preferred that perspective, because the other way around meant she was the first line of defense to keep him from walking out of here. He still planned to leave and he'd like for her to let him. Hell, maybe even come with him for a bit.

"It's been months, so the story is longer than we've got time for. I'm going for the highlights here." He thought hard about what it would take for him to believe, if their positions were reversed. "Last time we met, you were in a rush. I'm going to point out that I took you at your word, with very minimal details, and I pulled back my team to let you and yours go on your way."

She gave him the barest nod. "You can start with the highlights and I'll decide if I need more before we move anywhere. Go."

Not exactly what he'd asked for, but he'd take it and make the best of it. It was what he always did.

"Meeting you was a wakeup call for me. I told you back then I didn't know about the captives on the plantation.

Withdrawing, then letting the authorities come in, was the right thing to do." He swallowed against the bitter taste in his mouth as he remembered his frustration. "Afterward, I reported back to my company and they didn't agree with my decision. Maintaining their relationship with a high-paying client was more important than questionable ethics, as they put it. They considered my actions a dereliction of duty."

It'd been a load of bullshit. What was worse, he had to admit he'd been inclined to turn a blind eye and give the same reasoning in other situations before that. Throughout his career, he'd been focused on contracts for the money and building his reputation in the private sector. He hadn't thought beyond the immediate objectives in any given contract, mostly security, to what the client might be trying to secure. His integrity had been about being trusted to fulfill a contract, executing it with excellence. But that'd been for black market goods, inanimate objects or animals. He drew the line at the buying and selling of human life.

"I was reprimanded and demoted." That'd angered him, too, because he'd worked hard to rise up in the organization.

She shifted her weight from one foot to the other, looking like she wanted to say something, but she didn't.

He took a guess at what she was thinking and waved it away with his free hand. "I don't regret it. I did the right thing. Then I gathered intel on you and your team, because I wanted to know more about who broke through my security plan."

It'd been a point of pride and a warped sort of goal to find the team that'd bested him. He'd also been intrigued by her. He wanted to know more about how she fit into her team—not the lead but a strategic asset. She was a sniper but her team all worked with dogs and her dog hadn't been with her when he'd first met her. Obviously, the GSD was with her now. Why had a sniper gone into search and rescue? How had she become a working dog handler? It was possible, just unusual, to change career paths that drastically and he was fascinated by the questions she inspired.

"Search and Protect Corporation." Honestly, he didn't like the name of their organization at all; too snappy. "You get paid to use dogs for search and rescue. Don't people usually volunteer for that kind of thing?"

"We are contracted to locate and extract high-value hostages from extremely dangerous situations, the kind that require infiltration and a decent amount of firepower on the way out." Her response was quick and pointed, but matter-of-fact. "Most of us have also volunteered in the case of major disaster."

Cool and calm. He liked to poke until he got a glimpse of temper in people, figure out what it took to get them fired up and potentially distracted. She was not an easy target for teasing, and he liked the challenge she posed. "Uh huh. Back then, we never would've met if my client hadn't started it all. I had to backtrack to figure it out since my team wasn't part of it."

She didn't respond, didn't even move.

He shook his head. "A group of scientists conducting interviews in Honolulu's Chinatown, researching human trafficking on Oahu and in the Hawaiian islands, and the client couldn't keep his cool. He made a bold move, snatching those scientists right off the street. He was lucky Hawaiian police were stretched thin at the time, or maybe he'd set up a distraction somewhere else. Either way, he didn't take time to find out who any of the scientists were before he had them taken. If he had, maybe he'd have realized one of them had family on the island. And if he'd followed up, he'd have figured out that family was you. If he'd asked my team to look into it, we'd have advised him against that kind of activity. He brought you and the police down on his head and my team had no warning. Maybe it was sheer luck Mali Siri evaded his goons and got to you for help. But even if she hadn't, I think you'd have come looking for her."

She interrupted her roving vigilance of the approaches to the room to give him a hard stare.

Oh yeah, he hadn't been sure this woman was related to the research scientist who'd escaped the client's kidnapping attempt over six months ago, but now he was. This woman's glare meant death for anyone breathing wrong in her little sister's direction. "So the client brought all this on himself. Once you'd extracted the scientists and gave the police the evidence they needed to search the rest of the plantation, you'd damaged operations, badly. My company was intent to make it up to the client by taking a more active role in re-establishing his human trafficking operations, with me assigned to the team in my demoted status. I declined and quit."

"Might want to choose your next place of employment more carefully."

It was his turn to glare at her. "What about you? Are you sure your missions will always keep your conscience clear? Do you really think you people will always be the heroes? You work with local law enforcement, plus that task force organized by the Hawaiian government. You do some work with the US military stationed on the islands, too, right? Police, government, a lot of people want to believe they're always the good guys, but they hire private contractors like us for the work they never want to tell civilians about."

He expected her to get angry. He wanted to see how she'd handle it, whether she'd lash out at him or get up and walk away. Instead, she only tipped her head to one side as she looked at him, a tired sadness in her eyes.

"It's not always as clear as 'good guys wear white.' I've got a thing for the anti-heroes, honestly." The corner of her mouth lifted in a hint of a smile. "Our backgrounds are accessible for most intel searches so I'm assuming you know I was military in the past. I got myself an honorable discharge so I could make my own choices. The only thing Zu promises me is that I will always have a choice when it comes to the missions we take on. I do what my conscience tells me is right. Can you say the same?"

"I could still be employed with a lucrative income. I'm here instead. Everyone has a choice, darlin'." And he'd get to why shortly, but with this woman, he thought his motives mattered as much as his perceived actions.

"Your team didn't respect yours. You were out of a job when you said no."

Jason shrugged. "Would you want to keep working with a team if they took a mission you decided you wouldn't?"

"It depends." Her expression remained enigmatically neutral. "So far, we've never disagreed that completely. I guess we'll see if the day comes when Zu's ethics have shifted completely away from mine."

The point was, her commander had given her the ability to choose without the threat of being tossed out of the team. Jason could see there was a difference. He filed it away to chew on later. It meant something, but he wasn't sure if he was understanding it completely.

"Why do you think you're in danger here?" She glanced away from him, out the lanai door and down the hallway. She was still keeping watch, keeping in mind his concern for his safety. Even if the background on why he'd come to the island was pertinent, she hadn't been distracted from her main line of interrogation.

He quit trying to suss her out for the time being and got to the point. "They were happy to let me leave, and if I'd gone back to the mainland or even out of country, there'd be no issues. But I didn't. I came to Big Island when I heard the client was replaced and the ring's new boss was assessing his properties here."

Her gaze returned to him.

He nodded. "Yeah, the organization you damaged is under new management. This morning, there was more security than there should've been for a simple taro farm, even with "stock" as part of the work force. I'm guessing his added security caught me snooping around the perimeter. I was too low on sleep and should've rested before trying to check out the area, but I didn't think there was time. I took the risk and it was a bad call. I couldn't have been unconscious long. They were probably checking back with the main team to figure out what to do with me when you arrived. They can't just let me go without some kind of retribution for being where I wasn't supposed to be. Hell, they could even suspect I led your team to them."

Her lips pressed into a hard line. "So you expect them to come here to shut you up."

"Possibly permanently, if they think I've been talking to you." He figured the minute she'd taken him into custody he'd become a dead man. He wasn't angry with her for it. He'd have done the same if their positions had been reversed. It was just a truth and he'd prefer to do all he could to remain among the living.

"Fine. I get how you ended up here. Why did you come?" She crossed her arms. The motion did wonderful things to accentuate her generous bust line.

He carefully kept his gaze up and trained on her face. "It didn't seem prudent to remain in the immediate vicinity on Oahu, at least in the short term. While I was staying out of sight and out of mind, I figured I'd do some digging."

He'd grown complacent in his old role with his former

private contract organization. He'd thought of himself as good enough. The Search and Protect team had proven back at the plantation over six months ago that he and his team hadn't been. From that perspective, he'd deserved to be demoted, not because he'd stepped aside after meeting her. "I needed to sharpen up some of my unused skill sets and...I wanted to do something to balance out the karma for contributing to the trafficking our client was doing. I was a part of it, even if I didn't know. There's no way I can make it right to those people, so I looked for other people I could help."

He paused. He wasn't good at admitting that kind of thing. He did what he did and he usually didn't bother to explain himself. Arin kept her gaze on the approaches but her mouth relaxed. He pressed on. "One of the first things the new guy did was plan to clean house on a few strategic distribution points that might be particularly vulnerable to discovery by law enforcement. That's why he's inspecting each of his properties. I tried to get ahead of that to save as many people as I could. I came out here on my own and figured if I could lead them out, I could call local law enforcement to come get them. I made it past the outer perimeter just fine but I hadn't acquired line of sight on my objective when I was hit from behind. I woke up here with you."

Her attention sharpened. She'd been maintaining watch on the approaches via the hallway door and the exit out via the lanai, only sparing brief moments to look at him throughout their conversation. Now she honed in on him specifically and the sheer intensity of her focus brought the world around him to a standstill.

"The people you were looking for. Where are they?"

Cold washed through him. "I was assuming you and your team extracted them already and came across me in the process. You didn't find them yet?"

CHAPTER THREE

Arin grabbed the satellite phone and called her team lead.

"This is Alpha." Zu came across curt, his tone sharp. That was a bad sign.

She tightened her stomach, bracing for an impact even if this one wasn't going to be physical. "Alpha, this is Charlie."

"Go ahead."

"Our guest is awake. We've got a problem." In the aftermath of the plantation incursion over six months ago, a brave young woman had given her testimony and intel on the human trafficking ring. In return, Arin had made a promise to look for a specific person on this mission. Among the captives, there was a boy. Lost. Now he might be gone forever and Arin would have to kill the hope in his older sister's eyes. "Our target's management may have decided to liquidate our objective. We need to find these people and get them out."

From his seat on the bed, her guest extended his hand to catch her attention. When she made eye contact with him, he mouthed the words, "South Quadrant. There's a set of sheds hidden in the tree line."

She relayed the information. Damn it. South was part of the sector she and King had been searching. She and her canine partner might've found them by now if they hadn't stumbled across this man and had to leave off their original objective.

Frustration and anger smoldered in her chest and she breathed in slowly through her nose to get a leash on her temper. She didn't let the anger go, though. She'd make use of it later.

"Those sheds might be housing a lot of people." She hoped not, but humans forced into manual labor weren't provided much in the way of shelter. They were given the bare minimum to keep them alive and able to work, which kept them too weak to rise up against their captors or run away.

"Copy and confirmed." Zu paused. "His intel is accurate. We came across the structures."

She waited. Zu wasn't a man for many words to begin with and when he was angry, he took his time to get his temper under control, too.

After a moment, Zu continued. "They're not housing anymore. They've become a mass graveyard. The dogs hit the scent trails a few minutes before you called. The teams are looking for survivors. We need to know what other intelligence he can provide."

Ah, shit. She clenched her teeth against a wave of guilt. Too late. Would she and King have found those poor people in time? Was the boy, Huy, among the dead?

She turned and studied the man sitting up on the hospital bed. Zu's last statement had layered meaning. There was a distinct possibility the man she had in custody could've done it all before he'd been taken out by one of his own teammates. He could be a trap all on his own. "Understood. This location might not remain secure."

"Can you move him?" The question came across sharp.

"We've got our hands full here but we need answers. You got this on your own?"

"King and I have this." Yes, she worked as part of Zu's coordinated team but she needed little oversight and could work as a solo unit if needed. Her independence was part of the reason Zu had brought her in first when he'd started building Search and Protect. They were a small organization, designed for maximum flexibility based on the needs of the contracts they accepted. Zu had intended for them to take mostly international black ops, specializing in locating missing high-value VIPs and extracting such hostages. If taking this stranger off the grid could help their investigation, then she could separate from the team for a short time.

There was a lot she could learn just by spending time with a person. And if he wasn't forthcoming, then she could employ a number of techniques to find out what he knew even if he didn't intend to give it up.

"Check in." Zu didn't say when or how often. It was understood that she would when she could. He ended the call without further instruction.

She lowered the satellite phone, acknowledging the man who was about to be her mission for the near future. However long it took to get the answers she needed from him. "I'll take you to a secure location if you tell me what happened back at that farm."

It would help if he had the face of an angel. Then she wouldn't trust him at all. But no, he was all hard lines and sharp features. Devastatingly striking. He had an even, medium skin tone that would've allowed him to pass for any number of ethnicities. If he was any kind of actor, and she'd bet he was excellent, then he'd be an asset to someone. She'd worked for a few private contractors in the past that'd snap him up in a hot second. His only limitation would've been the fact that he wasn't the type to blend into a crowd. He was an obvious predator and he stood out among the sheep.

Sadness flashed in his eyes. "I'll tell you everything I know, right up until I went unconscious."

Maybe he was a good liar, too. But he hadn't promised her anything and she took note, because a promise was a specific kind of thing to her. It was good that he hadn't tried to make one.

"Fine. We're leaving." She approached him warily and unlocked the handcuff tethering him to the hospital bed. It wasn't as if she'd expected it to hold him anyway. If she'd wanted to secure him, she'd have used zip ties. A lot of them. No, it'd been more to warn the nursing staff that he was a suspect, not a target for flirting.

Tossing him a plastic bag containing his shirt, pants, and whatever he'd had in his pockets, she moved to the door out to the hall and closed it. "King, *volg*."

Her partner moved silently to her left and came to a heel. He sat and looked up at her, ready for her next command. She kept watch on the approach from the garden through the lanai.

At the edge of her peripheral vision, the man swung his legs over the side of the hospital bed and stood cautiously. Good. He wasn't stupid enough to push a concussion. Rushing when your head wasn't right could result in a face plant on the floor. It was better to keep moving, even if it was a little slower, than end up unconscious and possibly dead.

He began dressing. "Surprised the nurses didn't cut my clothes off me. My name is Jason, by the way. Jason Landon."

While he had his hands occupied with clothing, she reached for her rifle and slung it over her shoulder. Normally, she'd have put it in its soft case to avoid freaking out non-combatants in the hospital. But the man was tense despite his bantering tone, and he was dressing as fast as he could. He wanted out of here with a real sense of urgency.

"You probably know mine." The question was, how much intel had he managed to gather about her and her team?

He chuckled. "Yeah, but reading it isn't the same as hearing it and I'd like to try pronouncing it the way you do."

Point to him. People tended to apply the pronunciation they were used to based on their native language, wherever they were from in the world. Her name was Thai and she noticed when it was pronounced incorrectly.

"Arin Siri. The doctor declared it unnecessary to slice your clothes since you were just dirty and not covered in blood. The nurses giggled unbuttoning your shirt and pants, but kept it professional." She reopened the door to the hallway and stepped to one side to see far down the end in one direction, then shifted her position to see toward the entrance to the emergency room. King rose to stand on all four paws but otherwise maintained his heel position at her left. At the entrance, the local policeman was still at his post, relaxed and leaning against the wall. "Clear to head out."

"Thank you, Arin." Jason had come around to sit in the chair she'd been occupying to get his boots on. He said her first name slowly, taking care to pronounce it as *ah-Rin* with the soft *ah* in the first syllable and the accent on the second rather than turning it into Erin or Aaron the way many tried to. Once his boots were on, he looked up with a grin. "So? You're not going to tell me to come with you if I want to—"

"No." She cut him short. Added point to him for doing a decent job on her name but it wasn't going to get him far. She also docked him a point for the over-used movie reference. "You can stay, and if you're telling the truth, you can die. I also don't do celebrity accents."

He stood and held up his hands in surrender but amusement sparkled in his eyes. "Lead the way."

Great, she had a joker. This was going to be irritating as hell.

Still, the way he looked at her was different, like he was enjoying her company. He didn't seem put off at all. Normally if she cut off a guy trying to joke around or make a pass, the rebuffed man turned sour at best, or called her a bitch for the rest of the mission. She didn't care as long as the job got done. But this was confusing and she couldn't afford it because she needed to get into his head.

As quickly as possible.

* * *

Jason checked the approach from the garden yet again. He didn't just look out the lanai to the paths and walkways. He scrutinized the slightly overgrown hibiscus and other flowered shrubs, raised flowerbeds, anything in the courtyard that could create a dead space where an attacker could hide. He also checked what he could see of other rooms and windows, even the roof.

His former employer didn't have a sniper on payroll as far as he knew, but he'd been gone a while. The roster could've been updated. With luck, they wouldn't have hired on any new contractors yet, which meant he had a reasonable idea of what kind of people they'd send for him. All of those would choose a more direct type of confrontation.

His gaze fell on the woman at the door leading out to the hallway. Arin. She'd pronounced her name with a lilting, tonal quality to it. He wasn't sure he'd reproduced it so the planned to get it right. He'd never mistake her name for "Erin," having heard her say it. Her name was new to him, one he'd never heard before, and he thought it matched what he had seen of her so far. Unusual. Lovely.

She glanced back at him. "With me."

She slipped out and he was right on her back, not close enough to trip her up but she would be able to reach back and touch him without looking if she needed to. Maybe he was closer than he needed to be, but he wanted to be ready to move with her if they had to dodge at any moment. Besides, he figured he might not get as good an excuse to be in her personal space later.

Despite their proximity to each other, they walked upright with normal posture and a seemingly unhurried but brisk pace. Arin crossed ground with a purposeful stride and a confidence he very much appreciated. One or two nurses saw them and opened their mouths to question them, but seemed to think better of it. He couldn't see Arin's expression but he guessed she looked no-nonsense and maybe a little scary.

He chuckled silently. There might've been a few sharp words exchanged while he'd been unconscious. Arin seemed to have the hospital staff downright intimidated.

As they approached the emergency room entrance, she slowed and nodded to a police officer. The officer straightened from his relaxed position against the wall and returned her nod. She didn't say anything, only turned sharply to head down a different corridor.

"My vehicle is parked outside the emergency room," she informed Jason in a low whisper. "Seems clear, but I want to get an alternate look at the area before we actually head to my car."

Sniper.

She preferred long-range surveillance. She'd also be sensitive to the possibility someone else would be watching her, or more accurately, looking for him. He appreciated her forethought and didn't comment, only stayed with her. The area between his shoulder blades itched and tension was building in his chest. He wanted out of here and the smartest option was to do things her way.

The hallway was windowed along one side, letting in natural light from the outer room and offering a view out to the emergency room waiting area. There were a few potential patients in the rows of seats and a single person sitting in triage off to one side. He spotted two men sitting in corner chairs, as far away from either the entrance or the doors leading farther into the hospital as possible.

"Two. On our left." Jason murmured the warning to Arin. "I don't know them well, but I recognize them. They're former teammates. Nasty assholes."

"Understood." She didn't change pace, but in one smooth motion she had her sidearm in her hands.

Jason judged the distance to the end of the windowed portion of the hallway and wondered if the glass was bullet resistant. It was fairly likely. Hospitals tended to install bullet-resistant glass around emergency rooms and nurse stations as a reasonable security measure that wouldn't impede or degrade services.

The nearer man caught sight of them as Jason was finishing his thought. Arin had her sidearm pointed to the ground at her side and she didn't change speed, but she turned her head to look directly at the man.

"Tweedle-One sees us." Her tone was conversational, even mildly pleased. "Let's see what they do. Oops, we've got Tweedle-Two's attention, too."

"We're not going with the original characters?" Jason asked, amused. He liked the way she was handling the situation. She wasn't just by-the-numbers and calculated. She had a sense of humor.

"Eh." Arin continued to scan the hallway ahead of them

and check on the two men now watching them through the glass. "There's never just two and they always want a battle."

"Ha." Jason wished for a sidearm of his own as Tweedle-One and Two rose to their feet.

They started to raise weapons.

"Go." Arin motioned ahead of her and pushed him into a run. "End of the hall and to the right."

Cracks radiated out from two points of impact in a web pattern as bullets struck and lost their momentum as their energy was absorbed by the layers of tempered glass and laminate.

Jason bolted, not because he was following her order but because it made sense. Arin stuck close at his side. She didn't open fire and he approved. As long as the glass held out, the now-shattered portion provided a partially obscured line of sight. If she'd have fired, she would only have helped to take down the barrier between them. Better to move and get out of sight.

"Chances they have backup?" Arin asked. King kept pace beside them as they ran, unphased by shots fired. The dog acted like a MWD—military working dog—even if he was supposed to be search and rescue. Jason wondered how much additional training the Search and Protect Corporation had for its assets. Dogs suited for multi-discipline training were hard to come by.

He scowled. "Possibly two more. They'd be on the main exits."

"Police will slow them down. There's the one we passed and the one stationed just outside the ER entrance." Her tone had turned grim. "We don't need a body count today. How badly do they want you?"

"I'm not worth killing police." At least he didn't think so. He didn't want officers down because of him.

They came to the end of the hallway. She slowed just enough to kick the emergency exit door open, setting off the alarm. Then she continued to the right as she'd directed. "That'll bring police backup."

He eyed the fire alarms at intervals down the hallway ahead of them. "Fire alarms will add to the first responders on their way, more confusion to cover us."

"No."

Seriously? He glared at her.

"Local law enforcement is on standby nearby so the security alarm on an emergency door will bring them. We don't want other first responders in danger. The fire department would have to respond to a fire alarm and the hospital staff would have to follow procedure." She pulled up short and opened an inner door, motioning him into a stairwell. "I don't want to trigger an evacuation and have patients out there."

Ah. He swallowed his initial irritation. He'd thought only about the benefit for him and her. He hadn't considered the well-being of innocent bystanders. Fuck. He was used to assuming that that was someone else's priority. As long as he'd been careful never to directly hurt an innocent, he'd considered himself a good man. She was showing him how to think above and beyond the current objective, even in a tight situation where fast thinking was paramount.

He'd made some choices to help people and that was why he was in this situation at all. Was he doing this for just the one effort or was he going to adjust the way he did everything moving forward?

Food for thought. Later.

They reached the top of the stairwell and she paused at the door, crouching low as she motioned him to the side. He'd already positioned himself where she needed him to be, but he liked that she'd made no assumptions. Quick, efficient, clear in her communication. All that and she had a very nice behind, too. He did as she asked while she cautiously opened the door. King was crouched at her side, ears forward and nose twitching as he eagerly scented the air coming in through the crack.

She studied the outside and glanced at her dog several times. "Clear."

Jason wondered how much she relied on her dog to tell her if people were in the vicinity. At least, that was what he assumed had transpired. He'd never worked with dogs in his previous jobs. This one seemed to be in telepathic communication with her the way they moved so closely together.

They moved out onto the roof, sticking close to the outside wall of the roof access at first. There was little cover but it was easy to see no one else was up here. Wherever the other potential threats were, they hadn't chosen the higher vantage point and there were no trees near enough to hide shooters either. In the distance, sirens were growing louder and louder.

"Stay here." She paused.

"Please."

She shot him an irritated glance. "Excuse me?"

He was relatively certain they had the extra few seconds and if he let her continue giving him orders, they were going to have a misunderstanding. He wasn't always going to just do what she said. If he followed instructions or orders, it was out of a mutual respect. They were still building that. "It's a general courtesy. You're not my commanding officer. So yeah, I'll stay here and watch your six for you... if you say please."

She narrowed her eyes. "Please."

He nodded with a grin. Oh, he had no doubt he was going to pay for that. But it was important to establish this balance between them if they were going to get to know each other. And more than ever, he wanted to know Arin Siri.

She looked at her dog and gestured toward Jason. "*Bewaken.*"

The big dog sat and turned his full attention on Jason. Well, shit. He had a babysitter.

She didn't wait to see how Jason took it. Instead, she moved toward the far end of the building, overlooking the outside of the emergency room. Stopping short, she unslung her rifle and proceeded forward on her belly, using her elbows and knees to take her forward while still remaining as low to the roof as possible. It should've looked awkward but somehow, she was amazing to watch in motion. Once she reached the edge, she studied the area. Shouts were coming from the parking lot below. The local police were facing off with suspects. It could be Tweedle-One and Two or it could be more men who'd been waiting outside.

After another moment of observation, she moved back from the edge and sat up. She shouldered her rifle and stabilized herself, finding a target through her scope. Time seemed to stop as she calmly took aim. Then she fired and a man screamed.

She hadn't taken a kill shot. A moment later, she fired again and a different voice shouted in pain. Two hits, neither fatal. Shouts from the police made it clear they were moving in to take the downed men into custody.

She backed farther away from the edge and pulled a radio from her shoulder harness. As she switched it on, police chatter became audible. She returned to Jason. "That's four in custody and the local police will confirm when the area is secure. We'll wrap up the loose ends and head down to my car."

Jason stared at her. "You just shot two men and they're not going to hold you for questioning?"

She didn't even blink. "Nope."

CHAPTER FOUR

Arin pulled her rented Jeep up to the small parking area in front of her current bolt-hole and glanced at her passenger. Jason had settled into the passenger seat and snored through the last several hours of driving. It'd provided a helpful counterpoint to how damned hot he was in profile—sexy scruff, strong jaw, and all.

He might not have really been sleeping, but he'd made a good appearance of it. And hell, maybe he had slept. Blindfolded as he was, there hadn't been a chance for him to enjoy the scenery along the way. She didn't particularly care. After having a terse discussion with the law enforcement at the hospital, who'd required a little nudge from the Hawaiian government task force to expedite the statement they needed from her, she'd taken herself and Jason away from the scene as quickly as possible. Raul would smooth any ruffled feathers. It was part of his job as liaison for Search and Protect with the task force itself. Getting out of there had still taken longer than Arin liked.

She'd checked her vehicle carefully for any tampering and

left the premises, then swapped it at a car rental for a new Jeep. King had taken it all in stride, simply napping in the back. But Jason had grumbled once he realized she sucked for conversation when she was driving. Actually, she considered herself particularly bad at random chats in just about any situation. After a few tries, he'd tired of being shut down and tipped his head back to nap away the impromptu road trip.

He'd stopped snoring as she'd rolled to a stop. When she put the Jeep in park, he lifted his head. "Are we there yet?"

Even his voice was sexy when he woke up. And the effect was definitely unique to him because she'd woken up with her share of partners over the years—though none since she'd moved to Hawaii—and she didn't remember liking a voice quite so much as his. He had a hint of a South African accent, and it paired with the mellow timbre of his words in a seductive way.

"We're here." She hopped out the driver side. "King gets out first, then you."

"Do we both get to take a piss?" Jason called out as she walked around to the back of the Jeep.

She opened the back and murmured a quiet command to let King hop down. Her GSD disembarked and stretched briefly, with a big yawn, then followed up with one of those all-over body shakes. When he looked up at her, it was with a wide doggie grin. She smiled back at her partner. He was always ready and willing to work.

Shutting the back, she circled around to the other side of the vehicle and opened the passenger side door. Despite his blindfold, Jason turned his face toward her. "You didn't answer my question."

Behind her, King found himself a fern and lifted his leg. Jason tilted his head at the following sound of trickling relief and grimaced. "Aw, c'mon."

She sighed. "Hold on another minute or two and we'll find you someplace a little more private."

He smirked. "Suit yourself. I don't mind exhibition. I've got enough to flaunt."

She wrapped her hand around his bicep, or some of it. His muscles were more impressive than she'd admit out loud and her fingers barely got halfway around. "You'd only be show-ing off to King at the moment and he has a lot of practice with pissing contests. Let's just not."

She grabbed her duffel from the back seat and closed up the Jeep, then took him by the upper arm again and started to steer him across the tiny lot.

"This would go better if I could see." There was a thread of irritation under his otherwise light words.

To be fair, they were walking over gravel. It sucked to go over uneven ground without being able to watch where you were going. She'd done it in the past. "Just another minute or two."

At the edge of the parking area were a series of paths. To the right, there was a larger walkway with good lighting. It led to the main house and check-in. She directed him to the left.

The gravel gave way to hard-packed dirt on the narrow trail, with only enough lighting to keep from stumbling. The tropical rainforest closed in around them and after a few steps, neither the parking area nor the walkway to the main house were visible through the thick ferns and falling dark-ness. She loved this place and the privacy it offered. A person could literally tuck themselves away and forget anything else existed. Yet it was only twenty minutes to the nearest Thai food restaurant. Not that her guest had to know that.

This was a hideout. A temporary place for her to rest when she was on a mission away from home for longer than a day.

She stopped him in front of her cabin and removed his blindfold. He could pretend to stumble on the steps and she wasn't in the mood to grapple with him if he did. But he remained where he was standing, rapidly blinking his eyes as he looked around and gave his vision time to adjust from the pitch black of the blindfold to the relatively bright light of the cabin porch. She caught herself staring, watching the dark rings of his irises widen and contract.

He glanced around, efficiently taking in his surroundings. "Looks like your tree house fell out of its tree."

She lifted her chin, shaking off her fascination. This wasn't the time. "Inside, please."

"Okay, okay." He proceeded up the steps without any further wise cracks. Once they were inside, he stood in the middle of the small space. "Cozy."

Yes. Both cozy and private, the way she liked things. What she didn't like was having to have him in her space. There hadn't been time to arrange for a separate safe house, so here they were, in one of her favorite hideaways, and she'd never be able to come back to this one again. Once someone knew about one of her places, she tended to change it up and never go back. It was just good practice when you wanted to disappear on a regular basis.

She'd spent some time working freelance after her military service had ended, and her looks, combined with her skills, had taken her into some actual cloak-and-dagger insanity. She'd taken a lot of lives and there'd been plenty of people happy to go after hers. Arranging bolt-holes while she was on a mission was a habit she'd developed to stay alive. Zu had given her a future with the Search and Protect team, with a decently longer life expectancy, but some habits were hard to break.

As much as she'd tried not to get attached to locations,

she did appreciate good accommodations. This place had amenities to make her stay comfortable if she had to be here for more than a few days. It was beautiful, peaceful, and with King's help, she could tell if someone was approaching with plenty of time to decide on a course of action.

Jason turned to her and waited for her to meet his gaze. She must've been tired to let her thoughts wander like that. It annoyed her, so she glared up at him. Damn, standing right in front of him, he was head and shoulders taller. "What?"

He lifted his wrists, bound with zip ties. "I could take a piss like this, but I was hoping for a sign of good faith."

She raised an eyebrow at him. "It was already a sign when I secured your hands in front instead of behind you."

Still, he hadn't tried to leave on the entire trip here. She'd secured his hands to reduce the chances of him killing her along the way. Not that he couldn't have managed it if he'd really wanted to; she could've done it if their positions had been reversed. But so far, he hadn't made a great effort to escape. It'd be interesting if she gave him more slack to try to leave.

The way he was acting, he really wanted to stick with her. It could mean he truly wanted to help. Or he could be trying to get close to one of the Search and Protect team for dangerous reasons. She was more inclined to believe the latter rather than the former. Maybe.

She didn't like being this indecisive. Taking a pocketknife from a handy pouch on her shoulder harness, she sliced the zip ties holding him. "Fine. Bathroom is right over there. Don't take long."

He made a show of rubbing his wrists. "How about I talk to you as I go so you know I'm still really in there?"

She glared at him. "I can tell the difference between water going into the toilet and running water in a sink."

He turned away and crossed the distance to the bathroom with his hands in the air. "I figured. Still, there are things you wanted to know. Why waste time since you're all tense?"

She was. There was no point in denying it. But she had every reason to be. His relaxed attitude only pricked her temper. "People died today."

The bastard stepped into the bathroom and only closed the door most of the way, leaving it cracked open. She heard every moment of him slowly unzipping his damned pants. And he even groaned as he let loose his bladder. "Standard action when there's a change in management higher up. Clean up any compromised locations and tighten up the paper trail. The new boss wants to get business back on track and that means he needed to reduce liabilities."

It took the entirety of his little speech for him to finish, too. It occurred to her that they'd had him on a saline IV at the hospital but neither of them had hydrated on the car ride here. She stepped over to the cube-sized refrigerator under the entertainment center and nabbed two bottles of water as the sound of running water in the sink indicated he was washing his hands. When he came back out of the bathroom, she held an unopened bottle out to him.

He took it with a nod and opened it, taking a sip. After a moment, he caught her gaze with his own, steady and...melancholy. There wasn't a hint of the teasing or humor he'd maintained over the last couple of hours. "I am truly sorry those people died. I was out there to try to save them. I'm still here now because I want to share what I know. Maybe they won't have died for nothing."

She studied him, considered the tone of his voice and his body language. She searched for a dozen different physical tells to indicate he was lying, but he was telling the truth. He just wasn't telling her everything.

* * *

"You're just going to leave me here? I thought we shared a moment there."

Jason scowled at the handcuffs chaining him to the foot of the bed. Seriously, it wasn't as if they could really hold him. But he stopped and considered his hostess. He'd meant what he'd said. He'd been out there trying to help. People had died anyway. Now, the only thing he could do was help her and her team take down that human trafficking ring by sharing whatever he knew. But it'd only help if she trusted the information he gave her.

Conversation was obviously not the only way she was going to find out what she wanted to know about him. Otherwise, she'd have grilled him the entire car ride. Instead, it seemed like she was taking in how he chose to deal with things. Testing him in little ways, maybe, but not with the malicious intent some people had. If anything, it felt like an invitation to a game and he was amused. So, how to deal with the handcuffs and give them both a path forward for an amicable chat when she came out to see what he'd done?

"For the next five minutes, yes, you can stay there." Her voice came through from the bathroom clear, even through the closed door. There were small spaces in the wall near the ceiling and he heard the water in the shower start flowing. After a few seconds, the scent of lavender and mint came into the room along with a bit of steam.

The thought of droplets of water running over her golden skin took over his brain and he was caught wishing she'd invited him to join her.

Great. Even inside the cozy single-room lodge, he wasn't crazy about being stuck standing in the center of the room getting more turned on by the second. He could pick the lock and get free, sure. But she had to know that. It was about what he would do next. He could leave. He could stay and poke around her private space like a creep. Or he could be even worse and peep on her in the shower. None of those things would win her trust.

"Do I get a shower next?" Come to think of it, he'd appreciate the chance to clean up. They must've wiped him down some at the hospital, but he could do with a thorough hot shower, too. The idea of her soaping him up was appealing, only trumped by the follow-up thought of returning the favor for her. His palms heated at the thought of lathering soap over her shoulders and down her back, up her flat abs and over her breasts.

Maybe a cold shower would be wiser. He was getting way ahead of himself and she hadn't shown any signs of interest in him.

He wanted her to be interested in him.

"You could." She paused. "A change of clothes would be a problem for you, though."

"Good point." And an effective way to cool his naughty thoughts. It was almost worse to get clean and put on dirty clothes again. He'd done it plenty of times in the past. "I'm considering whether it's better or worse to stay as I am. To stink or not to stink, that is the question here."

She laughed. "King could find you either way."

He glanced at the dog. The big GSD was lying across the door to the bathroom, head on his paws, watching Jason. The dog wasn't a threat at the moment. She hadn't given King the command to keep guard, so Jason could move if he wanted to. It was another hint that she was testing him.

He was entertained by this little game but she was going to learn he gave as good as he got. He let a little edge into his voice. "I asked to come with you. He's not going to have to come looking for me. I told you why I'm still here, too."

"True." Her response sounded non-committal.

Sure, he could cooperate and stay put, but he didn't want to be completely compliant. He wanted her to recognize him as a fellow professional, respect him as someone who could be a challenge in other circumstances. He was choosing to help her here and now. The time he spent with her here was his chance to interact with her and he intended to learn as much about her as he could while he was at it. He also needed to get her comfortable enough to let him give what help he could.

She seemed intelligent and jaded, with a respectable amount of experience gained in a dangerous way of life. She was probably a good judge of people and was likely right most of the time. He was tempted to surprise her a little in the way he handled these stupid handcuffs and let her know she was engaging in a meeting of minds. He wasn't a simple subject to study and he wasn't likely to do things exactly the way most people would. He liked to be surprising.

"So I've got two basic options here. Stay where you left me or get out of the cuffs and leave." He decided to switch gears, changing his tone to light and conversational. "Staying means I'm cooperating, A gesture of good faith and all that."

Presumably it'd indicate he was trustworthy. If he wanted her to trust him, that'd be the best option to show his intent.

"Sure." She sounded almost cheerful this time.

He chuckled. He was glad she was having fun with this. He liked that she was playing a little with him. "The other option is to try to escape. Which, considering the skills your doggie friend has demonstrated, would not only prove me to be untrustworthy but also stupid."

She didn't answer. Uh huh, she wasn't going to comment yet on whether she thought he was either of those things. Well, he was in the process of proving himself someone she could trust and the conversation in general should've already proven he wasn't just stumbling along with the course of events. He was thinking every step of the way.

"All in all, this is a kinder choice than the lady or the tiger for all parties involved." And he didn't deserve kindness at the moment.

Well, he was here because he did want to help. That meant getting Arin to accept him as a potential ally, someone she could work with, and he wanted to have a little fun in the process. He was going to stay on his terms, so the cuffs had to go.

Glancing around, he considered what might serve his purposes. She hadn't left any convenient bobby pins or paper clips around and he didn't have something suitable in his pockets. There was a small breakfast table set against one wall. Place settings for two had been arranged with care. He stepped toward the table and reached, just able to snag a fork. It was a decent piece of flatware, nice enough to look neat in a place setting and not so high quality that someone would want to take it home with them. For his purposes, it meant the tines were also reasonably easy to bend.

He picked the lock on his handcuffs with little fuss, then grinned as he stepped to the head of the bed and hung the open cuffs from the headboard. She could take that as any kind of message she wanted, but it amused him to see them up there, resting on one of the fluffed pillows.

The water in the shower turned off and he decided he wasn't going to get too comfortable. Lying on the bed was just asking for trouble. He didn't want to sit at the breakfast table either, with it pressed up against the huge picture window. There was nothing but rainforest out there but he didn't like putting his back to it. King rose to his feet and Jason made his decision. As Arin emerged from the bathroom, dressed in a fresh pair of pants and a plain tank top with a towel draped over her shoulders, he was waiting in the armchair by the gas stove.

She studied him, her gaze unreadable. Her hair was still wet. She must've finger combed it and twisted it to hang over one shoulder. Probably an easy habit to her and the effect was alluring. He had all sorts of thoughts of being with her on a beach or beside a lagoon, even in the water.

But first, he needed to convince her to work with him. Play came later, maybe. He did have priorities. He wanted this human trafficking ring damaged again. Shut down would be even better.

He smiled, deciding to go with a combination of confidence and charm until he had a better idea of what sort of attitude she'd work with best. "Macadamia nuts? They're covered in chocolate. Good snack to keep us thinking clearly while we go through what I know and figure out how it can help you."

He held up a couple of the snack packs he'd found in the basket on the table.

She smiled. Sort of. Okay, it was more like the ghost of a smile, there and gone again once he blinked. But she had at least a little humor and he was happy to see it. Their line of work was serious, yes. But he found the professionals he respected most, could work with the best, and genuinely liked on a personal level, were the ones with a bit of humor to balance the gravity of their actions.

He'd contributed to some horrible things and he'd go insane with guilt without levity to balance him. He wanted to help Arin and her team to make up for what he'd done, yes, and he also wanted to know what it was like to work with her. Get to know her better. And damn, get to know her personally.

She sighed and pulled her duffel close, reaching in and searching for a moment, then turning back to toss a neatly folded cloth at him. He raised his eyebrows at her and shook out the folds to figure out what it was. It might have been a pair of trousers but they were of very thin, lightweight cotton and the waist was huge.

"You could fit in here with three of your best friends." He peered around the side of the fabric he was holding up and caught her smiling again before she schooled her face to a more neutral expression. Ah, her mouth was a lot of fun to watch.

"Those are kangkeng le. Thai-style pants used by fishermen, historically. They're becoming more popular with people as casual loungewear, though. They're one size fits most and these are specifically cut to be one size fits Westerners, even." She gestured to the extra wide waist. "You step into them and wrap the extra material across the front, tie it off at the waist, and let the folded fabric fall over the top of the ties. I've been sleeping in them but they'll probably fit you, at least until we can throw your clothes into a washing machine and dryer."

"I appreciate it." He stood, taking his time as he did. With most other people, he moved slowly if he didn't want to scare them. That wasn't the concern with her. In her case, a fast move would push her into a defensive stance and then she wouldn't be open to letting him help. He wanted her to keep her guard relaxed. It was too much to hope for her to drop it altogether.

Instead, he strolled over to her, dared her to take a step back or push him away. She didn't move but she did glare up at him as he walked right up to her. Toe to toe, she wasn't about to give even the littlest bit of ground. He grinned. "I guess I'll be spending the evening shirtless."

"I understand if you might feel too exposed." She responded in a completely flat tone. "Feel free to keep your current shirt if you like."

He nodded, never taking his gaze away from hers. "Noted."

"Fun and games aside. You only told me the highlights earlier." Her tone turned frosty.

"I haven't lied to you."

"Not directly, no." Her lips pressed together and her dark eyes lost their brightness. "But omission is almost as dangerous."

He recognized that look. It happened to him, too. The humanity leached away, leaving behind only snap decisions. It was the void a person had to find in order to do what was necessary. Those things could be defined as evil by some, but mostly, they had to be done. There was no leeway for ambiguity.

In this moment, if he wasn't completely honest, there'd be no way to gain her trust ever.

"I don't do morals and ethics." He searched for a way to explain. "I could give a shit about high concepts and ideals. None of those drive my decisions. I contract for work because I need income and I'm good enough at what I do to be paid very well. It's all very straightforward. But when I saw what I was protecting back on Oahu, I was pissed. I'd been a part of this nightmare for these people. I hated myself for it. I wanted to set some of them free, if I could. Get them help. Make up for the part I'd had in it. It's not saintly, and I'm not a drastically changed man with a cause now, but there it is. I thought I could do something by myself and I failed. So I'm here giving you everything I know about that shitty organization so your people can take it down and I can feel a little better. I'll figure out what's next afterward."

"That's selfish." Despite her statement, her shoulders relaxed subtly and she let her weight settle back on her heels a fraction.

"Yes." He leaned forward. "And there's also you. You were there over six months ago at the plantation, *doing the right thing*. I'm sure you wouldn't have let yourself end up in my position. Your team wouldn't have contracted with a client like that. Since then I've been thinking a lot, off and on, about what you would do and what choices you'd make. I met you for a few minutes and you changed my entire perspective. I'm not saying I became altruistic in a heartbeat, but I'm different and it's because of you. Here you are again and every minute I'm near you I want to prove to you I can be a better person."

She blinked, eyes widened. She was genuinely caught by surprise and her mouth dropped open.

It was too much of an opportunity to resist. He leaned forward, quick as possible, and kissed her.

CHAPTER FIVE

She could've stopped him, could've dodged or stepped back, could've lashed out. She didn't.

His lips were warm against hers for a split second, then when she didn't hit him, he pressed his mouth more firmly against hers and heat flared between them. Her entire body woke up in response. Her pulse quickened and damn it, even her nipples tightened. As she breathed in, she took in the spiciness of cinnamon and cloves threaded through the rich earthy smell of him. She couldn't imagine how he managed to smell good after the day they'd had, but he did. She groaned, wanting more.

He lifted his hand to her waist, starting to pull her against him and her brain caught up with the rest of her body. She placed her hand between them, flat on his chest, and pressed.

He stopped.

"This isn't going to happen." She said the words against his lips, killing herself as she did because she really liked the feel of their lips brushing against each other. It was painfully tempting. She wanted to open her mouth and let him drown them both in deep, carnal kisses. She wanted to feel his hands on her.

But what she wanted wasn't going to serve a purpose here and she didn't need to cloud her judgment. She was too hungry to enjoy without regretting it later.

A long moment passed in silence. He was the one to step back.

"I'll be quick." He turned on his heel and went into the bathroom. The shower turned on and she shivered.

Fine. She'd been enjoying the banter. The verbal sparring came easy with him and his sense of humor tickled her almost as much as it got under her skin. In holding her ground when he walked up to her, she'd been daring him to get closer. She'd left him the opening.

She was massively attracted to him.

Figuring out how far she could trust him and his intel should've been easier with a zing of chemistry to distract him. It wouldn't be the first time she'd flirted to get more information out of a person than they'd intended to give her. But she'd been lucky through the course of her career. She hadn't had to go past flirting and light foreplay to complete a mission. Intimacy, for her, was still personal. If she wasn't careful, she could be every bit as likely to be distracted. She wasn't willing to risk it right now.

"What do you plan to do next?" His voice floated out with the steam from the shower. "Are you in a holding pattern or are you investigating something?"

"I want to know what you know." She didn't bother to dissemble on that point. He was intelligent enough to figure it out. "And we'll go over it until I've got the details I need, even if it's information you didn't remember you had."

"Fun." The sarcasm was strong in his tone. "I'll go over

the intel I gathered to locate the farm and any information I had on other properties."

The water shut off and there was a rustle of fabric. She tried not to imagine what he'd look like all wet and toweling off. She failed. He stepped out of the bathroom a minute later, shirtless and in the process of tying off the waist of the kangkeng le she'd lent him.

Ohh. Say. Can. You. See…

He was glorious. She'd known he had an amazing build to begin with, but the muscle definition exposed by his current state of undress was mouth-watering. He was broad across the shoulders and heavily muscled through the back and lats with the kind of cut that made her want to run her hands all over him. And those abs…

There was a saying popular in the Thai dramas her mother liked to watch: "chocolate abs." Arin always cautioned her mother not to use the term, especially not in the US where it had a different connotation, but in those Thai dramas the phrase was intended to compare a man's abs to the subdivided sections of a chocolate bar. Very tempting. Personally, Arin liked the idea of chocolate abs much better than a six-pack. She was a lot more likely to nibble and lick a chocolate bar than the outside of a six-pack of tin cans.

He wore the kangkeng le low at his hips so she couldn't help but appreciate her absolute favorite spot. He had the deep definition V, leading from high on his hips down below his waistband. The kangkeng le was very lightweight and if the extra fabric hadn't been folded over where he'd tied the pants and lower, there wouldn't have been much left to imagine.

Heat rose in her cheeks as she realized she hadn't taken all of him in during her usual split-second assessment. No. Her gaze had lingered, and considering she'd denied him only a few minutes before, she was being rude as hell. She lifted her gaze to meet his. "I'm sorry."

He crossed his arms. Not a positive sign as body language went. "For stopping us earlier? Have regrets?"

"No." This time she was the one to lift her hands, palms open in a sign of peace. "I shouldn't have been rude just now."

His arms relaxed a bit, but remained crossed. "Appreciated. But you get that all the time, I'm betting."

She shrugged. "Not so much. I'm...off-putting."

It was true. She wore her attitude like dented plate armor and most didn't dare look long enough for her to catch them at it.

He grunted. "Why don't you find yourself a seat. We'll start this debrief, then we can figure out who is sleeping where."

Back to business and steadier ground. She nodded and sat on the end of the bed, cross-legged, leaving him the seat he'd chosen previously. He settled onto the chair, leaning forward and resting his elbows on his knees.

"I'll start from when I first met you and take you through to the last thing I remember before I got knocked out."

He started from their meeting at the plantation over six months prior and reviewed the same highlights he'd given her at the hospital with more detail; in particular, the intel he'd gathered right after the incident and in the weeks following. His former employer was exactly the kind of private contract company she wouldn't consider working for if she could possibly help it. The client, the owner of the plantation and head of the human trafficking ring, had retired in shame and been replaced. One bad guy down, but the actual trafficking ring was still in operation, just under new management. Jason had several names of business owners on Oahu, Big Island, and a couple others. She made a mental note to have Pua research them back at headquarters to confirm the intel and put a watch on them. But for the most part, he'd told her the pertinent highlights at the hospital. The nitty gritty didn't include any red flags for the team still searching Waipio Valley as far as she could tell.

Once he'd finished, she waited for him to take a sip of his water bottle, then she slid off the bed. "I need to check in with my team. Then, if you're up for it, I'd like to know more about this new management. Is this just one person? More? How much of a re-organization is this going to be?"

She was betting Jason wouldn't have had the chance to find out before he'd left, not with the way he'd protested, but he could give her team a few more leads specific to this line of investigation.

For his part, he only shrugged and sat back in the chair. Some of his attitude was coming back but there were shadows under his eyes and his bravado was starting to fade. He was tired. He was recovering from a concussion. Frankly, he'd probably had better days. Maybe she should let him have the bed. She could make a nest of blankets and pillows on the floor and rest just fine. She didn't plan to sleep anyway.

She glanced at King, lying on the floor at the foot of the bed. "*Blijf.*"

King raised his head, his ears lifting and forward as the dog watched her go to the glass doors at the back of the small room and slip out onto the lanai.

Outside in the night, she listened. It was quiet to a certain extent, but what reassured her was the natural rustling and abrupt calls of nocturnal creatures. The rainforest wasn't ever completely silent, especially at night. If it was, then she'd have been alerted to something out there that shouldn't be.

She turned on the satellite phone and contacted her team. "Bravo."

She scowled. It was late and Bravo, or Raul Sá, should be home. After all, his *fan* would be missing him. "Fan" was a Thai word for a significant other that was close to boyfriend or girlfriend, but Arin had learned it with a more committed connotation, like fiancée. Arin thought of Raul's partner in the Thai term because his fan was also her little sister and Arin wanted to know he wasn't choosing work over Mali without a good reason. "Bravo, this is Charlie."

"Good to hear from you. Status?" Raul sounded genuinely relieved.

"I was a little slow getting out of the hospital. King and I are fine. Our guest is in one piece." Ah damn, it might be her fault Raul was still working if he'd had to deal with the damage control after her precipitous departure from the hospital. She gave Raul a quick brief on the information she'd learned so far.

Her small hideaway wasn't soundproof. In fact, she liked it because she could hear so much of the surrounding rainforest. Jason was probably sitting inside listening to her relay exactly what he'd shared with her. She wasn't going to add her personal thoughts yet. She only gave Raul the facts as she knew them through Jason.

"I'll work with Pua to start investigating those names." Raul paused. "We got preliminary findings on the bodies from today."

She waited.

"The dead were all either old or injured previous to their demise." Raul sounded worried. "We've got teams at airports and potential harbors. There's a possibility those killed weren't worth transporting but the able-bodied are still out there awaiting transfer off the island."

"The boy, Huy—was he among the dead?" Hope flared. Raul knew about the promise she'd made.

"No. Not as far as we could tell." Raul gave the answer cautiously. "Arin, I know you promised Mali you'd do your best to help this kid's sister. Mali will understand if you don't find him."

She'd promised Mali she'd do her best. Her little sister and she had only rebuilt their relationship after long years apart, mostly because Arin had left home and hadn't kept a promise to come back to Mali. A little over six months ago, a weird quirk in life had landed them both on the island of Oahu. They were only just getting close again and Arin didn't intend to break any more promises. Ever.

"I'll see if our guest has any thoughts on likely modes of transport off the Big Island."

"Copy." Raul sounded resigned. Well, he was being as good as he could to both her and Mali and that meant he was staying out of it to let them work their issues out with each other. "Check back in, Charlie. Do not do this solo. There could be more than one unit can handle."

She ended the call without acknowledging. What she'd do all depended on what situation might unfold next.

* * *

"News?" Jason studied Arin's face as she came back inside from the lanai.

She had a pleasant expression on her face but it was frozen in place. It must be her version of a poker face. In the brief time he'd known her, he'd been fascinated by how animated she was in subtle ways. You'd have had to really watch her to notice. In this moment, her hint of a smile and slightly widened eyes had alarm bells ringing in his head.

"Hmm." She blinked. No change.

"Maybe I have perspective on it?" He wasn't sure why, but he didn't like being on the outside of her thoughts like this. He wanted her temper again, and the sharp-edged verbal sparring.

Her lips pressed together in a line, breaking the amicable expression she'd been holding. "I thought you told me as much as you knew about the farm before you went there to get those people out."

He took his feet off the ottoman and placed them flat on the ground again. He liked verbal sparring with her, but he also liked to be ready to dodge in case she made any sudden moves. She had that kind of dangerous feel about her and it was exciting, but it was also prudent to be ready for anything she could do. "I did, but new intel can always connect the dots where there wasn't a relationship before."

She considered. "Fine. Sometimes we don't know what's relevant without added context. I get it. The sheds you identified did contain people, but they were all dead."

He winced as she delivered the news. He'd guessed but hadn't asked her after they'd left the hospital. There'd been times when he'd walked among the bodies of innocent people in villages overseas. But this was in the US, and he'd been trying to get there in time to help those people. The bump on the back of his head ached and his joints creaked to underscore his failure as he leaned forward in his seat to rest his elbows on his knees.

The line of her mouth softened and she moved to sit on the edge of the bed again. "The medical teams have only identified old and injured so far."

He lifted his head and met her gaze, the weird weight on

his chest lifting. "There should've been young people, fresh workers. There were shipments as recently as the last several weeks."

She nodded. "We need to know everything you do about those shipments, or how to get more intel on them. Most immediately, are the shipments moving between islands by private plane or via ship?"

"Almost all transport is by shipping containers. Has to be." He thought furiously through everything he'd seen while he'd been on the job. "I was mostly on site at head-quarters, but we had a few people at the docks in Oahu to protect shipping containers in the area. If the boss had an airstrip, we weren't contracted to protect it, but I'm thinking it would've been too expensive to try to move so many people via air. You can't fit enough of them on a small plane to make it worth the trip."

"Plus you'd have to move them onto and off of the plane to other types of transport." Arin chewed her lower lip as she mulled over the possibilities. There was a red mark there already, turning a deeper purple. He wanted to kiss the hurt away. She was mean to herself and he wondered if she even noticed a small thing like that. But she was still thinking. "Shipping containers could come from overseas or go from island to island."

"Shitty way to travel." He made the comment light to hide his discomfort, thinking about what the people in the containers had gone through.

She narrowed her eyes. "Charming way to put it. Many don't survive the trip overseas. They took the risk hoping for a better life and those who did make it faced a living nightmare almost worse than the days at sea."

Red flag. He was enjoying pricking her temper on light topics but this was getting too close to home for her, if his research on her personal background was on target. Her little sister was a leading researcher on human trafficking in the Hawaiian islands. In fact, her little sister had almost been kidnapped because of it.

"Hey." Normally he'd let the person go on thinking whatever the hell they wanted about him, but in this case—or maybe with this woman—he wanted to make himself clear. "I get it. I do. These people came from dire circumstances if they've made the decision to take the risk. Hell, they even pulled together insane amounts of money to pay for the chance. They were duped and screwed on the other side."

"If you get it, don't make light of it." She was on her feet again and had stepped away from him. It seemed like way more distance than was possible in the single room. Her dog, King, got to his feet and joined her. Whatever the dog was reading from her mood, Jason might be wise to take the hint. The pair of them were looking more distant, unapproachable, with every passing moment of silence.

"You're right." He pitched his words quietly, hoping his sincerity would come through. "I try to keep a sense of humor because people like you and me, we're going to see things that only get worse and worse as we go through our careers. Keeping it light helps me stay sane but sometimes I get carried away. I'm sorry. I'm way out of my comfort zone here and I'm not even sure how I can help any of these people at this point."

She stared at him, those dark eyes unfathomable. "You came to this island before leaving Hawaii. You could've just cleared your conscience by terminating your contract and heading straight to the mainland. Why are you really here?"

It wasn't as simple a question to answer now as it had been in the hospital room. He wasn't going to insult her by acting like his initial answer was enough. "I told you; I wanted to try to help some of the people victimized by that godforsaken trafficking ring, and I meant it. A long time ago, I made the decision to leave the place I knew, looking for something better. Hell, at the time I thought nowhere could be worse than where I'd come from. Later, I learned it definitely could."

He paused. Unpacking the why of it all wasn't something he did, ever. Introspection was something he tended to avoid. Probably because he didn't like himself very much. But looking at her, sitting there, waiting and listening...She'd been judging him earlier for the way he made things into a joke. Now, there was no judgment, only listening. She was giving him a chance. If he botched this, she'd cut him out and he wasn't ready yet, not when these last several hours had been more interesting to him than any number of years he'd spent living. "As far as I know, there is no security that someone else gives you. Not family, not friends. Every company or business goes down over time, every community falls apart." He let a short laugh loose and swallowed when he heard how bitter it sounded. "You build your security for yourself. No one will wait for you while you do it. Everyone will move on with or without you. And I was okay with that. I was holding my own. But these people? They were trying to find better opportunities for themselves, too. Every possible chance for them to win that for themselves was taken away and I was part of doing that to them. I'll be going to hell for a lot of reasons, but it won't be because I contributed to this kind of evil."

There. He had next to nothing left in his mind but the memories he'd take away from the plantation and how they'd changed him. He remembered the looks on the faces of the captives. They'd been lost and brutalized. And as they'd been stumbling out of the building on that plantation,

Arin had been on a rooftop watching over them through the scope of her sniper rifle. Her mission had been completed and she'd lingered, even after he'd confronted her. She'd made sure someone was watching over those people until the police arrived on the scene. Then she'd vanished.

She'd changed him and he didn't even understand why. This was his chance to find out.

He cleared his throat and lifted his chin at her. "Why don't you tell me why you're here. Just the job?"

She blinked and her lips parted, her mask slipping away. He'd caught her off guard. Maybe people didn't derail her often, or it was possible not many tried. She didn't barrel ahead with her interrogation of his motives, though.

"I made a promise." Her statement was short, defensive.

He lifted an eyebrow. There was weight behind those words. Promises meant something significant to her. He filed that thought away for future reference.

"To family? A friend?" If this was loyalty, he could understand it in theory. He wasn't big on loyalty himself.

She shook her head. "A woman I barely know. She's an older sister and she doesn't have the means to find and save her younger sibling. King and I have the skill set. I promised her we would do everything in our power to find her younger brother."

He stared at her. She was absolutely dedicated to this promise she'd made to a person she barely knew. It'd make more sense if her promise had been made to someone close, but a stranger? Why? "The woman could be lying."

Arin nodded. "She had a picture or two. There are records. The circumstances around her involvement in this human trafficking ring aren't what most would expect. This woman wasn't running from war-torn lands or villages threatened by conflict. The oppression she left behind was more subtle in its iniquity. She was educated. She had student identification and a diploma from back home. We were able to confirm her records with the university overseas. She took what she thought was a job offer to apply her degree in a new career on the mainland and paid extra to relocate her younger brother with her. She was tricked and they were separated. Raul met her in a massage parlor on Oahu during our investigation leading up to the plantation raid, and she provided us with additional intel when we were in the planning stages for this mission. I made the promise because it's in alignment with the investigation. King and I can do this."

She'd made the promise because she was a big sister, too. He didn't have siblings and he didn't share a feeling of brotherhood with anyone he'd worked with to date, but he also wasn't completely lacking in empathy. Maybe what drew him to her was the fact that she didn't preach what she thought was right or wrong. She didn't put her opinions into words so much as she executed on them. She took action, and he admired her for that.

He shook his head slowly. "Honestly, I've never committed to help a single person the way you are right now. But I met you and haven't been able to get you out of my head since. Let's go find this kid."

CHAPTER SIX

Arin put the Jeep into park, well away from the lighting around the main gate to the Kawaihae Harbor. It was the middle of the night and headed toward the dark hours just before morning. They hadn't taken the time to wash any clothes, but she'd at least pulled a clean long-sleeve shirt on before pulling her protective vest over it.

Jason sat next to her, back in his dirty clothes. She glanced at him and he had a spark of mischief in his eyes as he gave her a quick smile.

This could be a trap.

Oh, she believed most of what he'd been telling her, even his motives for being here on the island. But believing him and trusting him were two different things. She didn't trust anyone easily. She'd either seen people live to regret trusting too much, die for that mistake, or experienced the former herself. Too many ingrained lessons in why not to trust anyone made her cautious even as she'd brought Jason along with her to the harbor.

Jason could've told her the truth earlier and still be capable of flipping his loyalties. Coming that close to being eliminated by his former colleagues could induce a change of heart, and he might be tempted to try to get back into their good graces by giving away her movements or the movements of the rest of the Search and Protect team. Whether his intentions remained helpful or turned treacherous, it was better to keep him where she could monitor his activities directly.

She'd checked in via text messages with Raul before leaving her bolt-hole. Raul and his team were searching Hilo Harbor and had turned up nothing so far. The next best option for the human trafficking ring was to try to ship their captives out of Kawaihae. If the boy she was looking for was still alive, he was most likely here for the moment. It would take Raul, the Search and Protect team, and the task force hours to cross the island to get here, and they couldn't risk taking local law enforcement resources away from the airports, just in case the main perpetrators tried to fly off the island. Huy and the other captives could disappear with the outgoing tide before search and rescue teams could arrive to start looking for them.

So she, King, and Jason were here ahead of the official search. She was also here without explicit orders, which could be all sorts of interesting. Creativity in high-risk situations was her specialty.

"This is unexpected." Jason rolled his shoulders as they met at the back of the Jeep. He stood back as she opened the trunk to let King out.

"How so?" She double-checked King's vest and made sure his digital camera was working. Footage caught by the equipment on King's gear could be valuable evidence later. It was above and beyond what most search and rescue teams might use, but Zu thought using it'd be worthwhile, considering how much they'd been collaborating with local law enforcement lately. Zu's Buck and Raul's Taz had been equipped with digital cameras, too.

"I offered to help and I'm glad you accepted, but I honestly thought we'd either be chatting all night, trying to get inside each other's heads or I'd be secured and tucked under the bed in your little hideaway while you hared off to go save this kid." Jason continued to warm up his upper body, swinging his arms forward and back in slight arcs.

"You wouldn't have stayed put." The image of Jason bound to the underside of the bed tickled her, followed by the very sexy image of him bound to the top of the bed instead. *Yeah, no.* It probably would've taken a while, but she was guessing he was resourceful enough to have gotten out of any number of zip ties eventually. Sure, she could've secured him well enough to keep him for a few hours, but this excursion would've given him long enough to have a change of heart and flip back to his former team. She wasn't willing to risk her chance to rescue Huy and the other captives.

"Probably not." He didn't seem to have a problem with being equally as candid. "I don't like to get bored. I also seem to have some people after me, so if you didn't let me help you then I'd have nothing left to do but get on with my life."

"Yeah?" Satisfied with King's gear, she kept him leashed and murmured a soft command to keep him at heel beside her. Then she started toward the gatehouse. "I thought you were working to lighten the load on your conscience."

"Thus the offer to help you," Jason responded easily. "If you refused, I couldn't do much more by myself and there's obviously an effort to erase me from existence. I like my life, so practicality would indicate I should move on."

"It's not too late to go now." She gave him the out despite

her earlier caution. He had every reason to leave if that was the way he was thinking. His staying was weird.

He had no reason to be targeting her specifically, as far as she knew. And she hadn't missed the way he'd looked at her every once in a while. His interest was very real, and very much in her.

"I'm here." He was cheerful about it. "Until the rest of your team arrives, I'd like to be sure someone is watching your six."

She strode toward the gate. They'd been in the parking lot long enough to be spotted by any cameras in the area. Unless the whole harbor was under the payroll of this human trafficking ring, any security should be fairly straightforward to talk to. She slipped through the closed gate—mostly meant to keep vehicles out rather than individuals on foot—and proceeded as if she was absolutely supposed to be there. Any attempt at stealth would make explaining her presence on premises harder later. Best to be open and obvious about her intent to the nice security cameras.

Jason kept up with her, staying on her right to give King room ahead and slightly to the left of her. The man's head turned as he kept an eye out for any movement in the darkness. Presumably, he wanted to warn of any trouble. He moved with assurance and an air of competence. There was no sign of his concussion impeding his perception or motor function.

It'd been her impulse to bring Jason along and he hadn't argued when she'd told him where they were going. He'd even agreed that this was the likely location to ship out the missing captives. She needed to decide whether to work with him or treat him like an extra liability—along for the ride only because it'd made more sense than leaving him behind. After all, even if he was being completely up front, she was twisting herself into knots anticipating the worst—and honestly hoping for the best. "I do fine on my own."

"I believe you do," Jason murmured. "But I'm here anyway."

His statement could've creeped her out. Instead, the tightness in her gut eased a little. For this action, here at the harbor, she'd work with him. It still wasn't proof she could trust him, though.

* * *

Jason kept pace with Arin as she continued through the harbor area. She walked with confidence, and with King next to her she looked like law enforcement even if neither of them was wearing a uniform. King was equipped with a military-quality vest, and the camera definitely made it impossible for someone to think of him as just a service dog. To be honest, service dogs weren't incredibly common on the island anyway, particularly at night, walking around a shipping harbor.

They reached the container terminal and Arin stopped, kneeling to whisper to King.

"Can't you just tell him to search for humans?" He couldn't hear what she was saying to the dog but he'd listened when she'd given commands. When it was time to do actual work, she spoke in concise, short phrases or single words.

Arin looked up, though she still had her hands buried in the dog's fur around his face. The overhead lamps produced catchlights in her eyes and he didn't think he'd get tired of the different ways light caught in her eyes, ever. She shook her head once. "Mmm. Not King. He needs a specific scent to track."

She shrugged out of the small backpack she'd been wearing and reached into the main compartment. Drawing out a gallon-sized ziplock bag, she held it low and opened it. King immediately stuck his nose inside, took a few short sniffs and one long one.

"The boy's sister had a T-shirt or two from their journey before they were separated." Arin shook her head. "It has her scent on it as well. There's a chance it'll confuse King, but I can give him another check if we get through the terminal here without him detecting anything."

She sealed the shirt away, tucked it into her backpack, and swung the backpack into place over her shoulders. "Ready?"

King was sitting, watching her, ears up and alert. He was visibly eager, almost trembling, and he looked *happy*. Jason wasn't sure how a dog looked happy when it was just sitting there, not wagging its tail or barking or hopping around in the middle of play. King was as intense as Arin and he projected sheer joy working with his mistress.

Damn. What was it like to enjoy the work you do the way this dog did?

"*Such*." She delivered the command in the barest of whispers. Really, only the dog had to hear it. Jason caught it because he'd been listening for it. He was going to guess it was German. He could be wrong, though.

Arin and King started forward together, systematically making their way down the rows of forty-foot containers.

"Sure he'll be able to catch a scent if what he's looking for is inside one of these?" He tried to give them room, but stayed close enough for conversation. He also paid attention to the direction of the wind and did his best to remain downwind to avoid adding his scent to the many others the dog was probably sifting through in search of the one he was set to find.

"Shipping containers aren't airtight." She was watching where King was going and also remaining vigilant to their surroundings.

He'd been doing visual sweeps of the area as well. He wasn't worried about someone who belonged at the harbor. A security guard or employee would approach them openly. It was more an issue of someone left to guard the human cargo. Whoever it was would be tucked away somewhere inconspicuous, easily missed by security. It could even be a member of his former team. Considering the shots they'd taken at Jason already, he wasn't eager to let them catch him by surprise again. He also didn't want Arin hurt by someone trying to get at him.

"So scent from inside could be detected from the outside." The rapport between Arin and her GSD was interesting. He hadn't had much experience on a mission with a handler and a working dog in the past. The sheer level of awareness she had for every nuance of her dog's posture and body language blew Jason away.

"They wouldn't have been loaded here, so there's no trail for him to follow to a container," she said almost absentmindedly. "He literally has to sniff each container on as many corners as he can reach for detection."

She delivered the explanation in a matter-of-fact tone, clipped and maybe even abrupt to some people's ears. It didn't bother him, especially after having spent the better part of the day listening to her. The edge always seemed to be on her words, but she didn't sound more irritable than any of their conversations earlier. She was . . . focused and driven.

"Seems like fun." He wondered if either of them ever relaxed. She'd been on alert and "working" in every moment he'd been in her presence so far, even when she'd been in the shower and she'd left King to watch him.

"For him, this is fun." Her attention never left King, but her lips took on a soft smile. "The best working dogs come from encouraging behaviors they already do naturally, instinctively. King is exceptional because he loves what he does."

And she loved her current work, too. Jason squelched a pang of envy. He liked getting paid, but he'd never been as into his job as these two were.

Abruptly, King sat and looked up at Arin.

"What's that about?" The dog was sitting upright, similar to when he'd been ready to start, and Jason couldn't quite figure out why King looked different. Maybe he was going crazy but the dog's body language almost shouted success.

She was suddenly excited, too. It didn't show in her expression so much as her eyes. They gleamed with a predator's anticipation and she had her firearm in her hands, pointed at the ground but ready. "He's found something. It's his passive signal."

"Does he have a not-so-passive signal?" Jason wasn't armed but he scanned the area around them again, trying to keep watch. If a threat was going to make itself known, it would any minute now.

"Ah, well, when he's chasing down a target, it's a different situation. Especially if he's off leash and possibly far ahead of me." She was checking out as much of the container as she could. It was positioned at a forty-five degree angle and flanked on either side by similar metal containers. "Depending on the terrain, King could get out of my sight. Then he'd signal with barking, both to bring me to him and to intimidate the target into staying put."

Jason wondered how often their organization was contracted to search and capture, rather than rescue. Arin's description sounded more like the latter than the former. Or maybe she was in an aggressive frame of mind. "But you didn't ask him to bring a target to bay."

"No." She shot a dark glance at him then turned her attention back to the shipping container. "King is my partner and smarter than most humans, as far as I'm concerned, but he's a dog. I don't ask him to do anything. I give him a command and he executes it, with excellence. Anything less and it becomes a danger to him and to me."

Jason grinned.

She looked up when he didn't say anything and caught sight of his expression. "What?"

"Oh, I'm thinking you demand excellence in all things, from yourself and others, and I've got some amazing fantasies in mind now."

He thought she might snap at him, maybe even hit him. Instead, she gave him the most enigmatic look he'd seen from her yet. "You're welcome."

CHAPTER SEVEN

Let him chew on that.

Arin didn't know why she was encouraging him. She shouldn't. But his charm was impossible to ignore and he'd been keeping watch alongside her. He'd been wary and careful, not projecting the anticipation of someone bringing her into any kind of ambush. Instead, having him at her side had been like having a partner, of the human sort.

Besides, he was an incredibly hot man and she'd seen him in various levels of undress through the course of the day. She had a few choice visuals to fuel her own fantasies for the future.

Turning her attention back to the container door was more of an exercise in willpower than she wanted to admit to herself. The door was fitted with a lockbox, which was basically a set of steel plates welded together to shelter the lock itself. This set up definitely prevented unauthorized access from someone trying to cut a lock off or jimmy it off with a crowbar. It was a good precaution in other situations but in this case, it meant she was going to have to pick the lock.

She crouched down to peer up into the lockbox with the light from her cell phone to get a look at the kind of lock she was dealing with, then she pulled her set of lock picks from their home in the shaft of her boot. King sniffed her shoulder, then turned and sat to keep watch on her six. He'd warn her of any activity behind her while she concentrated on the heavy lock.

"Do all of you know how to pick locks?" Jason moved to stand near King, covering her as well. Now, even if someone took a shot at her, it'd have to go through Jason first.

She hadn't thought to ask him for cover, honestly, but she appreciated the gesture. "I'm not sure, but it's a handy skill. I thought most people in security would know how."

He grunted, a noncommittal sound. "You're search and rescue, though. Aren't dogs your thing, more than keeping threats in or out of an area?"

"I'm a dog handler, yeah." The lock itself was heavy duty. It wouldn't be as easy as the average locks on doors or even regular padlocks. She inserted her tension wrench to get started. "I'm also a sniper, which you know if you were researching our team. It's not something I've tried to hide from my files."

"Snipers don't generally have to pick locks either." No surprise from him, though.

Then again, he'd also met her on the roof of a building providing cover to an extraction team. He'd seen her rifle then and again at the hospital earlier today. So it wasn't as if he'd have needed to look into the information available on her. She'd mentioned the intel and his research more to acknowledge he'd been looking into her background. Acquiring information on a person was a smart move when you wanted to know anyone in the private contract industry. Back at Search and Protect HQ, her colleague Pua was in the process of digging deeper into his background than most people had the technical skills to do.

"As to snipers and lock picking, you'd be surprised." She started simple, inserting a slender tool with a squiggle at the end—a rake—into the keyhole along with her tension wrench. She applied slight pressure on the tension wrench and started working her rake to find the binding pin. "It's all about finding the right location to set up and take the shot, and sometimes the right location is behind a locked door."

"So you learned to do this as part of your sniper training." He shifted his weight from one foot to the other. She didn't turn to look so much as hear his clothes rustle, but his presence at her back was almost warm.

"No." She found the binding pin and used the rake tool to lift it up gently until she was able to turn her tension wrench in the key plug just a bit. The rest of the pins would be easier from here on out. "My little sister was delighted to learn how to lock doors as a child. She figured out how to lock herself into bathrooms, bedrooms, cars. I learned how to pick locks as a result of babysitting her when we were kids."

He chuckled. "Sounds like an interesting childhood. Learn anything else while you were trying to watch out for her?"

"Lots of things." Patience, for one. Arin continued to work on the lock. This one wasn't easy and it was taking longer than she'd like. "When it came to learning anything, my sister set the standard to which others strove to achieve, myself included."

Finally, she was able to turn the tension wrench all the way and felt the lock release. She unhooked it and placed it on the ground, then put her tools away before standing. As she rose, she had her firearm in hand, pointed at the ground for now.

"I'd say you've been setting the bar for a lot of others, yourself." Jason stepped to the side.

She didn't answer. Instead, she lifted the latch and pulled open the container with her free hand, keeping the door between her and any nasty surprises.

Even as she pulled, she peered around the edge of the door. The interior was dimly lit and with the door open, she could hear the quiet whir of a few small fans. Sitting along the sides of the container were a dozen or more people, mostly men, all cowering from her.

King stood next to her at the ready, but didn't issue any kind of warning growl or bark.

She exchanged glances with Jason. He gave her a slight nod and turned to continue to cover them from anyone coming up behind them.

She pitched her voice to be as calm and reassuring as possible. Some of them may not speak English, so her tone was going to have to carry her intent. "It's okay. We're here to help. Everyone needs to stay calm and we'll get you to safety as soon as possible. But you need to come with me. Can you do that?"

She paused for a few moments, then repeated her message and waited for eye contact from each of them. They all met her gaze after some hesitation, but there was hope there and most of them nodded their understanding. None of them had any hint of malicious intent or the blank look of a sleeper.

"Is Huy here?" *Please let him be here.*

One boy sat forward. His face was streaked with dirt but he looked to be in his early teens. There was fear clashing with hope in the way he met her searching gaze, but he lifted a hand and nodded to her.

She smiled, lips closed, and hoped she still remembered how to smile gently. Kind and gentle weren't her forte, but this was a kid and he'd already been treated too harshly. "Kim sent me to find you."

Relief broke across his face with a tremulous smile at the sound of his big sister's name. He drew his knees up to his chest and propped his arms over them, burying his face.

Damn. The poor soul. She stepped into the container, to help him up maybe or to do whatever she could to comfort him. He was so close to returning to his family.

"Wait!"

* * *

Jason cursed as Arin didn't stop in time. Her foot came forward as she stepped and her shin contacted with something he'd only caught sight of a moment prior. The lighting over the container storage area hadn't been enough to catch it, but the added light from the battery-operated lamps inside the container had caught on the trip wire a little too late. She froze at his warning, though, and hadn't stepped fully through it. Maybe she hadn't triggered it.

Either way, he wasn't going to leave her there to figure it out on her own.

Jason kneeled just behind Arin, taking a closer look at the space where she was standing. "Stay right where you are."

He quickly but carefully moved ahead of her, careful to avoid the trip wire and look for any secondaries. Followed it around the container. The people inside scrambled to get out of the way.

Frustrated, he growled. "Stay calm, people. Try to stay toward the center here."

If they panicked and started darting around in the close space trying to get out, one of them could blow them all up. This kind of situation was hard enough when he'd been the only person close to the device he suspected was present.

The more people trapped nearby, the worse the odds were of them all walking away.

Behind him, Arin repeated his instructions with her calm, low-pitched voice. Hearing her and seeing her remain exactly where she was seemed to help the others get their shit together. They followed the instructions and gathered in a tense group at the center of the cramped space.

She had a way about her that made people want to follow her lead. Jason was as susceptible to it as the rest of the poor bastards in this forsaken box, and he was going to think about exactly why later. Right now, he only knew he didn't want to leave her, and she wouldn't leave these people, so Jason was going to have to clear the container so they could all walk away.

He figured the best he could do to keep building their confidence in him was to focus on his goal. At the moment, that was following the trip wire. It led him to the side of the container and into a box rigged to appear as another battery-operated lamp and fan.

"The good news is I've found an IED." He kept his tone lightly conversational, his posture relaxed. It'd been a while since he'd had to deal with an improvised explosive device, and considering their current company, it might be best if they didn't recognize the acronym he used. It was a hope, anyway. The harsh reality was that IED was a well-known acronym even to non-English speakers who came from areas subject to constant warfare.

Arin didn't let on the severity of the situation either. She kept her voice pleasant. "How is that good?"

"Because you initiated the trigger mechanism, but it hasn't gone off yet," he responded, sounding cheerful. He was actually pretty happy about it. The alternative would've been for them all to have been blown to bits by now. He'd take their being alive as a positive and investigate why so they had a better chance of staying that way. He carefully studied the area around the box, watchful for additional trip wires. "But it will eventually, so it's good I found it."

She was quiet for a minute. "What's the bad news?"

Satisfied that the immediate area was clear of any additional trip wires, he conducted a visual assessment of the box itself. Then he lifted the cover slightly, running his fingers around the edges as he looked for a deadman's wire or some other form of tamper protection. It took precious time to locate and disable. Finally, he began to remove the cover, gingerly handling it by the edges, and exposed the device. Its mechanics were straightforward and its maker hadn't bothered with any other cover than the box in which it had been placed. "There's a time delay on the mechanism. It's doing some sort of countdown now that you've triggered it, but there's no convenient display to show me if we have minutes or seconds or anything. I'm working to disarm but I need you to get out in case I don't defuse this in time."

"No."

He'd been expecting her to say something else, so it took him a precious second to absorb what she'd said. "You're kidding."

He couldn't spare the time for an argument with her, so he kept his mind on his work. He stared at the mechanism, taking in every detail he could and considering how it contributed to the overall setup of the device. It wasn't about recognizing a bomb. Every maker put his own special touch on an IED, and the making of them constantly evolved. He needed to apply knowledge accumulated from learning a variety of techniques and seeing them over the years. It helped that he'd survived to apply what he'd learned.

"Can I evacuate them?" Her question angered him because

it meant she was still with him, inside the likely blast radius and in danger.

Staying near her had been a game before, good intentions and clearing his conscience, but now she was remaining with him—with all of them—because she was that damned good a person. The risk didn't make sense in any normal person's head and her virtue made him livid. "Not until I defuse this one and verify there isn't a secondary device set to catch them on the way out. There could be another trigger somewhere. You can look for one. Or there could be a hostile outside, watching from a distance, ready with a manual trigger to set this off as soon as he sees us trying to run out of this container. As long as we're in here, anyone watching will think we haven't discovered it yet. They'll wait to trigger the trap."

"But if you don't disarm this, won't we be screwed anyway?" She was being very sensible considering the situation, projecting a steadiness he admired.

He'd seen plenty of soldiers who could manage gunfire and hand-to-hand combat fine, but in the face of a bomb they'd lost it. They'd bolted or tripped themselves up and set off other IEDs. The trick to surviving this type of situation was to remain capable of thinking clearly, move with purpose, and be extremely lucky. She had the first two qualities. He was hoping his history of luck would be enough for all of them.

"This is why I told you to get out." He wanted her to back away, get to a reasonably safe distance. He wanted her safe. "You're on the other side of the primary trip wire. You could step out and make it look like you and your dog are doing another sweep of the area."

If someone was watching them, there was a chance they'd wait to see what she was up to. They might let her walk away. Or they might take a shot at her, but those were still better odds than her staying in here.

"I won't leave these people. I just told them I'd get them to safety." The woman was unflappable.

The mood shifted inside the container. They were listening and with her last statement, there was a collective sigh released as if they'd all been holding their breaths. Someone might have whispered thanks to some deity.

They should thank her.

He didn't argue further. If she left at this point, they'd just bolt after her. It was her they were listening to, her they'd follow. She was their beacon.

Instead of fighting her, he worked as quickly as he could. It was complex work and was never as easy as picking a certain colored wire. Seconds or minutes might have passed; he had stopped keeping track. He only worked as quickly and carefully as he could.

Finally, he drew a deep breath. "This one is clear. Everyone stay calm. Stay where you are. Try to keep as still as possible."

Arin repeated his directions.

He swept the container for any other signs of devices as everyone watched, their fear stretched taut in the air around them all.

Finally, he turned and met her gaze. If she was afraid, he couldn't see it in her dark brown eyes. She was rock solid and waiting.

"We're clear. Let's get the hell out."

CHAPTER EIGHT

Arin took a steadying breath as she slid into the driver's seat. Adrenaline had long since left her system, but she was still hyper aware and wound up. Just a few yards away, lights flashed from the police and ambulance units that'd pulled into the parking lot an hour ago. Raul and his canine partner, Taz, stood with the lead detectives sorting out the situation as paramedics saw to the newly freed people from the shipping container. She had King in the back and the all-clear to head out, but she needed a minute to find her calm before she started driving.

Jason opened the passenger side door and climbed into the seat with a similar sigh.

She shot him a look. "Are you okay?"

Actually, she wondered what he was still doing here. She'd half expected him to slip away in the fuss as the various teams had arrived on the scene. He'd accomplished what he'd come to do and he'd proven he hadn't been a part of a distraction or ambush waiting to happen.

He turned to her and raised an eyebrow. "Are you? Okay?"

He didn't say it in the bantering tone he'd been using before they'd walked into the shipyard. His tone was somber, serious.

Her gut tightened and she responded cautiously. "It's easier when I can take action in a situation."

Jason nodded. "It's tough, having to hold position and wait for the outcome of what someone else is doing. Being near an IED and keeping your shit together is not for the weak of heart. You were solid and you kept those people calm, too."

She looked away as heat rushed over her face. Compliments made her feel awkward. She took pride in doing her job and doing it well, but he was implying an impact on people. She didn't consider herself particularly strong when it came to people skills. Normally, she'd have left the conversation there. She wasn't big on sharing. But tension ran through the set of his shoulders and the upright way he was sitting. His hands were splayed over the tops of his thighs like he was trying not to let them ball into fists.

"I'm not satisfied." There. She wasn't sure why she said it, but it was giving voice to a feeling she'd thought would go away when she'd completed this mission.

"No." Everything she felt was echoed in Jason's voice. "I thought I would be when this was done. Case closed, time to move on. But the look on those people's faces…"

She nodded slowly. "It wasn't enough to free them now."

"I wish I'd gotten to them sooner." There was regret in his tone. "I wish I could wrap my hands around the neck of the person responsible for all this."

His words resonated deep inside her chest with the insistent hum she felt beneath her sternum. It was a need to take action. "I want this new boss."

"Get in line." His voice had darkened, turned grim.

It was an admirable sentiment, but she considered his chances alone. If she got in line behind him, she'd be stepping over his body to get to the man they both wanted.

"I'm about to start driving." She wasn't sure what she expected. Honestly, she was curious as to what he'd do. If he got out of the car, he was likely going to go his own way and there was no knowing if they'd cross paths again. She didn't really want that, but she couldn't think of a reason to ask him to come with her.

He froze for a long moment, even his breathing stopped as he stared out the window at the people they'd helped make safe. "So drive."

He was coming with her. Okay, then. The team didn't need her for the rest of the night or until it was time to debrief back at headquarters. There was time to investigate this pebble of an idea knocking around between them. She put the vehicle into drive and pulled out of the parking lot.

It was more than an hour before he said anything again.

"So what's next?"

Arin stilled behind the steering wheel. She pulled into the parking lot of her destination as she considered the answer. Maybe his question was more about their new location than the status of him being with her and King. She didn't have much of a sample size of conversation to go on to justify her hunch but he'd been tense the whole way. The scowl he'd been wearing on his face didn't seem to be a natural expression for him. She, on the other hand, could have a seriously nasty resting bitch face.

"Talk to me about why you're still here." A lot depended on his answer. She needed to determine how his intentions might align with the goals of either her team or the Hawaiian task force. Otherwise, there wasn't a real way to include him in their activities officially.

He didn't answer right away. When he did, there was reluctance in his voice. "I'm still figuring it out as I go. I'm not generally inclined to think hard about why I do what I do."

She waited. He could share or he could go on his way in the morning. She thought he was astute enough to know it.

"I know what it's like." He stared straight ahead as he spoke. "Not as bad as these people, but enough to have more of an understanding than most would of why they took the risk to find a better life for themselves. My world turned upside-down in my early teens and financial stability? Hah. My parents were scrambling to manage any kind of food and shelter. I had to leave if I wanted to make a life for myself because I was never going to get back the childhood I remembered."

"A lot of people leave home that way." She winced when she thought about the words. Too late. It'd come out sounding brusque, and she didn't want to make less of the courage it took to strike out on his own.

He only shrugged and gave her a half grin. "True. That might be what's bothering me right now. I left. They left. What happened to them could've happened to me. I went out into the world and I lucked out. I either found and earned opportunities or someone gave me a chance. A lot more doors opened to me because I spoke with a level of education and because of the color of my skin, but some of those doors could've been traps and I was fortunate they weren't. Those people, someone preyed on them. It goes beyond pissing me off."

His voice had dropped to a low growl with his last statement.

She nodded. The feeling was familiar. His motives for wanting to go after this new boss were clear. She was certain he could be helpful to the team, too. But they were both short on rest and she needed to get back to Oahu in the morning to debrief.

"For tonight, we're going to check in to this bed-and-breakfast." Best to share the most immediate next steps with him for now and not what she hoped would work out once she talked to Zu and Raul. Honestly, she was taking things one step at a time from here on out anyway. She needed time to process his actions back at the harbor. He'd made good on his word, but now she had a whole new set of questions.

Yes, they wanted this new player, the man who'd taken over the human trafficking ring, but they knew next to nothing about this new target. A new boss meant new plans and some reorganization, with reset business goals. She wanted to find out who this man was and delve deeper into what Jason might know about him.

She turned off the engine and pulled the keys, hopping out the driver side. He followed her example and exited the vehicle, meeting her at the back of the car and watching as she let King out.

"So did you already have a reservation here?" He seemed to change gears in conversation easily. Maybe he was happy to leave the personal discussion behind. She would be.

She shrugged. When she was on a mission, especially solo, she tended to set up multiple bolt-holes. When she was on her home island of Oahu, she didn't stay at her own home if a mission was going to take more than a day. There were limited choices on any island, even here on the largest in Hawaii, so she tried not to stay at the same places too often. Since she had joined Search and Protect, she hadn't had that many missions directly in the Hawaiian Islands until the team had begun working with the Hawaiian task force going after human trafficking.

Zu had chosen Hawaii as a base of operations for Search

and Protect to take on both domestic missions on the mainland and missions overseas, particularly in East Asia or Australia and New Zealand.

The current initiative was really spearheaded by Raul in his role as liaison to the Hawaiian task force. This time she'd been brought on as a supporting resource. Her caution in setting up multiple locales might have been born of old practices, but Zu hadn't ever asked her to change her habits. Her flexibility in being able to operate as part of the team or go solo—and in being able to change gears from one moment to the next depending on the circumstances—was one of her strengths.

Jason didn't press her for more information on where they were. Instead, he fell in next to her as she and King walked toward the main entrance. He hadn't visibly wrestled with any reactions or shown any signs of added irritation, but he wasn't relaxing either.

Fine. She missed the joking and teasing earlier. No way was she going to admit it out loud, but it'd been an odd kind of fun.

He continued to play a follower as she checked in and headed up to the room. It was almost dawn but they'd both need rest before they caught a flight later in the day to get back to Oahu. It'd been almost twenty-four hours since she'd found him and it felt like days. She put the key in the door lock and glanced up at him, serious expression still in place, and caught him wiggling his eyebrows at her.

She couldn't help it. She chuckled.

She opened the door and sent King ahead to clear the room with a murmured command. Jason remained just inside the door as she and King completed their sweep.

"Clear."

"Do I not have a room of my own because you didn't

have time to make reservations for two separate rooms?" He leaned back against the door frame, crossing his arms over his chest. Muscles in his biceps and forearms flexed, and her mind blanked for a moment out of sheer admiration.

She lifted one corner of her mouth. "I'm not footing the bill for your accommodations."

Most of the reservations she'd made would go on for another few days, simulating a stay for a different length of time than she'd be on the island. It was her standard practice on travel. If it was longer than her actual stay, it was an expensive precaution, but one she'd found worth the investment several times over. Initial information searches would try to locate where she'd been based on when they thought she'd arrived and left. Nowadays, it was easy to check in or out remotely.

He huffed out a short laugh. "I'm not going to assume this is an invitation. What patch of floor do you want me to take?"

She gave him a full smile this time. Too many people in their business did make a large number of unwise assumptions, or they didn't care to wait for invitations. "You don't want to stay up and watch the sun rise?"

He shrugged. "Since you didn't blindfold me on this ride—and I appreciate that—I can say for certain that we're still on the west side of the island. There's not going to be a great place to watch the sunrise over any of the nearby beaches. I'm also going to take a shot in the dark and say you wouldn't bother with checking in to any kind of room for the night if all you planned to do was watch the sunrise. This is Hawaii. Plenty of people just park their car at some beach and doze until the sun comes up."

"True." Ah, hell. She wasn't going to sleep until she understood more about why he'd gotten back into her car.

He was an experienced professional in the private security field. If he'd wanted to go after this new boss on Oahu, Jason could've tried to do it solo. He might have contacts in the industry who owed him favors and would come to the islands to help him if he made it a personal quest. But he hadn't. He'd stayed with her and she wanted to know why. She was also tired of standing, so she sat on the edge of the bed. Unfortunately, this new room didn't have a convenient armchair for him to sit in while they continued their back and forth commentary. "Look. I'm good at light conversation and detailed debriefs. I'm not good at real conversation where I just blurt out what I'm thinking because it invariably comes out sounding wrong either in phrasing or tone. And yes, I've thought about the way it happens a lot. I'm short on sleep and I never had many filters in the first place. I've got more questions for you."

He stared at her across the few feet from where he still leaned against the door frame and she sat on the bed. The distance closed without him moving an inch. He just dropped his arms and hooked his thumbs into his pants pockets. "Ask. I won't lie, but I won't promise I'll answer you either."

King looked at each of them, big ears swiveling in minute adjustments as the dog considered them both. After another moment, her partner settled for lying down on the floor at her feet with his black and tan body placed definitively between her and Jason. Obviously, King was in for the conversation but didn't have the energy to remain at attention without a command either. But the dog was relaxed. He sensed no tension or immediate action from Jason.

"You originally indicated you were here on the Big Island because you wanted to help in some way before you left.

You did. Why are you still with me?" Well, that was question number one out of the way.

"That's a complicated answer." Jason drew the statement out, probably to buy himself more time to think.

"Fine." Maybe her tone was getting sharper but she pushed forward and asked her second question. Giving someone time to think was giving them room to lie, or at least give you the answer they thought you wanted to hear. "What was your problem on the car ride here?"

His eyes widened and his mouth dropped open briefly before he shut it again, his jaw tightening. "My problem?"

She almost crossed her arms over her own chest but resisted the impulse. If he was going to stay open to conversation, so was she. Maintaining body language was easy, trying not to be defensive at all was harder. "I recognize the silent treatment when I get it. What are we, twelve?"

He laughed in her face.

She hated when people laughed at her. It was one of the things that got under her skin in ways she couldn't manage to ignore.

"Okay, you said no filters. Same here. I'm too damned tired to think through my response so let's at least agree not to come to blows if what's about to come out of my mouth insults you. Agreed?"

She was already fighting down the urge to close the physical distance and throw a punch at him, but she wanted to know what he had to say. "Fine."

"Answer to both questions is you."

Nope. No matter how surprised she was, she was not going to show it. He could be baiting her to see if he could win her over by flattery. If his motivation was revenge for her part in the takedown of the plantation months ago, he'd have done something earlier in the day. It didn't make sense for him to have waited until now. So it had to be something else. She was going to wait for him to clarify.

He didn't keep her waiting long. "Yeah. I came here because I wanted to do some good to even out the awful. I contributed to the hell these people are living and I don't like it. But I wouldn't have known about it without meeting you, or at least I didn't know about it until I met you. I've spent months looking for more information about the business they were running, the high-level players, and you."

She wasn't a high-stakes player in this game. If he thought she was, he sucked at gathering intel. But his tone didn't indicate he was making that assumption. Instead, he was here, looking at her and the intensity in his gaze was... hungry. Heat rushed across the surface of her skin, everywhere, in response.

He lifted a hand and dragged his fingers through his hair. "I remembered your face. I didn't dig too deep in my research because I wanted to meet you and find out about you directly from you. Once I found intel on you, I looked for every image I could get my hands on to be sure I'd found the right person. Last thing I wanted to do was introduce myself to the wrong woman. Pictures don't do you justice. There's nothing I found that could stand up to my memory of you in motion. Yeah, I came here to help those people, but I was also hoping I'd find you again."

* * *

There it was, out in the open. If they'd worked in any other career, his actions could've been considered stalking. Who was he kidding? No matter how professional the approach, running background searches and pulling up intelligence on any person was a type of stalking. She could kick him out immediately, or she could beat him to within an inch of his life, then eject him from her presence. He'd gotten a read on her—seen her in action—even back at the hospital, and she didn't shoot to kill if she had a choice. She was very effective at incapacitating her targets, so he didn't think she would kill him for looking for her.

Of course, if she decided to, he might not hold it against her.

She stared at him, her dark brown eyes serious. "Me."

"I'm sorry." He wouldn't insult her with anything less than a sincere apology. "Meeting you the one time stuck in my head. I got more than curious about you. I wanted to meet you again."

Now he had, and he'd seen her take the lead in a combat situation at the hospital, then again searching for those captives at the harbor. In each situation, he'd been drawn to her confidence. He liked intelligent, capable people in general. Pack those qualities into an amazing body like hers, and he was hooked.

Her lashes came down and then she opened her eyes again, her gaze somehow softened an infinitesimal amount. "I ran queries on you, too."

The statement coming from anyone else might not have meant what he hoped. It could've been an acknowledgment between two professionals of precautions any of them took when they came in contact with a new player. The more you knew about possible threats, the longer you stayed alive. But this was Arin and her tone—her body posture, the heat in the way she was looking at him—said more.

"We're not on opposite sides." He made the statement quietly. She was a smart operative and trust didn't come easily with any of them.

After a long moment, she spoke, "Tomorrow, we'll head

back to Oahu. There'll be a debrief at my headquarters and I'll propose going after this new boss. You want to come with me?"

"Yes." Definitely. A thrill ran through him at the thought of going after bigger quarry. It had taken something out of him to see those captives traumatized and afraid. "Rescuing those people, it was a good thing. I'm glad I was there. But I'm still pissed as hell and I want the person responsible for so much suffering."

"Ditto." She cracked a smile then, a fierce one.

He stared.

"What?" Suspicion crept into her gaze.

He didn't want that, so he blurted out what he was thinking. "You're beautiful."

"You're kidding." Now there was a spark of temper, too.

Oh no. He was going to be clear here. "I'm not. No mind games. I just sincerely looked at you at that second and I wasn't thinking anything else. Just that you are beautiful. True story."

Her cheeks flushed an amazing shade of dusky rose.

She stood and snapped her fingers. King scrambled to his feet, surprised, and she sent him into the bathroom with a whispered command. She closed the bathroom door, then walked back to Jason. She had his absolute attention. "In this moment, tonight, I believe you."

He got her. Tomorrow or a week from now or years from now could be a completely different scenario. He wasn't about to ask if she chose these kinds of liaisons often and he was pretty sure she didn't care if he did either. It didn't matter because this was about to get amazing.

He waited. She was in the lead here, and he did not want to misinterpret what they were doing, not in any way.

She stared up into his eyes, some decision made. He

wanted dearly to know what she was thinking but he was also drunk on her proximity. It took all of his self-control not to reach the bare inches between them to pull her against him. Still, she held back.

"No strings, no complications," she whispered. "Just this now and when we're done, that's it. One time."

He didn't trust himself with words so he nodded. He wanted her, badly, and he'd enjoyed his share of one-night hookups but he was sure this, she, was going to blow his mind. He wasn't going to mess this up.

She rose up on the balls of her feet, leaning her hands on his chest, and touched her mouth to his. Just the brush of her lips set him on fire. He opened for her and she tilted her head as they both took their kiss deeper, their tongues touching and exploring. A small sound of approval came from the back of her throat and she moved closer, the soft curve of her breasts pressing against his chest.

He let his iron control slip a little and placed his hands on her hips, easing back to tease her with light kisses for a minute until she practically growled at him. Chuckling, because he wanted her to ask for more, he slid his hands around to the small of her back and finally pulled her body in close against his. He wanted to crush her against him, slam her against a wall, and do everything she asked for and more because he was sure she could match him and clash with him and match him again. But she hadn't asked yet. So he went slow, excruciating for him, because he was determined to savor every moment she gave him. He ducked his head and kissed her neck in the place just above her shoulder, paused, then very gently pressed his teeth against her skin.

Her hands fisted in his T-shirt and she arched her back. "Harder."

He bit her just hard enough to mark, not break skin.

She let go of his shirt and lifted her hands to either side of his face, kissing him hard. He kissed her back, fierce and hungry. He shifted his hands down to cup her firm behind, lifting. She responded by setting her arms around his neck and wrapping her legs around his waist, giving him her weight.

He moved forward until his knees hit the side of the bed, kissing her the entire way, and let them both fall onto the bed. When he reared back out of her arms, she protested and he grinned. He coasted his hands from her thighs up her sides and cupped her breasts. She lay back and arched into his hands until he squeezed. They both made noises of pleasure then and she put her hands on his wrists, urging his hands lower.

She helped him unbutton her pants and gave him a look saucy enough to stop his heart as she wiggled out of them. He bent to kiss the black satin and lace of her panties reverently. He was definitely going to make the most of this, if it was going to be a one-time thing, and he'd do his best to make sure she remembered it with a smile, too.

He slid his lips over the edge of her panties and pressed his thumb against her center, gently moving in small circles until the satin went wet. It took no time.

"Now." She lifted her hips.

"Not yet." But he did take the hint and pulled her panties down and off, discarding them somewhere over the edge of the bed.

She might have growled at him, or the closest a human could come to growling, and the sound turned him on even more if that was possible. He spread her thighs and encouraged her to lift her knees, then he bent to taste her. She jumped as he put his mouth on her.

He froze, hovering over her. "Does it hurt?"

She was panting. "No. It's so good. I'm just...really sensitive."

Oh yes. "I'll be careful."

He didn't promise to be gentle. He licked at her in a hard, long stroke and she threw her head back, a yelp escaping her. But she reached down and buried her fingers in his hair, encouraging him.

Yes, ma'am.

He feasted on her, learning every fold of her most intimate and sensitive places. He licked and sucked, figuring out what would make her buck in his grip and writhe under his touch. She was incredible, strong and gorgeous and vibrant under his hands and mouth and he wasn't sure how much longer he could resist being inside her.

He slid a finger into her and almost lost it as she stretched around him. She was tight.

"Do you want to play more first?" He ground out the question because no matter how strong she was, how much she could take a beating in their line of work, he did not want to hurt her in this.

She tightened around his finger, making a cat-like sound of pleasure. "I'm not willing to wait anymore, Jason. Come inside me, please."

Her last word broke him. She wasn't begging, but she'd asked him sweetly and the contrast with her sharper temper sent him past coherent thought.

He stepped away from her and got out of his own clothes in record speed. He only paused when he realized she was watching him, and he let her get a good look at him from head to toe as he reached into one of the cargo pockets on his pants for a condom. Ready for any situation.

Her gaze dropped to his erection and he felt himself grow bigger than even he thought possible. He had the condom on in a fraction of a second. Then he climbed over her, coaxing her knees apart again. She reached a hand between them, helping to guide him. Once he was at her entrance, he nudged until the tip of him was inside her and she dragged her fingertips hard down his back. She didn't scratch—she was being careful of him too—but she was digging into his flesh in the hottest way.

He pressed into her slow, gritting his teeth as he struggled for control. She felt so good around him, tight and hot. Finally, he was deep inside her, his entire length, and she had her legs wrapped around his waist.

"Ready?" He whispered the question next to her ear and she nodded into his shoulder.

He pressed into her slow and drew back as she gasped. This was so much more than he'd anticipated, and they were both about to lose their minds. He pressed a kiss against her temple, then he slid into her again. Then again, harder and harder as she matched him. She ran her hands over his torso and back, nipped his shoulder as he thrust into her. Their shared rhythm picked up speed until they both crested in mingled shouts.

Minutes later, they lay entangled on the bed catching their breath. He savored the feel of her in his arms, trying to memorize every moment. This had been insanely good and he wanted to remember it for lonelier times. He was too deep in the feeling of this thing between them and he reached for a lighter mood. "Am I still sleeping on the floor?"

She laughed, cuddling into his chest. He really liked that she cuddled. "No, but we both need to wash up and let King out of the bathroom."

He lifted his head so he could look into her face. "Round two in the shower?"

CHAPTER NINE

Arin positioned herself to have simultaneous line of sight on approaches into the Search and Protect office space and out the window to the small courtyard downstairs. Most of the Search and Protect office space was defined by floor-to-ceiling ballistic glass walls, which made her current situation easier. Internally, stylish graphic patterns printed on the glass provided a modicum of privacy for the offices while still allowing for judicious visibility at certain heights in case of an incursion. The effect was sleek and professional, very corporate yet practical for the defense-minded. Each of the Search and Protect team members had an office, even if they spent most of their time away on missions. Pua, their communications specialist, was the only one of them that came in every day.

The exterior of the building was harder to make secure, though. Just outside the windows was a wall of concrete fashioned into a surprisingly delicate latticework. It kept the office building from looking boring and also served as a kind of sunscreen so the hot tropical sunlight didn't bake the interior. People inside could still see out the windows, but the latticework created a partially obstructed view of the courtyard at just about any angle.

Fortunately, Jason was being smart and remained seated on the bench in the shaded corner where she'd left him before coming upstairs. They hadn't been tailed on the way from Honolulu International Airport and the courtyard was reasonably secure. She'd chosen the spot because it wasn't completely exposed but still viewable from where she was standing. She was less worried about him being vulnerable and more curious about whether this was the moment he'd choose to disappear. Sure, he'd said he wanted to come with her and join any effort to go after the new person in charge of the human trafficking ring. But now she'd learn whether he was the type to change his mind once he'd had time to cool off. If Raul would stop ranting at her for more than a minute, she'd tell her teammate about Jason.

"Why didn't you withdraw from Kawaihae Harbor and wait for an EOD unit? You and King are search and rescue, not explosive ordnance disposal." Raul was still on a roll, pacing as he spoke. He wasn't the type to yell, but his voice had dropped at least an octave, and he definitely had a whole lot of emotion packed into his tone. He'd been worried about her and she appreciated it, even regretted it. So she'd been letting him vent while they waited for Zu to arrive from another meeting to begin the formal debrief. "We both know bombs aren't in your past experience skill set, either. King isn't even an explosives detection canine."

Raul had a point. Their dogs were amazing in the range of their training and abilities, but they couldn't do everything. Neither she nor King were explosives specialists. "Those people would've tried to run if I'd left them. They wouldn't have believed me about the explosives and they'd have taken the risk, hoping for a bluff. They'd all be dead and the container terminal at Kawaihae would've taken some serious damage."

Raul stopped in his tracks and glared at her.

She lifted a shoulder and let it drop. "The task force you're assigned to has strong political backing from the state of Hawaii and some funding, but it's not well enough funded to absorb that kind of cost."

Raul scowled. "Since when do you care about budget? Pua sent me the invoices for the rooms you reserved on Big Island. Did you have to reserve three different places?"

She'd have been amused but she and Raul were both used to directing conversation. They might've backed off the more sensitive topic for the moment to regain steadier ground, but he was still after something from her and it wasn't a debrief. The time for that would be when Zu arrived at the Search and Protect offices after his other meeting. For now, it was just Raul working off the worry he'd carried through the night.

Raul cared about people and expressed it. He was good people.

"All three places have a policy to only charge for the first night if I'm a no show." She kept her words light but she couldn't quite manage a reassuring smile. Old habits were hard to let go, especially when they'd kept her alive in darker times.

"No one is trying to kill you anymore." Raul made the statement gently, but his gaze was direct and his jaw set in a hard line. "Those missions are done, and the people involved who might be carrying a grudge? They're dead. You walked away from all that."

She'd left a trail of corpses in her wake. It all seemed like a story from some thriller, and their conversation sounded like something out of a movie.

Restless, she dropped her hand to her side and King stood from where he'd been lying at her feet to push his muzzle into her palm. She'd spent years working freelance without a canine partner. It was wonderful to be able to trust unconditionally again.

"I reserved the rooms just in case because I was uneasy when we were planning the mission," she admitted, then she shook her head quickly. "As it turns out, it's a good thing I did. I used two of those places."

"Where is our new friend, by the way?" Raul's tone was light but his gaze was sharp.

"Right where I can see him." She tipped her head to indicate her view of Jason, still sitting in the courtyard.

Raul sighed. "What would we do if someone took a shot at him right now?"

"I don't think they're actively hunting him at the moment." She reached up and tugged a lock of her own hair as she shared what she'd been thinking. "They were tying up loose ends on the Big Island. He'd been knocked out at the scene and they came after him at the hospital. But if they were looking for him after that, they didn't find us while we were in hiding and they didn't leave guards at the shipyard either. Maybe they didn't think he'd come looking again after he'd been left for dead the first time."

Or maybe they thought he was likely to leave the island posthaste, happy to have survived both getting knocked out and the hospital incident. Question was, did his former teammates really know him? Was she getting to know the real him?

"Okay, so he's not at risk at the moment." Raul was ready to move on. "And the IED at the harbor was impersonal, meant to destroy evidence if the container was discovered before they could move their assets off the island."

She nodded. "If we hadn't disturbed it, there would've been no danger. It was my fault we started the timer."

Raul joined her by the window, looking down at Jason. "And he disarmed it. What are the chances?"

"I thought about that, too." Hell, she was still thinking about it. It was a possibility, even after what she and Jason had shared, that it was all an act. She didn't think so, or at least she hoped not, but she'd be stupid not to consider it. "Explosive ordnance disposal isn't that uncommon, though. It's a valuable skill set in the private sector. It just takes a special kind of crazy."

Raul sighed. "The last thing we need in Search and Protect is more crazy."

"We're all our own special kind of crazy, though." This time she let herself be a little wistful as she spoke. "It's a prerequisite to fit into the team."

"But you weren't working with the team last night, Arin." Raul craned his neck to get into her line of sight, despite her still looking out the window. "What I'm worried about is whether that IED is a signature precaution we're going to see in the future as we go after more shipments full of people. It means we'll need bomb squads. You and King need to stop rushing in on your own."

"We weren't alone." She'd been giving Jason a chance. Whether he'd taken the chance to take her out or disappear, she'd have been less surprised than what he'd actually done. "He did prove more helpful than I'd expected."

When it came to most people she encountered in the world, she tended to keep her expectations low. He'd exceeded her expectations and maybe won a bit of her trust. Now, he was more dangerous because she wouldn't just be learning something new about him if he turned out to be playing her; she could end up dead.

"You didn't have to go to the harbor to test him or to get any more information out of him than you already had." Raul's words brought her back from her internal confession. "Don't use this guy as a distraction tactic. What were you there to do?"

Raul already suspected the answer. He needed confirmation. As a friend, and he was her friend, she owed him at least that. "I made a promise to Kim. I was looking for her brother. I didn't want to come back here and tell her we were close and lost him."

"Kim." Raul sounded lost. "A woman I met during that undercover investigation in the massage parlor. Since when did you make friends with her?"

It hadn't been just a massage parlor. It'd been one of the fronts for the human trafficking ring under the old manager. Women had been forced to work there, giving massages and sexual favors to clients. Raul and Zu had gone in undercover to find out more about the operation and potentially where a group of kidnapped scientists were being held. After the Search and Protect team had literally blown up a portion of the human trafficking ring headquarters, local authorities had raided the massage parlor, too, based on the evidence Raul and Zu had provided. Since then, the research program Mali worked for had converted it into a legitimate massage therapy business.

Arin shot him a glare, then resumed watching Jason. "Mali and I go in once in a while. Kim's happy to have gotten certified as an actual massage therapist and not having to provide side services. She asked me to look for her brother and I promised her I would."

The weight of Raul's stare was almost tangible on her skin. "It's not like you to make promises to acquaintances."

She didn't answer him.

"Mali knows you can keep a promise, Arin."

She shook her head. "No, she doesn't. She thinks promises are those light things everyone makes to everyone else and as long as there's a good reason, promises can be broken. But there aren't good enough reasons in the world for me leaving her when I promised I'd always be there."

"You were kids."

"We're not now. And the promises I make are much more serious." Finally, she turned her gaze to Raul and let him see how dedicated she was to this, because anything having to do with her sister meant everything to her. "I made the promise in front of Mali and I kept it. I found Kim's little brother for her and damn it, I wasn't going to let him blow up after all that."

Raul opened his mouth, closed it, then started again. "Okay. Mission accomplished. I get what you were trying to prove to Mali and I'm not sure she gets it, but that's between you two. What are you doing with him now?"

Well, there was what she'd *done* with Jason. That wasn't happening again no matter how much the memories had tried to pop up at the most random moments throughout the morning. But she had no idea what would come next. She kept expecting him to leave and he hadn't.

She shook her head. "I don't know."

* * *

Jason sat in the courtyard, watching Arin's shadow in the window. At least he was pretty sure it was her. The bright daylight outside and the concrete framework made it hard to see into the windows from the ground. It was a smart design for an office building and a good choice for a private contract organization like Search and Protect. Good security started with basic considerations in architecture and layout. It was enough to deter the casual observer or amateur investigator.

Still, he had a good idea of which floor the Search and Protect offices were on and she'd worn a light yellow shirt into the office this morning. The silhouette in the window had been there a while and seemed to be wearing yellow.

He had a duffel with gear and clothes back on the Big Island, complete with a small set of binoculars. They'd have come in handy right about now. He'd also look like a creeper out here if anyone saw him using them, but it wouldn't have taken more than a moment to confirm it was Arin he was looking at. Then at least he'd have been able to settle the nervous twitch he had from being left here for who knew how long it'd be.

But his duffel was lost somewhere back near the taro farm on Big Island and he didn't have access to any of his stuff. He didn't like losing the identification and money he'd had in there, but they could be replaced, as could his clothes and gear. For now, though, he was stuck with the tourist T-shirt and canvas pants Arin had bought him at the airport this morning. Great.

He didn't have to wait here. In fact, he'd had every intention of flying back to the mainland once he'd gotten those people out of the taro farm on Big Island. He'd figured a bunch of them showing up at the local police station would've caused a big enough fuss for him to get to the airport and off the island before anyone actively mobilized to look for him. Nothing had gone the way he'd envisioned. All things considered, he was lucky to be alive.

He glanced up at the window yet again, then scanned the courtyard and all potential entries to the area. He probably wouldn't be alive if it hadn't been for Arin and her team.

She had some uncanny timing when it came to life-changing moments.

Besides, he couldn't get her out of his mind. His palms heated as he remembered the impossible softness of her skin under his hands. Her pleased sighs whispered through his mind. It had been a one-night thing, a glorious encounter. He'd guessed they'd be good together. Hell, he'd entertained more than a few fantasies in the months before they'd run into each other again. But being with her had been beyond good, and any fantasies paled in contrast to the vivid reality of her.

So yeah, he was glad to have the chance to go after this new boss at the head of the human trafficking ring. He also wasn't ready to leave when he'd only just gotten to know her. Everything about Arin Siri made him curious. Physically, she was amazing to be with, both in bed and in action. Her confidence was inspiring, born of years of experience and excellent competence. She had a contrary streak and a quick temper. He'd learned those things in the space of a day or so. How much more would he discover about her if he stuck around for one more day? It'd be worth it to find out.

A shadow shifted near one of the corner entrances to the courtyard and Jason frowned. "Been looking for me long, Moz?"

The other man stayed back in the breezeway area, approaching only close enough to have a talk without either of them raising their voices above a conversational volume. "Nah. We've had eyes on this place since they hit the taro farm on Big Island. Heard you were here and came out to have a talk. Our new client doesn't like the way these people have been making problems for him. What's this company called? Lost and Found? Suits you."

Jason chuckled, remaining as outwardly relaxed as possible. Still, he kept watch for more ex-teammates at the other entrances and in the windows of the buildings creating the courtyard. He didn't think his old contract organization still wanted to eliminate him; otherwise Moz wouldn't have confronted him directly. They'd just make the hit and leave the premises. "Clever. Have you been waiting to say that to me? Next up is a crack about lost and found being where unwanted things get left, isn't it?"

"Relax, man. If you were supposed to be dead, you would be. No one is paying us for the hit, so you get to stay alive. This time, you're the messenger." Moz held up a photo between his middle and forefingers, then tossed it at Jason's feet. "This is our next target if the Search and Protect team doesn't back off. You let your new lady friend know. Maybe she'll believe you don't have anything to do with it, but I wouldn't risk it if I were you. She's frigid, from what I hear. It'd be better if you delivered the message and left."

Jason left the photo where it was. Instead, he kept his gaze steadily locked with Moz's. The other man had a lighter build and thinner face, with eyes set far back into the hollows of his skull. As Jason continued to stare, Moz paled. Jason let his lips spread in a wide, mirthless grin. "I'm not afraid to pass on the message. But whether I leave or stay, you might not want to meet me in the middle of a mission. We're not on the same team anymore."

Considering Moz's choice to stay, because the money was better than being a fucking human being, Jason doubted he'd ever be on the same team as Moz again. Jason made it a personal policy not to say never, of course. But it was extremely unlikely.

"Whatever." Moz backed away too quickly for it to be anything but a retreat. "Make sure the bitch gets this pic."

Jason waited a solid count of ten after Moz had gone and

the courtyard was quiet again before he bent to retrieve the picture. He lifted it gingerly, making sure to handle it by the edges. They might need forensic evidence from the photo or something. He had no idea, but he sure as hell didn't want to mishandle anything. Once he got a good look at the picture, he scowled. This was not going to go well.

The person in the picture was a woman, maybe in her late twenties. She had golden skin toasted by long hours in the sun and a sweet smile highlighting a round face with dark eyes. In the background, Arin stood in the shade of a tree with her dog looking at the main subject of the photo with the softest expression of caring he'd ever seen from the normally sharp-tempered woman. This was a recent photo, presumably taken with a telephoto lens if Arin hadn't spotted the photographer and King hadn't alerted them either. The woman featured front and center in the picture was her little sister.

Mali Siri was a target again.

CHAPTER TEN

Arin emerged from the building in the breezeway, scanning the area in an arc from the parking lots on one end to the courtyard where Jason still sat waiting. She hadn't seen anyone else from her vantage point, but his posture had changed a few minutes ago. Then he'd started talking to someone. It'd taken a minute or two for her to reach the elevator and get to the ground floor. Whoever it was seemed to have left before she'd gotten outside.

She paused in the breezeway for a moment, wondering if she'd made a mistake in her split-second decision to leave King upstairs. Her canine partner was an extension of her, but she didn't like to become too reliant on him. They would be an even more skilled pair if she continued to challenge her own situational awareness, rather than allowing his to become a crutch for her. Besides, this was a brief check. She didn't expect to engage in an actual altercation. For all she knew, someone had brought their dog to the office and taken it downstairs to relieve itself in the courtyard, pausing to talk to Jason.

Instead of going directly to him, she lingered and extended her senses. She listened for footsteps, voices in conversation outside the normal cadence of lunchtime chatter or sounds that didn't belong. She also paid attention to any odd silences, checking for the absence of birdcalls and songs in the presence of a predator. The scents of plumeria and tuberose filled the air from the courtyard, but there were no odd hints of smoke or gunpowder. If there'd been someone strange here, she couldn't catch a hint of whoever it was.

So she walked down the breezeway and into the courtyard, taking her time so she could continue to take in every available visual. Jason remained where she'd left him, outwardly relaxed with his hands resting on the tops of his thighs.

Her heart rate kicked up as she looked at him. He appeared to be just fine, no signs of injuries, not even a rumpled shirt or mussed hair to hint at any kind of scuffle with anyone. In fact, his hair was the perfect kind of stylishly disheveled she liked to run her fingers through. He gave every appearance of a man taking advantage of the peaceful courtyard for a quiet break. She wasn't sure why she'd been worried about him.

His gaze rose to meet hers as she approached and locked on with an almost tangible impact for a full second before breaking contact. She had to force herself to maintain her awareness of their peripheral space as she continued toward him instead of continuing to stare at only him. At a distance, he was a striking figure. Close up, he was breathtaking. But his expression remained bland. This was new and she wondered what was behind the carefully neutral look on his face.

"I had a visitor just now." He didn't waste any time, but he kept his voice low and pleasant, as if he was just telling her about some random, friendly thing. "An old teammate decided to drop by and pay me a visit."

She came to a stop outside of arm's reach and within the shelter of an office building so she wouldn't be as visible to anyone looking down into the courtyard. Jason's visitor had to have done the same. "Interesting. How did your friend know how to find you?"

"He wasn't a friend." Jason delivered the clarification with a chillingly nice tone.

Ah, she should take note. She really liked the effect his tone had and would try to strike a similar note in a future conversation. She kept her own voice sweet. "Question still stands."

Jason tapped the edge of what looked like a photograph against the top of his knee. "It was more of a coincidence. They're keeping watch on the office building because your team has been actively clashing with one of their clients. They spotted me and took advantage of the instance to come have a chat with me."

"Well, you're still alive. Not that I'm disappointed or anything, but why did they not try to kill you? Or are you here because you're still working with them and they want you here?" She could dance around an obvious point with the best of them but she preferred to put things out there and handle them directly. And she was not alarmed over his well-being. Not at all.

Liar. She'd just rushed down here why? Because something had been off, amiss, not right. She hadn't known what it was, but it'd been concern for him that'd rushed her.

He didn't need to know all that. Not yet.

He stopped sweeping the courtyard and met her gaze for a long moment. "I'm here because I want to be. We can talk about why again if you want, but there's a more urgent issue.

I am not here to sabotage you and I am not trying to infiltrate to learn some piece of information. I really did leave my prior contract and I am a free agent. Right now, I have some intel that's of real value to you and I want to help. What'll it be? Are you going to trust me enough to bring me in, sit down, and address the situation I've got to tell you about, or are you going to shut me out? If it's the second option, I'll leave. No hard feelings."

His gaze held hers and the connection sizzled. She parted her lips to sip cool air in through her mouth, wishing for the hot pressure of his lips on hers. Every fiber of her being was responding to him, and not in a strictly business kind of way. This was a tightly focused, serious facet of him, and she was caught up in the urgency he projected. It wasn't panic; it was a need for immediate, decisive action.

That, she could do. She shoved thoughts of kissing way to the back of her mind before she let on to him how much she wanted more of him. "Come with me."

She took him into the building and up the elevator. He said nothing along the way, keeping the photograph facing away from her. When they exited the elevator, she patted him down before they entered the Search and Protect headquarters. He didn't protest. It might've been uncalled for but he had admitted to meeting with one of his former teammates and she hadn't been keeping eyes on him every second. It was a real possibility that he had acquired a firearm, and she wouldn't be responsible for letting him into their offices with one.

"My office is over here." She gestured to one side and King was visible in the doorway like a confirmation of her statement. She'd left him on a command to stay, anticipating she'd only be gone a few minutes, so he was exactly where she'd placed him. At the sight of Jason, King's ears perked in a minute increase of alertness.

Jason didn't respond, only entered her office and waited, standing in front of her desk. His presence filled the small space and she tried not to acknowledge how very aware of him she was. It was a combination of his intensity and the physical attraction she still had for him. Damn, they'd enjoyed each other last night, and he was still in her system.

She let him wait another minute as she texted Raul to come join her and texted Pua to remain in her office with the door closed. When Raul emerged from his office a door down from hers, Taz at his side, she jerked her head to indicate her space.

She stepped into her office and released King with a murmured command, pausing to give him a brief scratch around the ears as she praised him. Raul and Taz came in behind her, making her usually generous office space a little on the crowded side. The square footage of the room could accommodate them all, but every one of them had a big personality. She opted to lean her hip on the end of her desk rather than sit behind it. She wanted to keep this collaborative; putting a desk between her and Jason wouldn't lend to that.

"Have a seat on the couch if you want." She lifted her chin to indicate the seating. "Or the chairs, but they're not as comfortable."

Jason opted for one of the chairs. Personally, she'd have done the same. People sank into the couch and struggled to climb out of it. The chairs offered an informal seating option without leaving a person floundering to get back to their feet.

Raul sat in the other chair facing her desk. Once all three humans were relatively seated, Taz and King settled at their respective handlers' feet. The two dogs were used to each other and well versed in working together. Even though they had lain down, their heads were up and their ears forward, indicating they were ready if their handler gave a command.

"All right, you're here. This is Raul Sá, one of my teammates." She tended to be concise with introductions and there was no need for Jason to know about Raul's current attachment to the task force put together specifically to combat human trafficking in Hawaii. Jason had been gathering intel on the Search and Protect team, so if he didn't already know the information, he didn't deserve to have it handed to him.

Jason appeared to recognize Raul's name, though. Jason leaned forward and offered a hand. "Good to meet you, I'm Jason Landon."

Raul took the offered hand and gave it a brief shake. "Not sure I can say the same. It seems you've stirred up things here."

Jason didn't take offense. "Looks like. It wasn't my intention, though. My former team is still on contract for private security with the trafficking operation you all blew up. They've got to compensate the client for the breach. In some cases, they take offensive measures to safeguard the interests of their clients."

Arin narrowed her eyes, focusing on the photograph still in his hand. "They want us to back off, so who are they threatening?"

It could be Pua or any of them…

Jason placed the photo on the desk where both she and Raul could see it. "I believe this is Mali Siri, your sister."

Arin didn't see red the way some people did. Instead, the world took on crystalline clarity and a cold calm settled over her as she embraced her growing rage. "I'll kill them first."

* * *

Jason had expected death threats from Arin. He didn't expect to hear the sentiment echoed by her colleague, Raul. Jason was confident Arin wouldn't actually shoot the messenger, but he didn't know Raul well enough.

"Where is Mali now?" It'd be best to get them both focused on actionable tasks so they didn't do anything too decisive or drastic.

"She's actually on her way here." Raul ground out the answer as he pulled out his phone. "She was going to pick me and Taz up for lunch."

Arin remained silent. An interesting range of expressions had crossed her face in the courtyard but the minute he'd put her sister's photo on the desk, she'd shut down. He didn't blame her, but he very much wanted to get back to whatever had been going through her mind downstairs at some point. There'd been heat in her eyes and her lips had parted in a way that would've had him on his feet and pulling her in for a mind-blowing kiss if he hadn't had urgent news to tell her about her sister.

Damn it.

Apparently, she had no issue with her teammate going out with her younger sister. Jason was unsure how to proceed. It wasn't his business, but he wondered how Arin felt about it. Family stuff got complicated, especially when family got mixed up with work. Maybe the Search and Protect team was more closely bonded than just people drawing a paycheck from the same company.

"Hey." Raul had his phone to his ear. "Where are you?"

There was a pause. The phone's volume wasn't turned up enough to overhear anything. Whatever the answer was, Raul visibly relaxed. "Good. No worries. See you soon."

Raul ended the call and got to his feet, his dog following suit. "She just walked into the lobby. She's literally here. I'll go meet her at the elevator and hustle her into the offices."

Arin was practically vibrating with controlled anger and Jason wanted nothing more than to reach out and touch her. He wanted to soothe her or unleash her temper to help her let off steam, do *something*, and either option was equally tempting. He didn't think she wanted to be distracted, though, so instead, he took a good look around him. He was betting every transparent wall of the place was made of ballistic glass. He'd want the target inside, too. That was some lucky timing.

"This isn't an active threat yet." Arin made the distinction as Raul was leaving the office. "They want Search and Protect to back off. Otherwise, they wouldn't have given us this warning. They'd have taken her out as a message instead."

Jason waited until her teammate and his dog were out of earshot. "I get why you're upset. I expected him to be a little more objective."

She shook her head once. "Nope. Raul and Mali are a couple."

Maybe Jason should've looked more closely at the relationships between Arin and her teammates. He wouldn't have done anything different, but he liked to know these kinds of things. It would inform his decisions moving forward concerning Arin and Raul. "I knew you and Raul had worked together multiple times in the past. I gathered you were close friends. I didn't make the connection between him and your sister. How is he still alive?"

He posed the question as half joke, half serious. If Jason had been eyeing the little sister of any colleague as skilled as Arin, he'd have approached the situation with extreme caution. Sure, normal people wouldn't kill a person out of hand for their interest. But people in their line of work weren't exactly normal.

He was awarded a slight lift at the corner of Arin's very lovely mouth. "They were long distance for quite some time and kept it discreet. She's only recently returned to the islands and they've both been dedicated to their jobs. If you were looking into the Search and Protect team over the last six months, there might not have been a lot of activity to tie them together until the last several weeks."

"I appreciate you giving me the out when it comes to my ability to gather intelligence." He was still irritated he hadn't made the connection.

"We all have our strengths." She let the comment drop, with the obvious follow-up going unsaid.

"Ouch." He was relieved, though. If she was verbally sparring with him, she wasn't going to go on a rampage for the moment. "I'll work on it. In the meantime, anything I'd recommend to protect your sister is likely stuff you're already thinking, so what's realistic considering her personality, her job, and her boyfriend?"

Arin looked at him then, really saw him. "You want to help."

"She might not be a target if I hadn't helped you find those people at the harbor on Big Island." He was making a habit of feeling responsible. It wasn't the wisest thing, in his opinion, but it sat better with his conscience. "And she matters to you."

He held Arin's gaze for a long moment. He wanted to ensure her little sister stayed safe, not because he knew much of anything about Mali Siri, but because she was precious to Arin. He was developing more feelings for Arin than he'd had time to process but he'd seize the moment for now and think it through later. He didn't want regrets if he walked away from all this, and he was damned sure he wasn't going to meet anyone like Arin ever again.

"What's with the sour faces?" A sweet voice called out in advance of Mali Siri entering the office.

Jason cleared his voice, suddenly faced with the sisters in close quarters. If Mali was beautiful in a still photograph, she was light and energy when she was in motion. Her face was rounder than Arin's and she was a couple of inches shorter, built more slender than her older sister. Where Mali gave an impression of delicate—almost fragile—sweetness, Arin was all fierce strength and fluid readiness.

Jason glanced at Raul and gave the other man a nod. Anyone who could survive with these two in his life was to be respected. "I still want to know how Arin let you live."

Raul cracked a grin.

Mali stopped and blinked at Jason, watching with widening eyes as he rose and held out a hand. "Jason Landon, miss. Pleasure to meet you."

Mali glanced at Arin. Her older sister lifted her shoulder a fraction and relaxed again. The exchange took a split second, then Mali gave him a brilliant smile. "I'm guessing you know who I am. It's nice to meet you, too."

She took his hand and gave him a real handshake, not as firm or aggressive as her sister's, but not one of those limp noodle handshakes either. Mali was a woman who knew her mind. Apparently, Arin was a sister who respected Mali's choices. Raul, in consideration of both women, was a lucky man.

"We've got a situation coming up and it'd be good if you could plan to stay in this weekend." Arin made her suggestion a balance between casual and serious. "Raul and Taz will be with you and it'll be good quality time."

Mali started shaking her head before Arin completed the

last sentence. "I've got a special brunch this Sunday. It's been planned for weeks and there are academics coming in from the mainland and overseas. We've got representatives from East and Southeast Asia. This is key to my work and I have to be there."

Jason expected Arin to tell her to cancel it. Instead, Arin closed her eyes briefly then reopened them and shifted her gaze to Raul. "Would it make sense for the task force to put in an appearance?"

Mali looked from Arin to Raul as Raul leaned back against the wall just inside the door. "It could. We could amp up security for the event and I could be with her the entire time."

"It's mostly indoors on private property, not in the city," Mali offered quietly.

She'd apparently picked up on the gravity of the situation. Jason considered the information he'd pulled up on the incident six months ago that'd triggered the Search and Protect team's incursion on the plantation. His former employer's client and the ill-advised decision to have a group of scientists grabbed off the streets just for conducting interviews of prostitutes in the area. Mali Siri had evaded the kidnapping. It was one thing to read about the young woman and another to meet her.

"You're still conducting research even after the incident in Chinatown?" He winced once he asked the question. It was one thing to be forthright with Arin, but her little sister was a civilian. She might not appreciate being reminded of a traumatic incident.

Mali's expression darkened but she didn't appear hurt or about to cry. On the contrary, a hint of her older sister's steel glinted in her dark eyes. "Absolutely."

"Oh." He probably sounded dumbfounded and he didn't

mind. Frankly, he was impressed. Arin had her integrity and moral code. Her sister had her determination and conviction. They were a potent pair of siblings.

"Once I was safe, I asked the Search and Protect team to help me find my colleagues." Mali lifted her chin. "I've been conducting research on human trafficking in various countries for years. I wasn't going to leave my colleagues with traffickers."

It had to have been a frightening time and she might've had to argue hard to get the Search and Protect team to help one person without some sort of sponsor to back the contract. Mali Siri had been through a lot. His respect for her fresh, positive personality moved up a few more notches.

"Can you work remote the rest of the week and only leave home for this event?" Arin asked.

"I can make it happen." Mali didn't even fight her. "But I want to know what's going on."

"We're still figuring out the scope of it." Arin tapped the picture on the desk. "But someone wants to use you as leverage to make us back off."

"Does this have to do with the group of people you kept from exploding at Kawaihae Harbor?" Mali asked.

Jason cleared his throat. When Mali looked at him, he grinned. "I disarmed the bomb."

"Uh huh." Mali was clearly loyal to her older sister and possibly not impressed by technical details.

"He did," Arin confirmed. "Without him, those people would've died and there would've been serious damage to a section of the container terminal."

Apparently, they were not going to mention how Arin and King would've been blown to pieces as well.

"We're helping the rescued people find shelter for the time being here on Oahu. Kim has her little brother back."

Mali beamed at Arin. "You should stop by the massage ther-apy place. Kim wants to thank you personally."

Arin shifted her hip on the edge of the desk. Her cheeks flushed dusky rose. "I made a promise."

Mali nodded, still smiling. "I want you to come to the brunch too, please. There are people who should meet you, understand the work you and Raul have been doing. They're very against the idea of private contractors—mercenaries—and I want them to meet you, so you're people in their minds and not names on an invoice. Come and I promise to work remote, stay home, follow every security precaution you and Raul ask me to until whatever threat is out there is done."

Well, that neatly guaranteed a cooperative charge.

"Agreed." Arin's demeanor had warmed by several de-grees and she almost sounded cheerful.

"Wear a dress." Mali held up a finger as she added the re-quirement.

"Excuse me?" Arin pinned her little sister with a sharp look.

Mali airily continued. "Please wear a dress and do some-thing nice with your hair. Give King a bath. You're not supposed to look like you're working even if you're always working. When you show up like you're on the job, you make some of the rescued women and men nervous. Even the professors and administrators stutter because you have this resting stern look. It's like a bitch face, only you make someone feel like they did something wrong."

Jason knew exactly what Mali was talking about, but there had to be a catchier phrase for the expression. Resting enforcer face? No. He'd have to think on it and come up with something good.

"I look like what?" Arin didn't sound surprised, though. If anything, her voice was muted.

"You're intimidating." Mali made the statement matter-of-fact.

The words stabbed Arin in the chest. Maybe Mali didn't see the effect but Jason did. Arin withdrew, pulling deep into herself. What was left was a pleasant-faced mask. "I'll do what I can."

"She'll have a date," Jason interjected. No way was he going to leave Arin to navigate this social thing without a wingman. Raul was going to have his attention on Mali, so obviously her longtime friend was not available.

"Oh!" Mali looked at him and studied him in a new light. He could practically see the gears turning in her head. "Yes, a date will make a big difference. I'll update the guest list. Thank you!"

Arin sighed. "It's all set, then. Why don't you and Raul make arrangements with your offices and head home?"

Mali took one handle of her tote bag off her shoulder and started searching inside the bag. "One more thing."

Her head and at least one arm disappeared into the tote. Jason chuckled silently. It was like the bag defied the laws of physics. How did Mali find anything in there?

"The whole reason I came up in the first place was to give you this. I saw it at a recent fan convention and knew it was perfect for you. It's a companion book to a really popular comic strip." Mali held out a slim hardcover book.

Arin took it, looking at the cover, her face unreadable. "Thank you."

CHAPTER ELEVEN

Seventy Maxims of Maximally Effective Mercenaries."

Arin cringed as Jason read the title of the book her little sister had given her. Happily, her apartment was only a mile or two away so this was going to be a very short car ride. They'd driven straight from the airport to Search and Protect headquarters; otherwise, she normally walked to the office building.

"I checked online to figure out what this is. It's part of a sci-fi webcomic. I might start reading it online. There's years' worth of funny there." Jason chuckled, paging through the book. "You know, I can see why she thought of you."

"I am not a mercenary." Arin bit off each word. "I've explained this to my sister—and our parents—over and over about private contract work. But they've never been able to get their heads around it."

"I think she gets it." Jason waved the book. "This is definitely a funny read. Probably funnier if you know the comic."

The necessity of being vague about exactly what kinds of things she did on contract didn't help. Years ago, when Mali and Arin hadn't had as positive a relationship, Mali had landed on the perception that private contractors were mercenaries, working only for the highest bidder and with no morals or ethics to speak of. They'd been in a fight when Mali had said it. Arin had been hurt, maybe because the words had been too accurate at the time.

"I don't mind being called a mercenary." Jason seemed unperturbed and not the least bit ashamed. "Look, being labeled a merc isn't evil. Hell, I read books and watched movies as a kid and all I wanted to be was a mercenary. Ooh. This third one about ordnance technicians, yeah, that's me."

He was legitimately laughing out loud. She might hate him a little at the moment.

"You know, she left little sticky flags in here." Jason tapped the front cover of the book. "I'm guessing those are the ones she thought were particularly applicable to you. Number twenty-seven has a big sticky note, not just one of the flags. I definitely think it applies to you."

"I refuse to ask you what it says, and I am not going to read it now. If you keep this up, I might beat you with that book." She kept her attention on the road. It would've been faster, really, to walk the damned distance from the office building to her apartment. Traffic around Honolulu was evil. They had a very short distance to travel and all of it was stop and go, with too many rented cars on the road driven by tourists who didn't particularly care about their vehicles.

"Aw, c'mon." Jason finally set the book down. "These are all in good fun. Whatever issue you two have with the word *mercenary*, I'm thinking this is a peace offering. Your sister looks like she's realized a mercenary isn't a bad thing. You could do the same."

"It isn't the word *mercenary* in and of itself, it's the implied lack of scruples." Finally, she turned into the parking garage entrance for her apartment building. She didn't speak to Jason as she parked her car and let King out the back. He seemed content to keep reading and chuckling to himself. Which was fine, as long as he wasn't trying to make her listen to any of those…maxims.

She was opening her front door when he asked her a legitimate question.

"Why did you bring me here?" He respectfully waited inside the entryway as she and King cleared her apartment.

"Pua got on my case about hotel expenses when we got in earlier, before I debriefed with Raul, and the Search and Protect team does not currently maintain any safe houses. I found you, so you're my responsibility. Your team might not be trying to kill you anymore, but we don't know exactly what they do plan, either, so it's not a good idea to send you out wandering on the island. You can sleep on the couch." She closed the door to her apartment behind him and pulled off her boots, leaving them on the shoe rack in the entryway.

She slipped her feet into her own house slippers and snagged a pair of disposable slippers from her guest supply. Raul and Zu stopped in once in a while so she kept disposables in their sizes. Jason might need a slightly bigger size than Raul, but his feet were definitely not as big as Zu's. Arin halted her train of thought right there. She didn't want to go any further down the path of comparing shoe size between the three men. Just, no. "Shoes off, please. Slippers if you don't like cold floors. The ceilings and floors are cement under the laminate so the floors are always chilly in the morning, even here on the islands."

"Nice little place you've got here," Jason commented

once he had his boots off and stepped into the main living area.

"We only recently moved in. King and I don't need much space." She'd have been nervous if she had a bigger place, honestly. Too many rooms was a pain in the ass to clear every time she came home. Plus, she didn't like to leave rooms empty and unused. Previously, she'd been staying at the Search and Protect house, where their kennel master kept a couple of the dogs not attached to a handler. But that house was more of a gathering place for the entire team. This gave her more quiet time. "The living room has a sofa bed. It pulls out to queen size. If it's not comfortable, I've got Japanese-style tatami mats and a futon I could lay out for you to make up a comfortable crash space on the floor."

She had her bedroom and a single bathroom beyond this living area. The kitchen was a part of the open floor plan and was very efficiently designed to take up as little space as possible while still providing all the necessities to cook on a regular basis. This apartment was her hideaway, small and efficient without being claustrophobic.

"You know," Jason murmured. She wasn't sure he was actually speaking to her. "You are allowed to take up space in this world."

She decided to answer him anyway. "I do. This is mine."

His words were pushing at her, though, and she was defensive in response. Rather than say something cutting, she swallowed hard and looked away. It wasn't her intent to take a shot at him right now. He was a guest, for real, and she did want him to feel welcome.

"We're both short on sleep." She decided that was a safe truth, one that wouldn't hurt either of them. "And I'm betting we both want a hot shower. You can go first and I'll put something together for an early dinner."

Jason lifted an eyebrow. "Why not shower together?"

She wanted to turn him down outright. But when she glared at him, their eyes met and the chemistry between them ignited again. It really hadn't ever gone. It'd been a smoldering awareness between them whenever they'd been in the same room. She was exhausted trying to keep it shoved to the back of her mind, but her body was very aware of his proximity.

"Even if I said yes, we'd pass out from hunger." Her stomach and hobbit-style eating habits were the current voice of reason. Her mind was too busy imagining him in her shower. "Extra towels are in the cabinet and Raul returned your duffel bag, so you have clean clothes, right? There's a washer and dryer in the bathroom. You can throw your dirty clothes in there. I'll add mine and run a load of laundry tonight."

She had plenty of practical tasks to throw between them. She could keep this up all night.

"Even if I clean up, you'll still be a dirty lady." Jason stepped closer to her and his tone had gone deep and suggestive. "That's very tempting."

She opened her mouth, but the cutting retort she had stuck there. Sharp words came out of her as easily as breathing. There'd been moments, memories as far back as her school days, when she'd pushed someone away with hurtful words and it'd been too far. Now she was torn because she wanted him to back off, but she also hoped he would stay just close enough. Total conflict.

He stilled, watching her. "Are you okay?"

She decided to be honest with him, again. "I'm thinking too hard. People tend to get tired of it and find something more...amenable...while I'm doing that."

"Ah." There was understanding in his gaze and she wasn't sure if it was uncomfortable or a relief.

Nothing about how she was feeling at the moment was normal. He'd extended a blatant invitation, but she didn't know how to tell him what she wanted, only what she didn't. "I don't want sex."

* * *

Jason rocked back on his heels. As rejections went, her message should've been clear, but there was more. There was a maelstrom behind her dark eyes, and he wondered how many people had heard her words and walked away from her. He admired so many aspects of her, but he was starting to realize words were not her strength.

"Okay." As much as he wanted sex, it wasn't all he wanted, and he was still exploring what that meant to him.

"Please don't leave." Her voice came in almost a whisper and almost cracked at the end. The request cost her something, a barricade or emotional wall of some kind. Standing there, she was vulnerable and bracing herself.

Whatever he did next could hurt her and maybe she hadn't admitted the reality of it to herself, but the knowledge hit him in the sternum. Hard.

"Mind if I sit?"

She shrugged, uncertain. This was definitely a new side of her.

He made his way over to the small sofa in her living area, making sure to face her as he moved and not give her his back. He guessed she might've seen people's backs too often in her life as they went on with their own lives and hadn't noticed how very alone they'd left her.

"Why don't you join me?" He patted the cushion next to him. "We can turn on your television and relax some. We were up before dawn to catch the flight over here from Big

Island and you seemed like you stood through your whole meeting with your teammate. Take a little weight off."

He figured coaxing her to relax was like approaching a tiger or other large predator. He went with the cautious, non-threatening approach. Of course, if he was too nice, she might get her back up again just because she'd be suspicious of his motives. Every person had layers of trust and comfort and with Arin, those were interlaced with a hell of a lot of personal defenses. He'd be stupid to assume he'd earned his way through all of them.

"Look, there's a lot going on." There was the defensive tone. She wrapped her arms around herself. "I need to process it all, not lose my mind."

A zing shot through him. It was damned good to know he could do that to her. He'd love to do it to her again, when she wanted it. Instead, he raced through the possible responses to figure out how he could keep her from withdrawing completely. "How can I help?"

Her fingers clenched harder around her upper arms as she hugged herself even more tightly. "Not sure. I feel like I need to let off some kind of steam or I'm going to explode."

Anyone as dangerous as Arin Siri had to find a release valve, otherwise she'd blow up and there could very likely be an inordinate amount of blood and/or body parts involved. He understood, because he faced a similar problem.

She did move, finally, and when she came to the sofa he was almost surprised. He'd already been formulating a plan B. She sat facing him, with one knee bent and pulled up against her chest.

He shook his head and enjoyed her puzzlement. "Turn around. I figure I owe you a lot and we're not at a bar, so the least I can do is give you a shoulder rub. I bet you're all tied up in knots."

After another hesitation, she shifted around and gave him her back. Another layer, but so far in his time with Arin, she'd been more willing to risk physical vulnerability than emotional.

He set his palms on her and started warming up the taut muscles across her shoulders. "Why was your sister at a convention that would have a book like *Seventy Maxims of Maximally Effective Mercenaries* for sale?"

Arin rolled her head, stretching her neck muscles as he kneaded the stiffness out of the area between her shoulder blades. "A lot of the victims of human trafficking come from overseas because the easiest targets are tourists traveling in places foreign to them. People go missing and anyone who cares enough to look for them is far away, in a different country."

She sighed as he hit a particularly tight spot. He resisted the urge to kiss the place, right in the curve where her shoulder met her neck. Instead he continued to carefully stretch and ease the tightness there.

After an appreciative murmur, she continued, "But some victims are taken right here in the islands. Locals go to the mall or attend fan conventions. It could be an anime or science fiction convention, any number of themed events. In a big place like that, people go missing. It's hard to track who a missing person might've interacted with at an event like that. My sister's organization works with con security to keep an eye out for those kinds of traps. I'm guessing the book was from some sort of comic con, or something."

"Interesting." Actually, he liked comics a little. "I've read some comics now and again. I've worked with people who had collections. I kind of envied them, actually."

"Mmm." She sighed. "Why?"

He considered it. "They retired after they made a decent

chunk of money. It doesn't take long in our biz if you don't have a gambling habit or anything. They had homes to go back to or plans to buy some place in line with their idea of happy."

"A lot of people have that idea of happy."

He grunted in agreement. "When you have a place to go to over and over, then you tend to accumulate stuff to fill that personal space. I don't really have any place I consider a home base."

She was starting to relax into his hands and it was easier than he'd thought it would be to converse, not just listen or make small talk, but actually trade back and forth. Being near her like this was another memory he was going to tuck away and pull out in lonelier days when his ambition took him to other places. It didn't escape his notice that she seemed better at answering questions than volunteering information.

"How do you make your home for yourself?" He wasn't sure she was going to answer, but he'd been curious.

She didn't pull away, but she tensed. "What do you mean?"

"This apartment doesn't have many personal belongings. It's not full of personal pictures or diplomas or awards, the way some people put their lives up on the walls. There's just a couple of items, like the little replica of the blue police box I can see on your nightstand over in the bedroom. Things with stories not everyone will recognize. But it feels like you when you walk in the door." He cleared his throat, uncomfortable, but he'd already started. If this was helping her let go of some of her tension, then it was worth it. "The two places you reserved over on the Big Island felt like you, too. It was like the minute you walked into those rooms, they were yours. It was nice."

There was a moment of silence, then she whispered, "Thank you."

They both said nothing and he focused on working the tension out of her shoulders. The tip of her ponytail brushed across the backs of his hands as he kneaded the tight muscles, and he thought about how glorious her hair was when she let it loose.

"I guess I've always traveled a lot. So if I'm going to be away from home, I pick places that match my mood." She tilted her head, first to one side and then the other, stretching as he worked.

"Ah." He started using his elbow to apply steady pressure to trigger points in an effort to get the knots in her muscles to release. "That's something I never really paid attention to. A hotel room is a hotel room to me, and I never thought about it as anything but a place to catch some sleep. I've even gone for those little cubbies in some countries where it's more like a drawer they tuck you into for the night."

She chuckled. "To each their own."

"But I only ever thought about the cheapest rate to pay for the bare minimum of what I needed," he clarified. "You actually live as you're doing things with your life. I like that."

This, settling on a couch with her and enjoying her company, was the best time he'd had in a freaking long time.

"Why are you so frugal about the places you stay?" She turned partly to look at him.

Oh no, that was too tempting, even if she wasn't trying to give him the come-hither look over her shoulder. He put his fingertips to the base of her skull, gently turning her head to face away from him as he worked on the delicate muscles of her neck. "Save money. I keep putting it away."

"For what?" she asked innocently.

He paused to consider. He'd never really talked about his end goals out loud to anyone. They were only half formed. Better to go with the short term. "To be my own boss. I'd like to work freelance and I need buffer to do that. Sometimes you have to front the cost of travel to do a job, then collect on completion."

"True." Her acceptance was a relief.

Maybe he wanted her to dig a little deeper, but she shouldn't have to. He just wasn't ready to offer anything more up right now.

"So why are you so grumpy about your sister giving you a gift?" Coming back to the topic of her sister might bring Arin's tension back a little but she did need to vent some, too. If he could help her let go of her tension and also work through some of the pent-up worry, it'd be better than her tensing back up later. "She thought of you and got you a thing. It does seem to fit you in a fun way, too. Why not read it?"

"She's a lot more considerate than she used to be." Arin sighed. As she tipped her head to one side again, her neck popped, releasing tightness right next to her upper spine. "She's an adult now, not the kid I remember, and she doesn't need me."

"Is that a bad thing?" Jason wouldn't want that kind of burden. It was why he hadn't been in touch with his parents since he'd left home. But maybe Arin was the sort to want to be needed by people.

"No," she admitted. "Not at all. I left home to go into the military when she was a teen. Well, maybe not even a teen yet, really. I kept in touch and even visited over the years, but never really came back. Then she went to college and we barely communicated besides the occasional email. She only came to the island recently. Interacting with her now, all the time, is taking more out of me than I can keep up with while I'm trying to adjust to her being an adult. It'd suck if I went on treating her like my kid sister. I keep catching myself and correcting."

"You wouldn't like it if the positions were reversed." If he'd had siblings, he wouldn't like it either.

"I wouldn't. I'm trying not to smother her either." Arin huffed out a laugh. "Intellectually, I know she's an adult and I mostly say all the right things as if she is all grown up, but deep inside I'm still trying to save her from bullies. Maybe because I wasn't around as she figured out how to handle them on her own."

Jason laughed with her. "In your defense, she seems to be a magnet for the sort of trouble a normal person isn't equipped to fend off on their own."

"True." Arin stretched forward as he started to work his way to her lower back. "But she has Raul. He's my best friend and he is absolutely capable of watching out for her. She is also above and beyond the normal person. She's brilliant. She doesn't need me, and we'd get along a hell of a lot better if I wasn't so used to making her my all-consuming priority when she's at the top of my mind."

Jason paused, both because he needed to pull his brains together when presented with her lean back and gracefully curved hips, and because he was trying to understand her thought process. "Are you saying you need a new hobby?"

Arin snorted. "I wouldn't put it that way, but yes. I need to let her live her life and get back to building one of my own."

"You've got a damned impressive career." He worked his way back up her spine and carefully kneaded the tight muscles under her shoulder blades. He couldn't get over how smooth and soft her skin was. He was incredibly tempted to kiss the nape of her neck, too, but he wouldn't be able to stop there, and she'd made it clear she didn't want sex right now. Besides, this was really nice as it was. "How much more do you want to build it up?"

"Establishing a career isn't the same as building a life for yourself." She leaned into his hands and he eased her back until she was lying against his chest. He dug his fingers into her thick, silken hair to give her a scalp massage, too.

"It's not?"

She turned her head, nestling more comfortably against him. "Not for me. There's . . . more."

He listened to her breathing slow and lightened his touch as she fell asleep. He wasn't sure he'd ever looked at life the way she seemed to. He was building the career he'd planned for himself. This was a small, unplanned detour and the way he was getting to know her was definitely more than he'd intended. But what was *more* going to mean to him?

CHAPTER TWELVE

Arin closed the trunk of her SUV and slung her beach tote over her shoulder. King bumped her left hip with his shoulder, lifting his nose to catch the breeze. As far as her partner was concerned, this was the closest he'd had to a day of beach fun in a while.

"Why? Why are we here?" Jason exited the vehicle, clutching a coffee in a paper cup in one hand. "And why were we up at oh-five-hundred?"

"Because I wanted to be on the road by oh-five-thirty. Hanauma Bay opens at oh-six-hundred and the parking lot is packed full within an hour. I wanted to get here before it got crowded. We're meeting a contact and it's better to talk to him before there are too many people around." She was inordinately entertained by his obvious dislike of mornings. They'd also slept for most of yesterday afternoon and the entire night. As far as she was concerned, neither of them should be operating on a sleep deficit at this point. True, they'd been on her couch the majority of the time, but she was still more rested than she had been in a while. Rested and...lighter in a lot of ways. She wasn't completely at ease with how much she'd shared with him yesterday, but she felt so much better. "Don't fuss. I stopped to get coffee."

Jason grunted his response, which she took to be something between a thanks and additional grumpy sentiment. She checked King's service vest, which clearly identified him as a working search and rescue canine, and clipped his leash on his collar. The leash was more for the people they encountered than to control King. He was excellent in his obedience training and well-practiced in working with her in crowds. But GSDs were big dogs and people remained more at ease around King when they saw him on a leash.

They'd arrived ahead of the crowd, right at open, so there was almost no line. Arin gave the person at the ticket booth a smile and paid the entrance fee. Next up was the educational video, which Jason watched at her side with minimal grumbling.

"You think they're going to update that video sometime soon?" Jason asked as they headed down the steep walkway to the beach.

Arin shrugged. She'd seen it and wasn't required to watch it again within the same year, but it'd seemed crappy to make Jason go in and watch it alone, so she'd gone in with him. "It looks better on a television screen than projected. State park facilities have to pick and choose where their funding goes."

"I guess." He looked out and down at the curve of beach and water below them, letting out a low whistle. "I've been on the island almost a year now and haven't ever been here. It's an impressive sight."

She agreed, enjoying the view. Hanauma was an almost complete circle, born of volcanic activity bursting up through the sea floor and the ocean itself, then subsiding. The waves had cut their way through the lower southeast wall of the crater and rushed in, forming the bay. Now, the water was a gorgeous blue green and clear enough to see the coral stretching out across the bay floor. The sky beyond the crater wall was mostly clear with only a few clouds overhead and in the distance. It was going to be a sunny, hot morning, perfect for snorkeling.

"It used to be even better for snorkeling but the coral has suffered bleaching from the warmer water temperatures recently." She frowned. "But we're not here just for the snorkeling."

"You mentioned there being an objective to coming out here."

He was a patient man; she'd give him that. It was a good thing, too, because she tended to wait longer if people nagged her too much. She was contrary that way. "We're looking for a contact."

"Ah." He didn't say anything further.

So they reached the bottom of the roadway in peace and she looked up and down the sand. "Honestly, this is the last beach I'd have thought he'd be at."

"Who?" Jason sniffed the air. "Also, I could definitely eat right about now."

"Snack bar is expensive." She searched around in her tote and came up with a small wrapped treat. "Here."

"Thanks." He took it and started to unwrap it. "What is this?"

"Onigiri. It's a rice ball with seasoning to keep it from being boring and some flaked salmon in the middle for protein." She loved onigiri and tended to make them for herself whenever she and King were going someplace relaxing for the day. This excursion was work-oriented, but they'd have to do some waiting and the surroundings made it a pleasure.

"Handy." Jason murmured his approval around a mouthful of rice. "Tasty, too."

Pride blossomed right below her sternum. She cooked for herself all the time, and it was nice to hear someone else enjoying what she'd made. "Trick is to have a fine sprinkle of salt on your palms when you're shaping them to have nice flavor on the outside. Not too much, though. They keep all day, depending on the filling. They're a great meal on the go."

Talking about onigiri made her hungry so she took one out for herself. This one was of plain rice, seasoned with a light touch of sugar and white rice vinegar to give it a subtly sweet tang. She'd steamed the rice the way she liked it, a little on the wet side but each cooked grain still tenderly distinct as she bit into her rice ball. She got a burst of salty sour as she caught a bit of the umeboshi. She liked to put one of the tiny pickled plums into each of her plain rice balls. They were tart and woke up her palate when she had them for breakfast.

"How are we going to find your contact?"

Thirty seconds earlier, she wouldn't have been able to answer his question. However, she caught sight of exactly who she'd been looking for and almost laughed. Of course he'd be there. "We're going to the information booth."

As she approached, Kenny looked up and saw her coming. He was forever unfolding himself from whatever chair he'd tucked himself into and by the time she reached the booth, she was looking way up at him. He was a tall man with a rangy build, all arms and legs and wiry strength. He reached out a long arm to gather her in and leaned across the counter to lightly press his forehead to hers. "Arin, lovely lady of doom, howzit?"

He gave her the same greeting whenever they met. Considering how they'd met, she did deserve it, so she didn't mind him calling her what she was. She returned the warmth in his eyes and his smile with one of her own. "I've got questions, like I always do."

Kenny laughed, the sound of it melodic in a soothing tenor. Listening to him speak or laugh or sing was like listening to a cello. "Don't I know it. Right on."

"This is Jason, by the way." Jason had hung back a foot or two, giving her the option to introduce him or not. She appreciated the consideration.

Now, he took a step forward. "Jason Landon."

"Good to meet you." Kenny was more reserved with his greeting to Jason, sizing the other man up. Kenny was distantly nice to everyone and truly warm to only a select few. She wasn't even sure he considered her a friend or someone he was willing to work with from time to time.

There was movement in the shade of the information booth and she glanced past Kenny. "How is Laki allowed down here? There's no pets allowed in the state park."

"Aw, now, Laki may not be a highly trained working animal like your noble companion there, but he has his talents." Kenny continued to smile, looking amused at some internal joke.

She scowled. "A pig who surfs isn't generally the kind of talent to get an exception."

"Park manager is a big fan." Kenny held his hands up. "Who am I to say? This is a good place to volunteer our time for a while. On the other hand, I thought your time was less fluid."

True. And she deserved being reminded. Still, she wasn't going to be derailed right away. "You two haven't been surfing here in Hanauma. How long's it been since you caught some waves?"

Kenny's normally coppery brown skin was a shade or two

lighter than the last time she'd seen him. Perhaps he hadn't been surfing as much recently. Not for the first time, she wondered if there was an active reason for Kenny's nomadic life on the island or if he just liked to be difficult to find on any given day.

"It's been some time." Kenny didn't seem fazed as he gave her his answer. "Now what can I do for you?"

"The trafficking business we were looking into some months ago, it's under new management." She tried to avoid exact timeframes. They were holding a normal chat, nothing for anyone passing by to listen in on. It was still very early and only a few serious swimmers or snorkelers were trickling down into the beach area so far.

Kenny clicked his tongue. "That job is not a position to be in for long, apparently."

"New manager got a few steps ahead of us on Big Island." She gave Kenny a brief, concise summary of what had happened there. "I need to catch up and even get ahead of him. Who is he beyond his name? Where's he from? What are his goals? What are some potential next moves? There isn't going to be a roadmap that gives us a step-by-step breakdown, but if anyone can search out all the whispered information out there and pull the pieces together, it's you."

Kenny placed his palm over his heart, long fingers spread wide. "You flatter me."

"It's not undeserved." She placed her hand on the counter between them. "And Kenny, this is about family. There's a threat to my little sister again. You were there for part of it. I won't allow them to use her as leverage."

"Ah." Kenny's expression turned sober, his full mouth falling out of the habitual smile. "Ohana is everything. I'll find what I can."

"We'll be here for a few hours, enjoying the sand and water.

Maybe we'll do some scent work with King when the sand gets hotter. It'll be good practice." Arin tipped her head to indicate the far end of the curved beach area. "Anything you can find this morning would give me a start, then maybe you could forward anything else you find to Pua?"

"Can do." Kenny's smile was back. "I might've set up a few laptops in here for just such a request."

"You're always prepared." Arin tapped the counter and stepped back. "Mahalo."

* * *

Jason watched the exchange between Arin and her friend, Kenny. Okay, and he couldn't help but check out the pig hanging out inside the information booth. Seriously, it had a dark bristled coat and rough features, probably born feral or from wild stock. The pig was small, half the size of King and, apparently, the pig could surf.

He was learning something new today and that hadn't happened often until he'd met Arin.

Or maybe he was just paying more attention around her.

He waited until they'd left the information center and headed across the beach. "So we're here for the morning."

"Yup." Arin looked out at the water. "We'll wait to see if he gets any immediate hits. It'd be too much of a giveaway if we came to talk to him and left, so we get a lazy morning. I cleared it with Zu."

Jason sat on one of the few patches of short, stubborn grass lining the beach area. "Sounds good to me."

A cat meowed.

Arin had been in the process of unrolling a tightly woven mat she'd carried in her tote. She turned at the sound of the cat. "Hey, Thug."

King watched but didn't make a move to go after anything, so Jason turned to check out the newcomer. He let out a low whistle. "That is a huge, fat cat."

Arin snorted and sat on her mat. The cat strolled over and sat next to her and her tote full of snacks. "There's some stray and feral cats down here. There's also mongoose, if you watch for them. This guy has been hanging at this beach a while. I think one of the locals said he's been around a few years, even."

"Long time for a feral cat." He studied the cat, who ignored him and King, pointedly pawing at Arin's tote.

"He does know where the easy food is." She didn't seem to mind, but she also didn't pet or cuddle the cat. She just sat there, knees drawn up to her chest, leaning forward and smiling at the thing.

He hadn't pinned Arin as a cat lover, but her eyes and mouth were softer around the corners. She wasn't scowling. Thug kitty had worked his way into her heart, and Jason was betting there'd be food for the feline before too much longer. "You're not a local, so did you grow up on the mainland?"

"Mmm." She murmured the agreement. "East coast. Normal childhood, nothing noteworthy."

"You seem to have a loving family, or sister, at least." He doubted he'd have a chance to chat with her sister, but watching Arin interact with Mali, then Raul, then Kenny, left Jason wanting more. They all had history with her. The time he'd shared with her had either been on the move, life-threatening, or mind-blowing sex. He definitely planned to coax her into more of the last if she was willing, but he also wanted to dig deeper. The bits she'd shared with him yesterday hadn't been nearly enough.

"I do. We weren't rich or anything, but Mali and I had what we needed growing up. We also had ambition and we each finished up schooling to get on to other things. What about you? Seems like I've been answering all the questions."

True, and he hadn't intended to hold back, really. No one had cared to ask him before. He was taken aback and…glad, at the same time, that she had asked.

Her history was a contrast to his childhood. "I grew up in South Africa, in Cape Town. My father was a businessman. We weren't rich and I definitely didn't suffer as a little kid, not by standards I've seen in other places, but my father lost his job when I was young and neither of my parents could get work again. Life got hard and we had to live without major things like electricity. We didn't just lose comfort items. My parents turned bitter, fought a lot. Once I completed compulsory education, I just continued with further education, determined to do other things with my life than be at home. As soon as I found an out, I left and didn't look back."

She rested her chin on her knees and sighed. "There are advantages to a clean break. I left home and came back for short visits, but never as long as they wanted me to stay. It got awkward. They kept expecting me to be the same, but I couldn't give that to them. I was even more decisive than they remembered, abrasive, harsh. They wanted me to go back to my old marshmallow of a bed, eat my favorite foods, wear the same style clothes. But I wasn't comfortable that way anymore."

He nodded. Service changed a person so they never quite fit back into the life from which they'd come. He would know. "Why did you leave home in the first place?"

Her lips twisted into what might look like a smile. But it wasn't. Not after he'd seen her real smiles. Her voice grew husky with sadness. "My parents, my sister, they're kind and gentle souls. They have good intentions and high expectations. But I didn't fit into the part of the world my parents had carved out for our family. I am neither kind nor gentle."

"You don't have to be those things to be a good person," he said quietly. "There's also a lot of things we can say about intentions."

She huffed out a laugh. "Yeah. Road to hell. I definitely took a long road trip and some of the places I ended up in were hell and worse. I was hungry to remake myself. I wanted to go into a crucible and come out free of the violent streak I had inside of me. I'm confrontational and contrary. I tried to get it all out of my system."

He stared at her until she lifted her eyes to meet his gaze, then he gave her a slow smile and put all the heat and desire he had for her into it. "I personally like all that about you."

She didn't answer, but a blush spread across her cheeks and her eyelids dropped to half-mast under his continued gaze. Good. He didn't want her to fight him on this.

"Those aren't issues." He leaned forward and put a hand out on the sand between them. "You tried to burn it out of you, fine. It's like cutting away a part of yourself. I like what you accomplished instead."

She blinked and her brows drew together. "What?"

Hah. He was glad she was listening instead of thinking up ways to refute his statements. "You honed your violence, made it something well-balanced and polished. Watching you in action is like watching a once-in-a-lifetime performance in a theater. Sure, other people can say the same words, go through the same motions, but anyone who witnesses you knows the moment is magic. They might never see your equal again."

She narrowed her eyes. "Possibly because I ended them."

He nodded. "Soldiers throughout history looked for that kind of ending. They couldn't think of any better way to go."

She reached out with one hand and touched a finger to a spot near his hand, drawing circles in the sand. "You make me sound like the Morrigan."

The what? He scowled. He was being serious, waxing eloquent even, and she had to throw him off his game. It was frustrating, but he also got a crazy kind of happiness out of it. "Here I was proud of myself for keeping up with the conversation."

She laughed, the sound of it expanding a warmth from his core out to his fingertips. "Brush up on your mythology. The Morrigan is from European myths connected to war and fate and death. My sister and I both had a thing for mythology growing up and I still like to read up on the legends of every place I go, if I get the chance."

He shook his head. "Always a learning curve with you."

And he liked it, a lot. He'd been growing stagnant before he met her. The people he worked with had all been the same personality with different names. None of them thought outside the box, but she was challenging in new and surprising ways. She tipped her head back, turning her face up to the sky. "We're both a long way from where we came from."

True. And her statement swelled in his chest, better than any "attaboy" from his former colleagues ever had. He liked her profile and wondered if she realized she was picture perfect at the moment. Leaning back, he propped himself up with his hands in the hot sand and enjoyed being near her. "We are."

"Personal history gets…too personal sometimes." She raised her head back up and looked out over the ocean. "I mostly avoid it if I can."

"I appreciate our talks so far, though." He didn't want her

to shut down or withdraw. She didn't sound uncomfortable, though. Just introspective.

"I do, too." The corner of her mouth lifted in a hint of a smile and she actually laughed, soft and almost to herself. "It's easy to share with you."

His heart kicked the inside of his chest. Damn, but he liked hearing that.

She looked at him then and her gaze seared right through him. "A little. I'm not keen on an overdose of the chatting."

He opened his mouth to respond but he had nothing. He had no idea what to say.

She released her knees and stood, brushing sand from her legs. King rose with her, shaking sand from his fur and causing Thug cat to give the big dog a hiss. "Let's go for a swim."

He rose with her. "Okay."

Sharing time was over. It would've been awkward to sit with her staring at the ocean or going blind looking out over the sand. Cooling off in the ocean sounded like a good idea.

"It takes a strong swimmer to go out past the inner reef but it's worth it." She raised her eyebrow and smiled. "You up for it?"

Glad for the lighter mood, he grinned back. "Hell yeah."

CHAPTER THIRTEEN

The water was warm as Arin waded in. She kept walking forward at a steady pace against the gentle waves. She stepped carefully to avoid the few rocks dotting the mostly smooth sand and headed out until she was waist deep in water. Then she stood there and savored the scent of ocean and the water swirling around her legs for a few minutes. Sharing so much had churned up too many emotions and she needed this swim to buoy her, find her peace with it all again. Even then, she might not have the courage to ask him more about himself. She preferred to learn from his actions as they moved forward and let his history come out without digging.

Jason caught up with her, a set of flippers, mask, and snorkel in each hand. "How did I end up paying for the gear rental?"

She grinned. "You're staying at my place for free, aren't you?"

He gave her a mock glare and handed over the gear.

Once they had flippers on their feet and fitted their masks

to their faces, she pointed to the right side of the bay. "There's a channel through the inner reef that opens out to the deeper part of the bay. Once we get through there, we'll keep to the right. There's better swimming to that side and less issues with rocks or changing currents."

He nodded. "Sounds good."

That was it for words for a while. They both got their snorkels into place with their masks and started swimming. The water was calm inside the inner reef, but there were already a lot of tourists in the water. That many swimmers churned up the sand and visibility was only so-so. It took some patience to thread their way through small groups of two and three splashing around and exclaiming into the water over the few brave fish feeding in the area.

It got less crowded as they approached the center channel, and they only had to wait for one other pair of swimmers to go by before they could swim through. Once they were clear, the water became cooler as the depth of the bay opened up in front of them. Coral was more vibrant in pinks and blues and there were more fish in this quieter and more wide-open area.

Arin took a moment to enjoy the view, then turned back to confirm Jason was still with her. He hung just below the surface to her right, the wide mask allowing a clear look at his eyes. He gave her a thumbs-up.

The waves were stronger here, pushing them back toward the channel, so she struck out at an angle to the right side of the bay. She loved swimming, stretching her arms forward and cutting into the water, pulling herself forward with every stroke. Water flowed over her skin in a cool caress. Brightly colored fish fed on the coral below them, unconcerned as they passed by.

She paused here and there to admire the sea life and each

time, Jason had given her a light touch to let her know he was at her side. He'd run the back of his knuckles over her shoulder and lightly tap her hip. When they saw a sea turtle swim by, he'd run his palm over the back of her calf.

Every caress had sent delicious shivers through her. Between the waves and his hands, her skin was hypersensitive and she was enjoying every minute of it. He was a strong swimmer, too, able to hold position despite the waves pushing them back and forth, easily avoiding being pushed into any of the shallows where they might end up touching and damaging the coral.

She was comfortable with him. Talking with him came easy and while she'd been unsettled sharing so much with him at first, she was feeling better about it. Partially because he didn't seem to be judging her or jumping to any kind of over-familiarity. He hadn't assumed he knew everything about her after the first heart to heart. He'd simply been interested to learn more. She was opening up to him, and she had a lot of reservations about it, but this feeling of...potential was something she didn't want to miss out on. It was like swimming out past the inner reef. She was more exposed, but the experience was breathtakingly rewarding.

Jason took the lead for a bit and she indulged in a few caresses of her own as he did. She enjoyed his body and he caught her hand, giving it a squeeze before he placed her hand firmly on his behind. She almost laughed into her mouthpiece.

A sea turtle joined them for a few moments, maybe curious. Arin had followed its dive to get a closer look at the coral when strange movement to one side caught her attention. She turned her head to get a good look and froze in the water, then she kicked back up to the surface.

Jason came up with her and spit out his mouthpiece to talk. "What's the matter?"

She took the time to clear her snorkel and then pulled her mouthpiece to the side. "Body."

He stilled, treading water to hold position. "Want me to signal the lifeguards?"

She considered. "I want you to get a look with me first. We won't go close. Just get a good look, then we call the lifeguards in."

"Okay."

They dove back down together and approached the body. It was a woman, stuck in the coral, arms waving in the rougher current. The corpse was mostly intact and couldn't have been there for long. But there were cuts on the extremities and they weren't bleeding anymore. It was amazing one or more sharks hadn't swum into the bay to investigate the body if it'd been in the water long enough to bleed out. Hanauma Bay had reef sharks and even the occasional hammerhead had been spotted in the past.

Maybe it was a drowning victim? They were very close to the Witches' Brew, one of two places where rip tides were a serious danger. But this woman wasn't wearing a swimsuit. She was fully clothed and wearing a familiar red yukata-style robe.

Arin hung in the water, committing as many details as she could to memory. She wished she had an underwater camera with her.

Jason tapped her shoulder. When she rotated in the water to look at him, he pointed up. She nodded and followed him back up to the surface. They both took long breaths. They'd been down a full two minutes, give or take a few seconds.

Giving her a grim look, Jason turned to face the shore and lifted an arm out of the water to wave down the lifeguards.

* * *

"You can't just take a day off, can you?"

Jason turned and scowled at Kenny as the tall man sidled up to them on the beach. The swarm of lifeguards and police had finished asking them questions. Now they were busy with body recovery or crowd control as a swarm of morbidly curious tourists tried to take pictures.

The man gave Jason an easy smile. "Hey now, I'm just sayin' our lovely lady of doom does have a thing for finding trouble."

"You're not wrong," Arin said calmly.

She stood next to Jason, one hand rubbing King's ears as the big German Shepherd Dog sat panting next to her. The sun was rising higher in the sky and it was getting to the hottest part of the day.

"No chance of getting a sniff of the woman to find out how she ended up in the water over there?" Jason figured the chances were minuscule.

Arin shook her head. "Not after she's been in the water like that."

"She wasn't a swimmer." His suspicion was mirrored in the faces of the police on the scene as a forensic team arrived to begin processing the body.

"She also might not be a random stranger." Arin made that statement in a very quiet voice. "Kenny, I'd appreciate it if you could get a hold of the report from the medical examiner as soon as it becomes available."

Jason turned and stared at her. No way was that going to become accessible to the public.

But Kenny simply looked out over the bay with a serene expression. "Right on."

Handy guy to know. Just how much intel could Kenny access?, Jason wondered. Neither of them was likely to answer him if he asked so he put a different question out there instead. "Who is she?"

"Not sure." Arin said the words slowly. "But the yukata she's wearing is from a massage therapy business in Chinatown. It's the place my little sister helped convert from a front for the human trafficking ring into a legit business."

Oh no. Jason studied Arin. She'd witnessed death up close and personal, but some hit harder than others. No matter how many times a person saw it, it didn't get easier.

"Is it the woman you know? The one who asked you to find her brother?" He kept his voice so quiet, it might've been sub-vocal, so he'd leaned in to be sure she heard him.

She shook her head slowly. "I don't think so. The victim looks too tall. But there was another woman there with that kind of long hair all coiled up in intricate ways. The water pulled a lot of her hair free but I still saw the hair ornaments. If it is the woman I'm thinking of, she was at the massage parlor before with Kim. Zu and Raul interviewed her. But I don't know if she was still involved in anything shady."

"Seems likely, considering her current disposition," Jason pointed out.

"True, true." Kenny leaned over and patted his pig on the shoulder, then straightened. "I'll find out what I can for you."

"Thanks." Arin raked her fingers through her drying hair. "Aside from this surprise, do you have any news for us?"

Jason was definitely interested, too, but he kept his gaze on the beach, scanning the paths and even the water for anyone who might be too interested in their conversation.

"Your new guy, we've got a name." Kenny wasn't speaking loudly but his voice was cheerful and rang with satisfaction. He really did seem to like finding information. "Mr. Jones."

After a second, Arin cursed. "Seriously?"

Kenny shrugged. "Hey. It's a good name, especially if you want to be hard to find."

Jason nodded. "You have a point. There's got to be countless people with the same last name out there."

"Right on." Kenny bent and picked up a decent-sized stick, then started drawing in the sand at his feet. "Your Mr. Jones hasn't had time to fully establish himself in the islands yet. He started by shutting down the most vulnerable, exposed points of the operation, just like you said. That was only step one."

"He needs fresh stock to replace the people he eliminated over on the Big Island, the old and the ones too sick to be able to work hard anymore." Arin followed the logic. "There might be more we don't know about."

Kenny made a sound of agreement. "He's also reaching out, trying to strengthen current connections and establish new clients. He's more ambitious than your old friend. He looks to be building up political support as protection."

"Ugh." Arin kicked up a small puff of sand. "I hate politics."

Jason grimaced. "Political connections could make things much more complicated and bury everyone in red tape."

She started gathering up her tote and towel. "We need to eliminate him fast, before he tries to make an example of Mali."

"Before he establishes political connections on the island," added Jason. There wasn't anyone paying attention to them, not on the beach and not in the water. He turned to Arin. "And before he gains new buyers."

She scowled. "We need to figure out where to find this guy."

"True." Jason added, "We need to take him down."

Kenny joined in with his cheerful attitude. "Ah, but it's

not just about getting him behind bars. You need to cut him off from his support and whatever person put him here on Hawaii. Too many powerful men succeed in continuing to do business as usual from jail."

"We can discredit him if we catch him this early, before he establishes anything." Jason resisted suggesting they just locate the man and erase him from existence. It wasn't easy to go the route of the ethical and morally upright.

"We need to discredit him with his backers and cut off his supply of workers to sell." Arin folded her arms across her chest as she stared at the dead body. "We don't know for sure she's a casualty, but if that's who I think it is, she wouldn't be on this island if it wasn't for that bastard. I am very willing to lay her death at his feet."

Jason was more than inclined to agree. In fact, he admired Arin's calm determination. Whether she had a contract or not, she was on a mission.

"I can keep looking for more info, but I don't have those answers now." Kenny sounded sad to admit he didn't have all the intel they needed.

"You'll find it." Arin leaned toward Kenny, briefly bumping him with her shoulder. "I know you will."

Kenny chuckled. "Right on. I'll contact you when I've got something."

CHAPTER FOURTEEN

"Mali checked with the massage therapy place." Arin dropped her phone into her lap and rubbed her hands over her face. "The woman I remembered, her name was Gigi. She hadn't been in to work in at least a couple of days."

Jason kept a close watch on the road and all approaches via the side and rearview mirrors. He was happy to be in the driver's seat and surprised Arin had taken him up on the offer to drive back from Hanauma Bay. "So the victim might be her."

"It's sounding more and more likely, but we won't know for sure until Kenny gets us the medical examiner's report." She sighed. "There's no reason the police would actually give it to us. We're not engaged in an official search and rescue operation right now and it'd be overstepping for us to officially request insight into an active murder investigation."

But wouldn't it be convenient if they did? He was kind of wishing a few things would come easy, just once in a while.

"Then we wait."

She huffed out a laugh. "Not my forte, but yeah. We fill in Zu and Raul, then we wait."

They fell into silence for a few minutes, heading down the highway back to Honolulu and Arin's apartment. A thought poked at him until he finally nailed it down. The first person she'd called hadn't been Zu or Raul. It'd been her sister. Thinking of family before anything else might make sense for a lot of people, but finding a dead body wasn't at the top of his likely list for reasons to call home to Mom and Dad. Unless Arin had been worried and used it as an excuse to check on her sister.

"You told me why you left home, but you didn't tell me why you left Mali." Jason probably should've stopped pressing Arin to give up information about herself, but he couldn't help it. She seemed amazingly complex, but really, she was deceptively simple at her core. Family, friends, the people she cared about came before anything else. She was a better person than he'd ever met in his life, if only because she didn't pretend to be good.

"I don't know what you're talking about." Arin turned her head and stared at him from the passenger seat, suddenly wary.

Yeah, mention her little sister and the protective shift came up. He didn't have any siblings to look out for and he didn't experience a particular need to see to his parents. They'd eked out their own lives for themselves and had been more than happy to be relieved of the burden of caring for him when he'd decided to leave. But Arin had a family and her sister, in particular, meant more to her than anything.

"You said you left, but why? And why are you still walking on eggshells with her now?" That's what was bugging him. They were both adults and Arin was still so careful in her interactions with her sister.

She hesitated for a long moment, then answered him. "She was afraid of me. Part of her still is."

Ah. That'd be enough to stab him in the gut. It must be torture for Arin. The one thing that could hurt a person more than anything else in the world was what they cared about most.

"What happened?" There had to have been a trigger, something that had pushed Arin into the decision to sever ties with her sister. He couldn't believe she would have left otherwise.

"I did." Arin let her head fall back against the headrest. "She's never been a sturdy person. As a kid, she was tiny and easily bruised, even breakable. She was bullied a lot, especially at friendly gatherings where all the adults hung out in the kitchen or living room and the kids ran around in the yard or basement. Bigger kids would do things like lock her in a shed and tell her it was full of spiders or shut her down in a basement with no lights on and tell her monsters were coming up the stairs. I'd come along and let her out, but I had to get the big kids out of the way first. She'd burst out of wherever they'd shut her and see me on top of some kid, punching the hell out of him or her."

"Sounds heroic."

Arin shook her head. "Mali didn't respond well to witnessing those things. She cringed and ran away, brought back adults. I'd get in trouble for embarrassing my parents. They'd wonder why I couldn't be a good little Thai girl like she was."

"Why would she get you in trouble?" Jason was honestly confused. The two sisters didn't seem the type, though he hadn't had siblings so who was he to say what siblings might try to do to each other?

"I don't think she was trying to. I think she was trying

to save the person I was pounding into a pulp." Arin's voice was melancholy. "I never got upset with her for telling on me. She was right about me being too angry to stop when it was enough. I'd always go too far if you left me to it. I think she worried my outbursts would be directed at her someday. Seeing me angry or violent upset her. Even if I lightly tapped her on the shoulder or bumped her, she acted like I'd truly hit her."

Jason swallowed growing frustration. He'd met Mali and he'd liked her. She was a brilliant woman and truly affectionate. Raul was obviously in love with her. But if Jason had learned this about the relationship between the two sisters before meeting Mali, he'd have thought some really uncharitable things about her.

"We're fundamentally different." Arin stretched her arms forward, then let them fall into her lap. "Her reaction to brute force wasn't bad in any way. It's just really hard to love your sibling when you're afraid of what she can do. It's different when Mali looks at Raul because she met him as an adult, came to accept him as an adult. How she feels about me developed when we were kids and it was more of an amorphous fear when she looked at me."

"So you left."

She nodded slowly. "I left her to face bullies on her own. My parents loved us, but they also went with the belief that she had to learn to persist through the tough times. They believed bullies would eventually lose interest and move on. And even though I promised her I'd always be there, I didn't come back home for good."

Because her sibling had been afraid of her. What would he do if he went home to his parents and saw fear in their eyes? He might turn on his heel and never come back.

Yeah, he could understand where Arin was coming from with her choices.

"If I couldn't work it out of my system, I figured I could learn better control. I was obnoxious with my bursts of temper and destructive behavior. I didn't like who I was, either." Arin gave him a real smile, one of peace, but there was still no happiness there. "I went away. That was the most important part. The military was the right place for me for years while I figured out how to be constructive instead of just stupid angry all the time. And my sister did get through the hard time in her life, too. She's never mentioned me breaking the promise, hasn't held it against me. But she doesn't have to. I remember and I want to make it up to her."

"I think you're amazing." He waited for her to scoff at him. He glanced at her before returning his attention to the road. She was blushing and he vowed to tell her more of what she deserved to hear. If she was embarrassed, she didn't hear it enough. "Seems like you achieved what you were intending. Why not be more proud of what you do in front of your family?"

"Because what we do is still the stuff of nightmares."

She had a point. Their line of work was risky at the least; more usually, it was dangerous and life threatening. Both of them had been doing private contract work for some time and tenure in their careers meant they had blood on their hands. A successful mission might mean they'd gotten in and out of a place clean, without being discovered. Or it meant they'd left a trail of bodies in their wake. The latter happened more often than the former, and he couldn't think of any civilian he'd ever met who could handle those details without being at least partly horrified. He wasn't sure he wanted to meet someone who wasn't.

He understood her being hard on herself. He didn't think about it often, but he couldn't remember the last time he'd thought he liked himself either.

"Hey." He waited until she turned her head to look at him, then dropped one hand down to rest on the center console between them. "You are fierce and confident, and you create safe spaces so those gentler souls you keep talking about have a place to be. You are amazing. Don't think anything less than that of yourself."

And he'd strive to be even a fraction as good a person as she was.

She sputtered for a minute. After a moment she placed her hand in his. "Hi."

He grinned. There she was. This was the woman inside all the prickly defenses. "Hi."

CHAPTER FIFTEEN

Arin stood tall, holding her head high enough to feel her neck lengthen and keeping her shoulder blades lightly squeezed to pull her shoulders back. She kept her rib cage lifted and her abdominals tight. Childhood memories of years and years of ballet, jazz, lyrical, and even hip-hop dance training ran through her mind. There'd been precious hours studying Thai traditional dance with her mother, too. Posture was an amazing thing. It could help her be ready to move quickly and fluidly as she needed, project confidence, give an impression of grace, or recover from a blunder, leaving any witness wondering if she'd tripped up at all.

Posture was second nature to her after fifteen years of dance. She barely thought about it in basic or combat training. Over the years, she'd kept up her stretch and barre exercises because they helped her stay fit and also brought her calm. She'd practice the few Thai dances her mother'd taught her when she thought of home. She'd never had to consciously make these corrections before entering mission-related situations. This was different. This was social and maybe it was just in her head, but she felt as if all these people would be judging her. But she'd promised Mali she'd come to this event full of academics, and she was going to make good on that promise.

Today, as Jason offered her a hand out of the car her sister had sent to pick them up, she ran through the mental checklist to be sure every aspect of her posture was appropriate to the situation. She wasn't wearing armor, no protective gear of any kind, only a simple swing dress in deep, sapphire blue sateen. The skirt was hemmed a touch shorter than the classic pinup look, swirling just below her knees. She loved the dress because it was wash and wear, for the most part, though it took a bit of steam or an iron when she traveled with it. It didn't require foundational garments, which was another bonus in the Hawaiian humidity and heat. The bold color let her get away with very little jewelry or none at all. Here, at this brunch, looking at the guests milling around the reception area outside the restaurant, projecting confidence was the best protection she had.

Well, King was on her left and Jason stood at her right. They were handy, too. Especially Jason, because he'd taken the time to clean up and she kept getting distracted by the temptation to nuzzle his cleanly shaven jaw. The earthy spice she'd come to associate with him was brightened by fresh herbal notes today and she could quickly become addicted to his complex scent. He was saving her from her own overthinking.

"You're stunning," Jason murmured and offered his arm.

Startled, she slipped her hand in the crook of his elbow. She'd had men offer her courtesies in the past, but most of them did it to put on a show. Jason made her feel as if he was doing it specifically to support her. It was nice. "These functions put me on edge."

"Same." He'd dressed nicely in slacks and a button-up dress shirt. For a daytime event, he was already looking formal. Most of the men in attendance were wearing crisply ironed Hawaiian shirts over khaki shorts.

He was still standing in place, though, and abruptly, Arin realized he was waiting for her to take the lead. She stepped forward and he moved with her, the perfect escort.

"Smells good." He leaned toward her, easily keeping their conversation between them while still giving a casually relaxed image. They were just two guests, heading into a thing. No big deal.

She was glad to have his company, even if he had inserted himself into her sister's invitation. Otherwise, Arin would have been tense and standoffish. She'd probably have ended up lurking around the edges of the gathering, herding sheep without meaning to. King would've taken his cues from her and walked around stiff legged, maybe even with his ruff on end. Instead, they were entering at an easy pace and she could think about eating, even. Food was good. She could always talk about food. "The restaurant here is famous for their prime rib. If they have kālua pig roast, definitely try some of that, too. It's worth elbowing people in line to go for the good main dishes."

"Noted." His voice was rich with amusement. "You can face down multiple gunmen, head into a potentially dangerous situation, even hold steady in the presence of an IED without breaking a sweat, but a crowd full of academic types has you stressed out."

"I had mission objectives in those other circumstances." She kept her voice low but she didn't blunt the edge on her words. He was teasing her but she was too edgy to take it with good humor. "Here, I'm just trying to be 'not intimidating,' however the hell I'm supposed to manage that."

"Not possible." He shook his head. "And with due respect to your sister, you shouldn't have to. There's people in this room who will be intimidated to find out you exist. Don't bother with any of their issues. Even if you tried, you couldn't stuff everything you are far enough out of sight to ease their insecurities. Trust me. If you want, we can go for scandalous instead, and they'll forget to be intimidated. I can think of a lot of naughty things I'd like to do to you in that dress."

She came to a halt in the middle of the room, startled. People were turning and looking at them. Conversation directly surrounding them had hushed to curious murmurs. Normally, it would have made her uncomfortable, but she was hung up on what Jason might do if she told him to go for scandalous. The temptation was almost irresistible.

"Don't look at anyone in particular unless they ask for your attention," Jason advised quietly. "If you look directly at them, they'll look away, and you'll look at them more and that's when they freak out. Let them get used to you surreptitiously. Besides, they're mostly staring at King."

Jason was probably right. King was a big dog and an excellent example of Eastern German lines. His back didn't slope dramatically down to low hips the way some GSDs did, and he wasn't built like a black bear the way other mainland breeders might breed their dogs. The black and tan coloring was iconic in its own way, but it was actually rarer to find in GSD puppies. King was classic and striking with the added interest of the vest identifying him as search and rescue. He was also a dog entering a venue where pets weren't normally allowed.

"It's too hot out to leave him in any car." She had no doubt King would maintain obedience and stay wherever she left him, but part of the trust between him and her was that she'd also look out for his best interest.

"I wouldn't suggest it." Jason slipped his arm from under her hand and snagged two glasses of sparkling wine from a passing attendant. He offered one to her. "We're not on duty."

No, they weren't. It was also easier to mingle with a drink or plate of food in hand. She'd gone unconventional and clipped her end of King's leash to the back of the belt matching her dress. If King had to bolt somewhere, her belt would never hold, but he was so good on leash it wasn't likely to be a problem. For now, she could keep some of his leash loosely looped over her left hand but she could drop it and he'd still stay with her. "I'm surprised there aren't mimosas somewhere."

Jason looked at her with interest. "You like them? I could keep an eye out for you."

"I like Bellinis better." She took a sip. It wasn't bad for a sparkling wine served at a larger gathering. "I prefer fresh peaches and simple syrup over canned. Mimosas are nice, too, but I like them with a touch of Grand Marnier to seal them and a lot of these venues just do the orange juice and bubbly."

"Good to know." Jason grinned.

"Why?" She glared up at him, suspicious. This time it wasn't a serious kind of suspicion, more like he was up to mischief and she had no idea when this was going to come back to tease her later.

Before she could press him to answer, her sister popped out of the crowd and approached. "You're here."

Arin lightly embraced her sister. "As promised."

Mali beamed at her. Dressed in a flowing wrap dress with a delicate floral pattern, she was a refreshing sight. Arin smiled back, glad to be the reason her sister was smiling. Raul came out of the crowd balancing two small plates in one hand and shook hands with Jason. Taz, his leash clipped to the back of Raul's belt in a method similar to Arin's, traded sniffs and tail wags with King. Arin was glad Raul had kept Taz with him, too.

Raul lifted the plates and wafted them under Arin's nose. "We've been quality-checking the buffet."

"Need help?" Jason asked.

"Sure."

"Let's all go." Arin didn't want to risk Raul and Jason wandering off. Mali had responsibilities here and even if she meant to stay, there was a high chance someone would pull her away for some other conversation. Arin had no issues standing alone, but she was more likely to intimidate someone if she did. It was better to use the men as buffers. Besides, they were headed toward the food.

* * *

Jason was bemused by Arin's nervousness. He was betting she could navigate the same kind of event without a hint of stress if she'd been on a mission with a target, either to extract information or perform some other action. It was because this was for her sister and Arin actually cared about the impression she was making on her sister's behalf.

Mali had rescued her plate from Raul and refilled it at the buffet as Arin acquired her own plate of savories. The two of them were a powerful pair and the servers behind the carving stations and other buffet areas were left with stunned grins on their faces as the ladies plundered the offerings on the tables.

Jason couldn't help it. He nudged Raul and jerked his head toward their respective ladies, currently chatting in front of and with the man carving kālua pig. He was piling more and more succulent pork on their plates to keep them talking to him. "They don't even know, do they?"

Raul knew exactly what Jason was referring to. "Arin can do it on purpose when she's got to, but she doesn't realize she does it unintentionally, too. Mali generally doesn't realize it at all."

"The cuteness is strong with those two." Jason didn't think it was wise to call Mali sexy. Besides, her attractiveness really did edge more toward an inherent sweetness. Arin was sexy, for damned sure, but she was also cute and didn't even know it. When the sisters were together, more of the cute side came out. It was like catnip to him and he kept fighting the desire to coax Arin into some secluded corner.

The ladies in question rejoined them and they all stepped over to a high-top table to set down their drinks and plates and eat standing. Arin wordlessly slipped a plate in front of him. She'd gathered a selection of the prime rib and kālua pig for him, as well as what looked like barbecued chicken and some spicy edamame. There were also scoops of poke and a handful of fresh vegetable slices.

"This looks great. Thanks." Jason was surprised, actually. He easily could have headed over to the buffet himself, but it wasn't likely Raul would go with him. Arin's gesture allowed him to stay a part of the group and he appreciated it.

"So would you call this a success?" Arin asked Mali.

Mali nodded, chewing and swallowing before adding, "Definitely. There's been good networking and information sharing going on. There's some interesting discussions and I'm seeing good mixing of our colleagues from the mainland with our local scientists and subject matter experts."

"Why did you pick this place? It's kind of out of the way." They'd had to drive through what looked like a residential area before turning onto the winding road. Jason had almost thought they were lost until they'd arrived at this location, tucked away in the tropical vegetation.

"It's mostly a wedding venue." Mali shrugged. "I liked it because we could accommodate all of the guests in this reception area with the balcony overlooking the gardens and pond. The view of the mountains is gorgeous, but if it rained, we'd still be fine in here."

"Good call." Arin nibbled on a piece of fruit. "It's also secluded. Not too many ways to get at you in this kind of area. I'm not sure how I feel about you exposed on the balcony though."

Mali sighed. "Raul already let me know how close to the windows and balcony I can go. He also took precautions as we were arriving. I've got a route I'm supposed to leave by if anything unexpected happens here and there's a police car in the parking lot."

Jason raised an eyebrow and glanced at Raul, who shrugged. "They're mostly there to be visible."

Ah. Raul wouldn't talk about it where anyone could overhear, but Jason would guess they were leaving through the service entrance in a different car with an undercover police team as escort. Security was their shared profession, after all. A venue like this only had so many options. Keeping Mali safe would be more about fast reactions and back-up plans than secret escape routes. Anyone watching Arin would've seen her shacking up with him and going out doing tourist stuff like snorkeling. Hopefully, his former team wasn't aware of the fact that he and Arin had specifically been the ones to find the woman's body at Hanauma Bay. Other than that, they hadn't given his former team any reason to take a shot at Mali.

"Someone's here to see you." Mali put down her fork and snagged Arin's hand.

Arin allowed her sister to tug her around and a few steps away. They were still close enough for Jason to overhear. Standing to one side was Kim and her younger brother, looking much better for having safety, means to get clean, and a few solid meals. There were still hollows under the boy's eyes, but those had no cure but time.

"Thank you," Kim said quietly, clutching her brother's hand. "I can't thank you enough."

"I'm glad you're back together."

Seeing Arin standing next to her little sister, talking to another pair of siblings, filled Jason with a surprising buoyancy that left him unbalanced. He hoped Arin was finding some peace by having fulfilled a few of the promises she'd made. She might be trying to make her sister happy, but he intended to focus on making her happy, for as long as he could.

"Kim is providing us with testimony on how she and her brother ended up here," Mali said, still holding Arin's hand. "She's contributing to our research while she continues to work as a massage therapist. The more factual accounts we have, the more we can learn from them and put preventative measures in place."

"Good." Arin's smile was a little wider than normal and her tone was pitched a little higher. She seemed like she was trying to sound positive.

Jason saw a matching effort from Kim. They'd left their home for a reason and there'd been at least some level of urgency, if not desperation, involved. Even if Kim had been tricked into thinking there would be a salaried position waiting for her on the basis of her education, there were others who simply pulled together their life savings and any funding they could scrape together just for the chance to get to the United States. There were still others who were kidnapped, taken against their will. Preventative measures and education would help, but it wouldn't erase the evil people did to each other. Jason was realistic that way. Human nature was the reason why he would always have new opportunities for his kind of work.

Kim and her brother excused themselves after another minute and Mali stopped to chat with a fellow researcher. Arin returned to Jason and Raul.

"Kid looks better," Jason observed.

Arin nodded.

Raul knocked back the last gulp of his sparkling wine. "Even if we shut down this latest group, there's more popping up. It's going to be an ongoing thing, working to help people like Huy and his sister."

It was like a game of whack-a-mole. Smash one group and another popped out of a hole someplace else. The islands were a gateway to the mainland for many trafficking organizations. Theirs was a long war. Raul seemed to be settling in for the duration and Jason wondered if this was what Arin might dedicate herself to as well, especially considering her sister's involvement.

Before, he'd only ever considered his own career path. Now, he had a vested interest in where Arin's career choices would take her. He wasn't sure how long they'd be spending time together on the island, but he definitely wanted to be able to find her again wherever they went.

"The research Mali is doing will help expand current programs," Arin said with a conviction Jason admired, maybe wished he felt.

Raul and Jason both nodded in response.

"Your Search and Protect organization has to stay in the black, though. You can't do all this work pro bono." Jason pushed his emptied plate toward one side of the table. "I got the impression your main contracts are for location and extraction of high-value targets, kidnap victims worth more ransom than most of these governments have in funding in a year."

Arin nodded. "We have standing contracts with the US government and take on more as the right ones present themselves. If a situation comes up, we're called in. We're not looking to get rich. Zu manages us so we can work with local law enforcement for a reasonable fee."

Jason raised his eyebrows. "You give the government a discount."

"Doesn't everyone in our line of work? It's all in the negotiation of the contract." Arin sounded innocent about it but their commander, Zu, was managing some shrewd diplomacy in what she'd described. Jason wondered if she had more involvement in the contract negotiation than she let on.

Raul cleared his throat. "With me on the task force, I get insight into the actions taken from a law enforcement perspective."

"And I supplement local law enforcement when I'm not assigned on the mainland or overseas on contract." Arin sipped at her sparkling wine and looked up at him through her long eyelashes. She was elegant and confident, exuding a spicy touch of danger. "Once we find and take out this new boss, I don't know if you'll be staying around or if I'll end up facing off with you in the middle of a mission again someday. But I, at least, will continue to find the lost people normal methods can't save."

God, she was beautiful.

CHAPTER SIXTEEN

Jason figured it was a good thing Arin hadn't planned to drive back to her place. By the time they got there, the drinks she'd consumed had worked through her system enough to open a floodgate of internal thoughts he might never have gotten to hear otherwise.

He was thoroughly enjoying every minute.

"I'm not endearing." She made the statement in a tone somber enough for him to wonder if her happy tipsy was taking a turn into moody. "Not like my sister. Every person in that place loved her. Not like other women, either. I'm decisive and stubborn and bossy, built like a beast and maybe curvy enough to be sexy, if a person is brave enough or stupid enough to tell me so, but no one has ever considered me endearing or...cute."

She'd left out fierce and full of vitality, charismatic and incredibly sure in her convictions, and maybe a little psychic considering his earlier comments to Raul. She was fucking inspiring. There was hurt in her voice, though, and a hint of wistful sadness he was surprised to hear. "Do you want to be cute?"

She glared at him, her cheeks flushed and her eyes glassy. "No."

She paused, and he could virtually see gears turning as she considered his question more thoroughly.

"Maybe, to the right person. Yes. Sometimes. Not most of the time. But sometimes."

He watched her stumble out of her shoes and drop them close to where they were supposed to go on a shoe rack, but ultimately missing her target. King was prudently hanging out in the living area and avoiding being underfoot.

Jason shook his head. "I'm confused."

"Most of the world can suck it. When those people say any woman is cute, they mean it as an insult. Hell, I've used it as an insult. I don't ever want to leave those people the opening to think of me as cute." She straightened and flipped her hair off her shoulder, heading toward her kitchen area. She pulled a saucepan out and lit the stove.

Drunk and playing with fire, especially on a gas stove, seemed like a bad idea. "Hungry?"

He approached her with caution, wondering if he could redirect her or at least help so she didn't blow up her apartment building.

"I'm obviously more inebriated than I usually get. Mali has a way better tolerance for alcohol than I do." She waved a packet of ramen at him. "It's been a few hours since we ate at the buffet, so I'm making myself a bowl of salty noodles to rehydrate and getting something in my stomach besides booze. You want some?"

Did she realize how generous she was? "Yes, please."

She turned back to her small kitchen area and opened the fridge. "We'll need protein. We should have some protein in this."

"Okay." He hovered near the stove, watching to be sure

there was actually water in the pot and that only the burner she needed was on and lit. She pulled a package of hot dogs out of the freezer and tore it open, then reached for a knife. He edged closer. "You don't need that."

She brandished the knife. "Stay back. This, I'm capable of doing, but don't get in my way. I need to do this without worrying about you."

"Standing right here and not coming closer." He had no doubts about her ability to handle a blade. It was just prudent to step back and give a cook some room.

In minutes, she had the hot dogs cut up into sort of long segments. If bite-sized was what she was going for, she might've overestimated the size of her mouth and his.

The water was boiling in the pot and she quickly tossed in the blocks of noodles from two packages. She emptied the seasoning packets in next and following up a minute later with the hot dog pieces.

"There's noodle bowls up in the cabinet in front of your face." She sounded grumpy, but he was glad she was letting him contribute. He'd expected her to shove him out of the way if she wanted to get anything.

When he complied and set the bowls on the counter, she murmured a quiet thanks.

Another two minutes and she'd split cooked noodles evenly into each bowl and poured the steaming broth over the top. Then she'd retrieved the hot dog pieces out of the pot. She must've done more knife work on the hot dogs then he'd realized because sections had curled up halfway along the lengths of each piece during cooking, so now they each had little hot dog octopi sitting on top of the noodles. She might've been tipsy when they'd gotten back to the apartment, but he was guessing she'd sobered up as she'd focused on cooking.

As she handed him chopsticks, he grinned at her.

She glared back. "What?"

"There are cephalopods on my noodles."

She scowled. "So? Food can be fun."

"You like to make food more than sustenance. Whether it's rice balls or late night noodles or whatever. You make it look appealing or fun or both and right now you've made hot dogs look like fancy garnish and you don't think you're cute." Jason lifted a hot dog octopus with his chopsticks and waved it at her. "You're prickly on the outside and I surely respect your strategic and tactical skills on the job, but you are cute in a hundred little ways. Someone else might blink and miss it, but I enjoy it."

Having said his piece, he popped the hot dog in his mouth before she could smack it off the end of his chopsticks. But she didn't take a swipe at him; instead she took her bowl and chopsticks to the breakfast counter. She hopped up to sit on the surface with her feet dangling and picked up the bowl with both hands to sip her broth.

He kept his mouth shut and shook his head. She was damned cute, but he wasn't going to push his luck and tell her again. They ate in companionable peace. Honestly, the ramen hit the spot and he hadn't thought he could be hungry again after the huge buffet. But it'd been a solid three to four hours since they'd stopped eating, done the requisite socializing, said good-byes, and finally gotten through the car ride home. He placed his bowl in the sink and turned, holding out his hands for hers.

She tilted her head. "What?"

"You done?"

"Yes." She drew the word out, still staring at him with suspicion.

He huffed. "You cooked. It's only fair if I clean. Besides, you're letting me crash here with you and I appreciate it."

She handed over the bowl and remained seated on the counter, watching as he made short work of washing the dishes and the pot. When he finished, he faced her again.

There she was, sitting neat as you please with her shapely legs crossed at the ankles.

He wanted her in so many ways.

"You are cute." The statement left his mouth before he'd had a chance to consider it and he realized restarting the line of conversation could darken her mood again. But he pressed on. "You're beautiful. You're amazing and I am incredibly attracted to you. I don't think you hear that enough."

She pressed her lips together. "Where have you done work?"

"Huh?" Apparently she'd hopped to a different subject entirely.

"It's your turn to share with me. People in our profession can find plenty of work on the mainland or we can work globally. You started in South Africa. It's hard to find the means to leave and make a new life for yourself, so I'm guessing you did various kinds of work there before you moved on, but where else have you been before you ended up here?"

There was no accusation in her voice. She seemed to get it, that he'd had to work in the grey area between legal and illegal, good and bad. Actually, he'd mostly not cared about the latter. He'd tried to stay on the side of legal once he could afford to.

"Hot spots, mostly. I went where there was solid money. I've been to the Middle East and Central Asia, gotten some experience in Eastern Europe, and done work in East and Southeast Asia." He'd need to have more time and be more sober to list his exact history. For years, he hadn't cared where he went so long as the job paid well. "I've worked a couple of times on the mainland United States and gone back to Asia before I landed here with this last private security firm. It was my first job for them and I doubt I'll be working with them again."

She nodded. "They did try to kill you."

He lifted his shoulders and grimaced. "It's a good thing I put queries out for new positions before I headed to Big Island. Proof I wasn't planning to stick around to become a permanent problem for them. It's probably another reason they didn't try super hard. They tried to scare me into keeping my mouth shut and leaving as soon as possible if I did manage to survive. But their primary specialization is actually security."

"You don't think they're really going to try to kill my little sister, then?" Arin's tone had dropped in volume to a deadly quiet.

He approached her, anyway. "I think they're using her as leverage to make you and your team back off. Which is exactly what you think. I wouldn't put killing past them and that's why I'm still here to help you make sure they don't keep going after her. But they're not as versatile as your team. They're good at surveillance but not good enough. I think you can go after their source of funding before they can crack the security around your sister to try to make you stop. I'd like to help if you let me stay."

* * *

Let him stay.

Arin was tempted to ask him how long he planned to. She didn't, because she wasn't prepared to hear the answer if it meant he'd be leaving right after they completed the current shared objective. She avoided past history and she didn't want to overthink the future either. His leaving right away was the worst-case scenario, but it was safer for her to assume it was the case anyway.

In the meantime, here he was in her kitchen, having just finished doing dishes. She'd watched him as he'd completed the simple task. He had a wonderfully broad back and his shirt sat across his shoulders just right. The fabric shifted as he'd moved, washing and drying, then putting things away. He was thorough and efficient in every way, wasting nothing, whether it was water on dishes or time in a tense situation.

She wasn't looking forward to seeing him go.

"I want a shower." She hopped off the counter. Pausing, she turned to look at him, still standing in the kitchen area, and let the happiness bubble up when she realized he was watching her intently. "Coming?"

She didn't wait for a verbal response. Instead, she headed for her bathroom before her deeply rooted caution took back the invitation she'd thrown out. Because she'd enjoyed being with him before and she wanted to again.

Stripping off her dress, she turned on her shower and stepped out of her panties. She ducked under the water as the bathroom door opened, then closed again. Instead of looking directly at him, she watched Jason strip out of his clothes in the mirror's reflection. He stood for a moment, gloriously naked and completely erect, staring back at her via the reflection.

"Hi." It was all she could think of. He short-circuited her brain in about fifty different ways and looking at him, all of him, her nipples tightened in anticipation and she was wet from more than the shower.

He joined her in the shower and she was glad it could fit

them both. Part of the reason she'd chosen this apartment was for the generous bathroom space. If there was one thing she indulged in, it was long showers or baths.

He stood behind her, placing his hands on her hips, and dropped a kiss on her shoulder. "Hi."

One word, spoken in his deep voice and with a hint of his South African accent, and she melted. She turned and pressed the length of her body against his, reaching up to wrap her arms loosely around his neck. He bent his head and they kissed, slow and hot...and fantastic. The hot water from the shower ran down her back, adding to the tactile stimulus as she reveled in the skin-to-skin contact with him. She was almost out of her mind already.

"Let's make sure you feel clean, so I can get you all sorts of dirty again." He held her against him with one hand at her back as he reached for her loofah with the other.

Instead of answering, because she was way too turned on to come up with a clever response, she helped him load it with liquid soap scented with lavender and mint.

He turned them both so his back was to the shower spray and started to lather her up.

Inhaling deeply, he made a sound of deep appreciation. "I can't get enough of the way you smell. It's this, all luscious and fresh, mixed with you."

She wasn't exactly sure he was making any sense but she was enjoying the way his scent mingled in the steam with hers, all cinnamon and clove spice and herbs. She closed her eyes and took it all in.

Mostly he used the loofah in long, gentle strokes. But he also used his other hand, paying special attention to her nipples. By the time he turned her around to lather her back she was awash in sensation, and she leaned against the shower wall to tease him with her behind. He teased her right back,

sliding his fingers along the inside of her thighs before coast-
ing his palms over her rear and up her back.

"Let's rinse you off now."

She went along with his prompt because it made her feel
good and because his tone made it a suggestion, not a command. They switched places and as the warm water washed
over her, she sighed with pleasure, leaning back against him,
very aware of the length of his erection against her back.

"You like the water?" He whispered the question in her
ear as he reached around to her front and dipped a finger inside her.

She gasped and clutched his arm, but he was relentless
as he pumped his finger in and out of her center. She let her
head tip back and to the side, exposing her neck. Without
hesitation, he dragged hot kisses from just behind her ear to
her shoulder. He slid two fingers inside her and began whis-
pering encouragement for her to enjoy. Listening his voice,
having the water run over her skin as his fingers were inside
her, she lost herself and came.

He held her through her orgasm, continuing to stroke her
and prolonging it. It'd been a staggering burst of ecstasy,
leaving her breathless. Drawing in steamy air, she looked up
and over her shoulder at him. "I'm clean but you promised
to make me dirty again."

He growled, releasing her and urging her to lean forward
and brace her hands on the opposite shower wall. The hot
water continued to fall over her lower back and behind. He
tickled her most delicate, very sensitized parts, encouraging
her to widen her stance. Then he put a hand on her hip.

"Steady?" His question was strained, barely coherent.

"Yes," she whispered over the sound of the water. *Oh yes.*

He used his free hand to guide himself inside her. He
entered her in a smooth, unrelenting push until he'd buried

himself to the hilt. She groaned, savoring the way he stretched her in all the right ways. "Feels so good."

His agreement wasn't in words so much as an inarticulate groan of his own. He started moving then, pulling out almost completely before sliding back into her. Her body tightened around him, so close to cresting again. She opened her eyes, staring at the tiles and trying to hang on this time, but he picked up the pace. He pounded into her hard and fast until her own cries of pleasure were echoing in the shower. The waves of sensation pushed her closer and closer until she crested into a second orgasm.

He stayed inside her through it and just as she shuddered through the end of her orgasm, he pulled out and came in a hot release across her lower back.

The only sound in the shower, then, was the falling water and their ragged breathing. After a minute, he helped her straighten to stand under the spray and said, "Now I get to clean you up again."

She laughed.

CHAPTER SEVENTEEN

Can I help you?"

Arin looked around the office area of the marine terminal service at Honolulu Harbor and gave the man one of her sweetest smiles. "I hope so."

Kenny had left her a message early that morning with a copy of the medical examiner's report confirming the body they'd found at Hanauma Bay had been Gigi. He'd also included a separate lead on an employee of this company, privately owned and providing support to container ships and tankers moving in and out of this major port for Oahu. The facilities here were much bigger than the harbor terminal they'd searched back on the Big Island at Kawaihae Harbor a few nights ago. The employee had ties with the human trafficking ring and he might've been involved with Gigi.

The office manager rose from behind his desk, then caught sight of King beside her and paused. "We don't allow dogs in this area, ma'am."

"He's a service dog." She didn't want to have to call up her contacts at the local police station to vouch for King as a working dog. Hopefully, this man would let it go. "I promise, we won't be here any longer than necessary. Maybe just a few minutes."

The man eyed King doubtfully. Jason seemed to be taking advantage of the man being so focused on her canine partner. He stood just inside the door, behind Arin, and said nothing as he did his best to be as uninteresting as possible. They'd both worried the man might be intimidated by Jason's presence but agreed it'd be better for them both to go in to ask questions. They could compare notes on what they thought afterward.

Arin decided not to wait for the man to agree to King's presence and pressed forward with her questions. "I was curious about your services. Do you provide the personnel to handle all of the marine cargo here?"

The man shrugged. "Yeah, for the most part. We supply ship and barge lines with both the personnel and appropriate equipment for handling cargo, plus processing documents."

"Do they handle the containers or what's in them, too?" She wasn't sure if there were subcontractors to the marine terminal wandering around, handling the contents of the containers after they arrived. She was hoping, for once, for a simpler organization. It'd make finding this employee a lot more straightforward.

"Both." The man puffed out his chest with pride, going into a sales mode. "Our guys are qualified to handle domestic and foreign containers, the container cargo inside, break bulk cargo, and more. Whatever you're shipping, our personnel can take good care of it."

"Funny you put it that way." She thought it was a coincidence. No person involved in the business of trading and selling human assets would be so obvious about it. "You have any new hires in the last several months?"

"You looking for somebody specific?" The guy wasn't stupid. He was getting suspicious and she wasn't police.

She shrugged. It'd be a waste of time to try to look harmless. Instead, she tried for nonchalant. "A friend of a friend. We've got a mutual new acquaintance in town and I wanted to reach out and make sure he knew. No one checks their voice mail these days."

"Huh." The man glanced at King and back at her. "No new guys recently but we do have a pretty high turnover rate. No one wants to work this job forever."

It'd be too easy if there were new hires. Of course it would be. So the person they were looking for had been established here under the old management of the trafficking ring and must be continuing to work under the new boss. "My friend has trouble sleeping. Any chance you have a person on payroll for a while who started asking for shift changes? Maybe not officially, just swapping with other guys a lot?"

Any movement of human captives would have to be in the dead of the night, during the graveyard shift, when there'd be the lowest possibility of witnesses. It'd be obvious if a person regularly worked the graveyard shift, but less likely to be documented if someone was just swapping shifts with a coworker here and there when shipments were due into port.

The man nodded. "A couple of guys swap shifts every once in a while. They have lives and sometimes they have things they can't get out of, like their wife or kid's birthday."

"Maybe he used to ask for overtime, but he gave up on that and just started switching shifts so he could work a different part-time job? It'd be more often than a birthday or anniversary." Asking for extra shifts would've happened when their guy couldn't find someone to swap with or when he got caught by surprise and a shipment was coming in before he could make arrangements. It was more noticeable, but he might not have done it often.

Arin was hoping for a hit. Nothing she was asking was too specific when taken separately, but her questions could give them a good lead when taken all together.

"I got a couple of guys who have other part-time jobs." He scratched the stubble on his chin. "Yeah, one used to always bug me for more hours. He doesn't anymore so long as he can find people to switch shifts. His whining used to be a pain in the ass so I don't have a problem with him swapping as long as they all take care of it among themselves and no one misses a shift."

Now this was a promising lead. She didn't ask for a name, though; after all, she was looking for a friend of a friend. "Any idea when he'll be in next?"

She and Jason had timed their arrival to be right around shift change. She was hoping they'd catch a lead coming off shift or coming in for the next one.

"Yeah. He just finished. Should be in the locker room getting changed." The man waved her and Jason back out the front door and came outside with them. Then he pointed at a door farther down the side of the building.

"I don't want to go lurking by the door. That'd be creepy." Arin bit her lower lip.

The man laughed. "Aw nah, but you ain't going to want to see any of those guys with no clothes on. They've got some hairy-ass sausages."

She was not even going to parse his warning. No. She didn't want a visual.

"I'll go call him out for you." The man waved for them to follow him.

The door to the locker room was at the other end of the building. One or two men came out as they approached but the manager didn't do more than nod or wave at them. When he reached the locker room, he didn't bother walking in. Instead he just opened the door and shouted, "Hey, Nick!"

There was a pause followed by various masculine comments Arin couldn't make out from where she stood.

The manager waited for her, King, and Jason to walk up to him. He scratched his head. "Nick was here and got changed, then said he forgot something out in the terminal. He left to go find whatever it was a couple of minutes ago."

"Oh." Arin kept her face sweetly confused as she considered the possibilities. He might've spooked if he'd heard them asking questions in the office. Or this man could've really forgotten something. Another option, which she would very much like to investigate, was that he could be checking on a shipment that had already arrived.

The question was, in broad daylight and with workers at this harbor around the clock, how would they investigate further?

"Why don't you leave a note in his locker?" Jason asked, waving a sticky note. "I'll ask the rest of the guys in there to step out for a minute."

He was proving to be a good human partner. He gave her and King enough room to work if they needed to, didn't make her feel as if she needed to manage him or get into a pissing contest every other moment over who was taking the lead. Pride or arrogance wasn't a thing with him, and he had no problems following someone else's lead, then stepping up when his skill set became the more urgent solution. Arin suspected he wouldn't have any problems finding a position with future private contract companies.

She gave him a look of honest relief. "Thank you."

Jason nodded to the manager and stepped into the locker room. As he did, she squelched an unexpected pang in her chest. Thinking about him finding a new position led to thinking of him leaving.

A few casual words were exchanged and a handful of men came out of the locker room, mostly dressed. One or two gave her a mildly interested look, but they generally didn't seem too curious. Jason popped his head out and motioned for her to enter.

The manager held the door for her but remained outside. "Gotta keep an eye on the office."

Jason was leaning next to a locker. When she approached, he pointed to the inside and murmured, "I asked a few of the guys which locker belongs to Nick. It's clean, as in no potentially explosive surprises, but not by any other definition. You and King need a scent, right?"

Arin glanced at the pile of discarded T-shirts at the bottom of the locker. "One of those'll do."

* * *

After a few minutes in the locker room they were free to start looking for "Nick," and Jason was eager to get moving. Finally, they headed toward the small parking lot as the manager returned to his office. Then they circled back around the building to use the locker room door as a starting point.

This part was Arin and King's specialty, so Jason was fine with taking a support role. He had fallen into a comfortable working rapport with the pair, and he'd even considered what it would be like long term. But this was temporary. He'd inevitably start to itch for opportunities to take the lead himself. Arin was a natural leader with the ability to analyze a situation and make split second decisions, executing them before too many variables changed. He had enough experience to stay out of her way, but he wasn't the type of operative to be happy in a supporting position for too long.

The way Search and Protect was structured, from what he'd gathered to date, each human/dog combination worked as a stand-alone team, but the teams could come together for a bigger operation under the command of Zu Anyanwu. Since it'd been Arin to break off and work solo on Big Island, Jason wouldn't be surprised if Arin might be another lead if multiple human and dog pairs were brought together in secondary fire team. She seemed to have an instinctive ability to monitor the state of the dogs around her in addition to the humans. Jason was fine around King, but he didn't know what the dog was communicating in the same way Arin or Raul seemed to understand their respective canine partners.

Arin rose from giving King a good, long sniff of the T-shirt she'd bagged and squirreled into her small backpack earlier. "We have to be fast. It's only a matter of time before security notices us in the terminal area. A dog with two people who aren't in uniform or work clothes will definitely look out of place."

"So let's be quick." Jason held out his arm to indicate she should lead the way.

Arin and King treated this search differently from the one back at Kawaihae Harbor. This time, King hit on a trail right at the locker room door. Jason supposed it was to be expected since they knew the man they were trying to find had recently been in the locker room, but there'd been a lot of guys in there and Jason was amazed the dog could sift through the scents to find the single one he'd been tasked to identify.

Jason followed a short distance behind as Arin and King followed the scent trail. Their target hadn't been trying to hide so it was a straightforward walk through the shipping container area. In the meantime, Jason kept an eye out for movement around and ahead of them. There weren't likely to be multiple hostiles, but remaining vigilant was always a good idea.

In the end, there was no need to wait for King to signal his find, because they were still yards away when a man came out from between container stacks and froze when he saw them. King's head came up as he sniffed at the breeze coming toward them, ostensibly carrying the man's scent. Arin saw him, too.

Then the man erased any doubt by bolting.

Jason ran after him, pouring on the speed to catch up before their target took too many sharp turns and lost them. Before the man could do more than dart between container stacks, Jason had him and took his feet out from under him.

A moment later, Arin and King joined them.

Jason looked up as they approached. "Why didn't you send the dog?"

He'd seen plenty of videos and even real life working dogs take down a running adult. King might be a search dog, but Jason was sure he'd seen evidence of bite and attack training, too, in the way Arin sometimes ordered King to stand guard. Generally, a dog trained to keep watch could follow up with a more aggressive action if the subject moved or tried to flee. He knew King also helped her clear rooms or spaces for unknown assailants, a more tactical behavior and not a task a search dog would normally conduct. Again, if they encountered a potential adversary, a dog helping to clear the room could respond with action more aggressive than just alerting Arin to the person's presence.

Arin shook her head. "We're not here on official police search. There could be legal action against King and it's my responsibility to protect him from humans, the ways they can twist a situation. You had it covered, so there was no reason to expose King to the consequences."

Her rationale made sense and he'd enjoyed the burst of adrenaline. She was so capable, he'd been mostly on standby. This'd been a nice change of pace.

Jason yanked the man to his feet. He had a few days' growth to his beard and was overdue for a haircut. His clothes were worn but reasonably clean, like he'd worn them repeatedly but at least had washed them between wears. "Look, tell us what we need to know and we all can go home."

"I don't know anything." The man's eyes were wide and he was shaking his head.

"You don't even know what we—" Arin started at the same time as Jason.

"Sure you do—"

They both paused and Jason looked at Arin. She nodded for him to continue. "Or you wouldn't need to run."

The man remained silent.

Jason got into the man's face, giving him nowhere to look but Jason. "Three questions. That's all. Answer them and you can go."

They'd agreed on the line of questioning on the car ride here. It'd been up for grabs as to which one of them got to ask but since Arin had been doing most of the heavy work, Jason figured he could step in.

The man's gaze darted left and right, anything to avoid direct eye contact. "Just three?"

"Three," Jason agreed. "You're not going anywhere until you answer them."

After another moment's hesitation, the man nodded.

"When was the last time you saw Gigi?" Arin's voice was flat, devoid of any heat.

The blood drained from the man's face.

"We'll know if you lie." Jason warned him. Technically, they might not but this guy was completely open and readable. He probably lost all the time in poker.

"It was an accident," he whispered. "The new boss, he sent her to me. She was supposed to do what I wanted. She said she was going to leave, go get a new job, talk to the police about me."

Jason tightened his grip on the man until he gasped for breath. Yeah, they planned to let the man go, but the police would know exactly where to find him, and they'd have the video from King's harness camera to prompt a formal confession.

Arin leaned close. "Are there any human captives hidden here now?"

The man's eyes widened.

"Answer the question," Arin snapped. Beside her, King growled on the tail end of his mistress' demand.

"No." The man stuttered out the response. "Not yet. Soon. I was checking to make sure I knew where to put the container. Preparing. I swear."

He turned his head from Jason to look at Arin, then King, then Arin again. "It's the truth."

Jason gave the man a shake to bring his focus back. "Where can we find this new boss of yours? Not the man you talk to. The real boss. The man who's going to own these people."

Arin was staring at the man with hardcore intensity. King was in the lower edge of Jason's peripheral vision and the dog was staring at their target, too. Arin and King in tandem were intimidating as hell, and they weren't even focused on him.

The man shook his head again. "I don't know."

Jason laughed in his face, making the sound of it deliberately ugly. "I think you're lying."

"No, no! I'm telling the truth!" Their man was all eyes on Jason now as the nearer threat. "The new boss, he likes the hostess clubs. You know, the private clubs where the ladies all stay with you as long as you want. Talk, laugh, treat you good. You want boys? They've got boys host clubs, too. He schmoozes and meets with important clients at the hostess clubs."

"You don't say?" Jason eased back and gave the man a look of mild interest.

The man nodded eagerly. "Yeah, yeah. He makes some of his girls work at one or two of the hostess clubs, too, as training, before they get into more serious work or he sells them."

So the new boss started the women he had light, with hosting and entertaining. Once they'd caught the eye of a few patrons, he sold the women into prostitution or worse. Jason was glad he wasn't working for a man like this new boss, however indirectly, and he was certain Arin and Raul would enjoy taking the boss out of his newly acquired position of power. He would be happy to help them.

"Bonus question." Actually, Jason had stopped counting because obviously their man was ready to answer anything to walk away from this. "Which club is his favorite?"

They were going to need to bump into the new boss, maybe set up a little conversation with him. As satisfying as it would be to make the man disappear, Arin and Raul were on the side of the lawful so they'd have to gather enough evidence to take him down legally.

"It's right in Honolulu." Nick screwed up his face as he thought about it. "Club's name is One in a Million."

"You stay right where you are. Don't move and my friend

here won't have any reason to start barking." She turned to King and gave him a quiet command.

King moved to sit, staring hard at Nick. There was nothing friendly in the canine's demeanor.

Jason appreciated that Arin had said out loud that King would bark, but he was guessing King would bark then do more if Nick tried to make a break for it. The expression on Nick's face showed a healthy fear that the big GSD might do a lot more, too.

Arin moved several yards away, out of earshot but still maintaining line of sight as Jason joined her.

Arin scowled. "If we confront this new boss, get him talking, we could get him to give up the information we're looking for." She paused. "Interrogation wouldn't work as well as tempting him with a distraction."

Jason considered where she might be going with that. While the idea of her dressing to tease the information out of a target had its allure, he didn't think it was going to work. Not that she couldn't do it well. There were women in their line of work who loved the mind games, did what they set out to do well, and Jason had utmost respect for their skill. Maybe Arin was one of them. But he had a different approach in mind.

Jason shook his head. "I don't think we need a woman to tempt him. He's a predator and he's got all the victims he needs. We need something else."

Arin stared at him. "What did you have in mind?"

"What's he looking for?" Jason grinned at her. "This guy supplies women and even boys as entertainment for all the high-paying clients, right? He's looking for the real players on the island and the high rollers. We need a whale."

CHAPTER EIGHTEEN

"Charlie here," Arin murmured the call sign into her comm as she kept an eye on Jason through her scope. She'd chosen her vantage point hours ago and settled in with her rifle. Happily, this particular host club was an open air lounge on top of a high-rise. She'd chosen a neighboring office building with a few of those rooftop decks for office workers to get some fresh air or take their lunch. She hadn't been able to access the topmost roof, but she'd found a good public conference room with a balcony to suit her purposes. It was a slightly higher elevation than the club and she had a clear line of sight to everything but the private rooms. "Juliett, I can provide cover as long as you don't go into a restroom or private area deeper in the club."

"Copy," Jason growled.

She allowed herself a smile. He didn't have a permanent call sign the way the members of Search and Protect had. For the purposes of tonight's activity, they'd simply taken the first letter of his name and used the phonetic alphabet, so J for Jason had become Juliett to the Search and Protect team on site, mainly her and Raul. Jason hadn't argued but he also hadn't accepted it cheerfully.

"I'm entering now. How do I look?" He emerged from the elevator out to the lounge area sharply dressed in a white dress shirt and black suit pants. Even though his outfit was simple, the way he wore it was breathtaking. He'd left the collar open to expose the hollow at the base of his neck and a hint of the definition across his collarbones. His broad chest filled out the shirt and he'd rolled up the sleeves neatly, exposing his sculpted forearms. His biceps bulged against the fabric of his sleeves. He'd slicked back his dark hair and his tan provided a contrast against the white of his shirt. There were black lights around the DJ booth and bar, so his shirt literally glowed. So did his teeth, when he smiled.

She couldn't resist. "But soft, what light through yonder window breaks? It is the east and Juliett—"

"Oh no." Jason stopped smiling, but otherwise continued his casual mingling as he placed an order at the bar.

Raul chuckled over the comm. "Bravo here. I'm all for chatter and keeping it light, but a romance?"

"It's not a romance—"

"Technically, it's a tragedy—"

Arin stopped short as she realized both she and Jason had responded. Jason laughed, directing it at a pretty little woman in a tight white dress. He emanated charm and she had to admit he had amazing charisma. There was no missing him, even in a crowded lounge area and watching him through the scope of a rifle. "Fine. I'll quit quoting one of the most well-known romantic tragedies."

Below, Jason allowed the white dress to lead him over to a set of couches. He lifted his drink to his mouth and murmured into his comm. "Wouldn't want to jinx this. That play didn't end well."

He had a point.

She settled in to listen as Jason guided the chatter of the woman in the white dress and a couple of her fellow hostesses. Each of the women varied in their conversational skills. The white dress was the lead, most intelligent, and had some skill in keeping people entertained. The others were all giggles and cleavage or suggestive caresses. They all hung on Jason's every word as if he was their window to the outside world. Even though this club featured hostesses on payroll—mostly identifiable because the patrons were almost exclusively men—these women weren't victims of human trafficking as far as Arin could tell, but she kept an eye out for the signs just in case. She had no issues with people hosting or escorting as a chosen livelihood. It became wrong when those people were forced against their will. The insidious thing about human trafficking was how much of it happened right in front of law-abiding citizens and no one believed it could possibly be happening in this day and age.

"I'm to make some new friends," Jason was saying. "Special friends."

"That so?" The white dress pressed her shoulder against his. "We aren't friends yet?"

Jason smiled at her and the fierceness of it sent a shiver down Arin's spine. He could project creepy like a pro. "You're nice. Wonderful, in fact. But I'm looking for a few friends who might be new to the island and looking for a...benefactor. They'd keep me company while I'm here on business and I'd see to it they have all the things they need."

White dress surprised Arin then, leaning back from Jason. "We don't need to be friends, then."

The woman started to rise and Jason caught her hand. She whirled and he let her go, holding his hands up to show he meant no harm. "Did I say something wrong?"

She glanced away, then gave him an equally insincere smile. "Not at all, honey. I'm just looking to help you find what you're actually looking for. There's a new guy over by the fireplace. He's brought his own party along with him. You might find your...new friends with him. But none of them work here."

"Thank you." Jason remained seated as the woman in the white dress stalked away.

"She definitely doesn't like you anymore," Raul commented.

"You only heard her." Arin tracked white dress for as long as she remained in view without taking her scope off Jason. "You should see her body language. She definitely has a distaste for our Juliett."

Jason had an arm around one of the giggle girls. "Aw, I can't blame her for leaving. There's so much excellent company here."

Giggle girl leaned her head in and rubbed against his chest. "Mmm. You want to buy another bottle of champagne?"

She was definitely a hostess. Hosts and hostesses made their commissions based on the bottle service each customer purchased. The more bottles they bought and the more expensive the beverages, the more the hosts and hostesses made. Their job was to keep customers engaged, entertained, and ordering more. Arin was almost sad the woman in the white dress had left. At least that woman made for interesting conversation.

But apparently, Jason had decided to send his giggling companions off with a pat on the shoulder blades. Instead, he sent a bottle of champagne over to the man their white dress friend had identified. A minute later he strolled over and was stopped by bodyguards.

"Are you kidding me?" Jason's attitude morphed, his tone full of entitlement and privilege.

The bodyguards didn't back down but the businessman stood and approached. "Who are you?"

Jason shrugged. "I'm a private security specialist and an entrepreneur. One of my lady friends over there told me you might be a businessman worth connecting with. I've been on the island almost a year, providing security services. I've been buying small businesses on the side and turning them over for profit, but I'm looking to diversify my interests."

The best lies came from as much truth as possible. At least half of what Jason had said was true. It was even possible he had a legitimate interest in entrepreneurship, too. If he did, she'd be curious to know what kinds of businesses he looked for. She wanted to know more and more about him, even if she hadn't admitted it out loud yet.

The businessman gave Jason an incredulous look. "And you came over here on the recommendation of a whore?"

Arin snorted. Their target was a winner, a real gem of humanity.

Jason's reply was smooth and unruffled. "I sent over a bottle with my compliments by way of introduction. Not interested? That's fine. Enjoy the bottle."

Jason turned to leave.

Their target placed a hand on the shoulder of one of his bodyguards. "Wait."

The bodyguards relaxed a fraction and moved back enough to give both men room. Jason faced the man again, his expression cold.

"Bruce Jones." The man didn't offer a hand, simply waited.

"John Smith." Jason didn't miss a beat.

Raul groaned quietly across the comm. "Mr. Jones and Mr. Smith."

Arin realized she was smiling again. Jason hadn't chosen

John Smith just because it was equally as generic. It was an alias used by one of her favorite science fiction characters. She wondered briefly if Jason really used the name sometimes or if he'd noticed the blue police box on her nightstand. "Common names, and at least one of them is an uncommon man."

* * *

Jason heard Arin's comment and smiled, making sure to look at one of the very young, almost too-thin women on the cushioned seats by the fire pit. People came in all shapes and sizes and normally, he wouldn't judge a body as too thin or too heavy if it'd been the person's choice. But these women watched the trays of drinks and food go by with an eagerness bordering on desperation and their collarbones stood out. He bet if he ran his hands along their sides, he'd feel ribs under the fabric of their very revealing dresses. He didn't think they'd chosen to go hungry for a desired aesthetic.

"Like what you see?" Their Mr. Jones brushed past him to resume his seat and motioned for Jason to join him.

The handful of women with Jones shifted to give Jason room and he settled in to see where this next conversation was going to take him. Anger at the state of these women could serve him well and when he smiled, maybe he had a predatory edge to his expression.

"Of course." Jason figured this was a man who liked to be complimented, either directly or indirectly. He had probably handpicked who would be accompanying him at the club tonight. "You're a businessman with exquisite taste."

Mr. Jones smiled broadly, wrapping an arm around the shoulders of one of his women. She gave him a smile after a brief hesitation, but he noticed it and gripped her shoulder. He wasn't a gentle man.

Jason only reached for a glass of freshly poured champagne with one hand and toyed with his phone in the other. He wasn't new to these games and it'd be ridiculous for him to give himself away by showing any kind of reaction. Besides, these women were probably treated far worse out of sight. A tight grip on a shoulder was the least of their hardships. It wasn't enough to break his pretense.

"So how do you imagine diversifying, Mr. Smith?" Mr. Jones was relaxed and watching him with a thoughtful gaze, maybe measuring the size of Jason's theoretical wallet.

Jason shrugged. "I'm learning more and more about the profit to be gained from buying and selling various assets."

Mr. Jones nodded. "If you're smart, it can be lucrative."

Jason lifted his glass, using the movement to draw the eye as he snapped a few pics of his target and the girls with his phone in his other hand. "That's what I'm hoping for."

"I happen to be a purveyor of various…assets," Mr. Jones said.

Raul's voice whispered across the comm. "Not enough. He's got to explicitly tell you what he can sell you and name a price, ideally a method of payment."

Sure. No problem. That wasn't going to be hard at all. Jason grimaced and placed the champagne on the ledge of the fire pit. "It kills me to admit it, but as I said, I'm learning. I've already made a few missteps because I thought I was making one type of investment and I ended up with a shrimp truck and a helicopter instead."

Mr. Jones frowned. "I prefer not to be obtuse."

Jason nodded. "I prefer not to end up with vehicles that stink of not-so-fresh shellfish. I understand it's rude of me to ask you to spell it out, but I'm a fan of clear communication."

Mr. Jones looked down at the woman he had pressed against his side. "Maybe we can't do business after all."

"That'd be a shame." Jason said, honestly, letting true regret color his words. The best lies came with true emotion. "You have some beautiful women here to take the edge off, though, and I'm sure you could find other businessmen interested in what you have. As I said, I'm learning, and I'm willing to hold onto my money until I'm absolutely sure I'll get my return on investment."

"I like you." Mr. Jones laughed. "You could be lying but you don't seem the type to waste time with it. You'll really stand up and walk away, won't you?"

"I don't lack for company at this club or elsewhere." Jason laughed right along with the man. Mr. Jones liking Jason wasn't a compliment, though. Jason had a strong need for a scouring hot shower after this.

"Mmm." Mr. Jones pressed a kiss on the curve of his woman's breast. "But they can all say no. What I sell, Mr. Smith, is the company of a woman for a night or a week or however long you'd like and she is yours to do with as you please. No conditions, no limitations. The cost increases, obviously, if you return any of my women unusable."

"That so?" Jason stilled, directing his angry stare at the woman across the fire pit from him. She shrank into the couch in response. "Just these women?"

"I have men, if you prefer." Mr. Jones's voice had turned silken, teasing.

Not enough to convict this guy. Jason wanted to know more from this bastard. Sure, it was tempting to save these women right here, but there were more on the island and even more on their way into this asshole's hands.

"I'm not looking for a one-time transaction, Mr. Jones." Jason tore his gaze away from the woman across from him and settled his attention back on his real prey. "If I engage in a business deal with you, I intend to become a regular customer."

Mr. Jones clapped his free hand on his knee. "Even better. I could use a business connection with security knowledge."

Jason laughed. "You've got enough hired muscle. My skills are more strategic."

"That would be a match for what I'm looking for." Mr. Jones scowled. "My former colleague had some trouble with security earlier this year, and it led to an unfortunate altercation with law enforcement. I enjoy my privacy and want to make sure nothing disturbs my business deals. So I'll appreciate your expertise."

"Perhaps we can come to an agreement to offer each other discounts on the services we can provide." Jason wasn't sure if this was going in the right direction. He needed to keep the conversation going until Mr. Jones incriminated himself. "Are you looking to secure a specific space now?"

Mr. Jones shook his head. "I'm in temporary space at the moment, but I have more…stock coming in shortly. Once it arrives, I'll be moving to a private property on the east side of the island. Not as isolated as my former colleague's place but better suited to my needs."

Jason nodded. "Well, maybe I'll take a sample with me tonight, and we can do a walkthrough of your property in a few weeks."

"Sooner." Mr. Jones was all business, crisp and driving toward a bargain. "My new stock could arrive within the week. It's coming on a container ship from Hong Kong, so the arrival date is not as specific as I'd like. But they're making good time and I want to be ready to receive those assets as quickly as possible."

Raul whispered over the comm. "Pua's got a lead based on the information you got from the guy at the docks cross-referenced with this. We've got a ship name."

That was fast. Both Kenny and Pua were turning out to be amazing information specialists. They'd been coordinating efforts, taking the tidbits of information Jason and Arin had been acquiring and turning those into solid leads. Search and Protect had some heavy-duty resources.

"Tomorrow, then." Jason glanced at the woman across the way.

"Ah, no free samples." Mr. Jones's voice turned hard.

"Name a price." Jason made a hungry noise.

Mr. Jones did.

Jason shook his head. "For that price, give me her and two friends."

Mr. Jones's eyebrows rose up into his hairline. "You think you can handle several?"

Jason didn't bother with any kind of leer. "Seven at a time might leave me too tired to arrive at your property tomorrow to walk the grounds. I'll settle for three tonight."

"Done." Mr. Jones sounded very pleased. "They'll meet you downstairs with one of my bodyguards. He'll see them into your car and take the payment."

Arin whispered into the comm, "Not exactly bargaining. I guess you convinced him you were an easy mark, definitely not a potential business partner. I'm betting he sends his goons after you to take your money without giving you the girls. You ready to be followed?"

Jason nodded. "Fine. I'll step out to make sure I have the cash."

Mr. Jones watched him as he rose from his seat. "You do that."

CHAPTER NINETEEN

"Juliett, this is Charlie." Arin didn't like what she was seeing and she kept this communication crisp, all business. "You have at least one of the bodyguards on your six."

"Copy." Jason kept it brief as well.

So far, their target was being predictable. She'd have preferred to have read Mr. Jones wrong.

"Juliett, this is Bravo. Try to be away from civilians when whatever this is blows up." Raul was gearing up with the task force on the street.

Raul had Taz with him, plus King in the surveillance vehicle. He wasn't going to be handling both dogs so King had to stay behind in the SUV. There were several police units readying for entry, too, and so far none of the revelers at the lounge about twenty stories up had any idea what was coming. Jason had to be careful to keep it that way even with a bodyguard following him.

Jason cleared the private tables and skirted around the dance floor, heading for a more intimate section of the club.

Cabanas lined both sides of a long pool, made for laps or relaxing.

"Juliett, this is Charlie. Ending up in the pool is ill-advised and I can think of three or four episodes of my favorite police procedurals where they tried it." Since she'd already warned him about his tail, she went back to the banter she and Raul used to help the tension as they all waited to see what the bodyguard would do. Jason had mentioned he was in private security when he'd introduced himself. Surely, the bodyguard didn't think another professional would be easy to surprise?

Apparently, the man did because he paused as Jason turned the corner and walked along the length of the pool, then sat on a lounge chair looking at his phone. Jason presented his back to the bodyguard, theoretically taking pictures of the view off the rooftop but really sending the images he'd taken earlier to Raul.

"Juliett, this is Charlie. He's approaching at a slow pace. He's not at an angle to see your phone screen and I think he plans to duck into one of the other cabanas if you turn around." Arin kept watch through her scope, keeping tabs on the bodyguard near Jason and to be aware of anyone else in the vicinity. "I detect no other people in the cabanas. Maybe those are pay to play."

Jason pretended to take a closer look at one of the pictures he'd taken and nodded to indicate he'd heard her, or at least she hoped she was reading him correctly. There was always an element of added risk when working with someone new. Even with standard communication and shared professional backgrounds, everyone had their own logic and individual quirks to how they chose to convey information via body language.

The bodyguard continued an attempted stealth approach

on Jason as Arin watched and wondered about the point of this. He could be trying to rough Jason up and scare him into working with Mr. Jones. Maybe threaten the fictional John Smith into keeping his mouth shut about whatever they'd been discussing. Worst scenario would be to try to eliminate Jason, but she had a clear shot with minimal winds to take into account. If Jason couldn't neutralize the man, she could. Depending on what the man did next, she might take the initiative.

The bodyguard closed the distance with Jason and opened his suit jacket, clearly showing his shoulder harness and gun. "You're not very good at private security, are you, Mr. Smith?"

Jason jumped as if surprised and shot to his feet, dropping his phone on the lounge chair between them. He immediately held his hands out. "Whoa. What? Look, I don't want any trouble."

"Mr. Jones wants those pictures you took with his girls deleted." Bodyguard still hadn't drawn his weapon, probably relying on the intimidation of having it to be enough to cow Jason.

"Juliett, this is Bravo. We've successfully received and downloaded here." Raul kept his message over the comm as quiet as possible. Their comms were the best in the private sector and Pua had them carefully calibrated, so there was no chance the bodyguard would overhear and realize Jason was wearing it. Raul was speaking low and calm to avoid distracting Jason too much from the current situation. "It's fine if the phone is a loss."

Good. Arin suspected that Jason was the type to take a chance on a rash action if he thought he needed to save the images on the cell phone. Raul had mitigated the risk. This was another reason she was happy to be working with

Search and Protect. Her teammates didn't settle for competent. They thought beyond reacting to the current situation and got ahead of it.

"Fine. I'll delete the images." Jason reached for the phone.

The bodyguard reached for his gun. "Don't. I'm not going to give you the chance to back them up before you delete them. Back away and let me have the phone."

Too late for that, but it wasn't likely the bodyguard was going to know how to check whether the images had already been backed up.

"Juliett, this is Bravo. We're ready to enter the club. Neutralize the hostile with which you are engaged and maintain your position." As liaison to the Hawaiian task force coordinating with police, Raul was technically the lead on this operation and Arin went silent to avoid excessive chatter on the comms.

Jason stared at the bodyguard. "Copy."

The bodyguard wasn't quick on the pick-up. "What?"

It'd been stupid on the bodyguard's part not to have finished drawing his gun. They were only a few feet apart—out of arm's reach, yes—but the man hadn't left anything close to the proper reactionary gap. The bodyguard had grossly underestimated Jason, maybe due to Jason's bulk or just out of dismissal of the majority of people out there. Either way, the bodyguard had made too many mistakes.

Jason shot forward, over the lounge chair, grabbing the man's wrist as he went for his gun again and using forward momentum to pin the man's arm to his chest. Jason slid to one side and around the man to get behind him, then wrapped his free arm around the man's neck. It wasn't a perfectly secure hold, but Jason was still in motion, using the man's distraction at having his airway cut off to weaken his hold on the weapon. The bodyguard tried to step into Jason, but Jason moved with him and allowed them to both fall on the lounge chair behind them with a simple ankle block. They hit the lounge chair hard and it gave out from under them with a crash. Jason grunted on impact. Then he was rolling with the bodyguard, going for a more secure hold.

Raul's task force entered the club from the elevator and the stairs, ordering guests to crouch down and remain in place. A few broke and tried to run, but they had no place to go on the rooftop. The task force had the place secured in moments.

"Juliett, this is Charlie. You have two hostiles approaching." The other bodyguard and Mr. Jones had edged their way through the initial chaos and the two of them were trying to slowly back out of the club area unnoticed. Their path was taking them around the corner in the direction of the pool and Jason. "Finish with your dance partner or you will be outnumbered."

"Negative," Jason grunted. He and his opponent rolled dangerously close to the pool edge. "This is harder than it looks."

"Bravo?" Arin asked as the other bodyguard and Mr. Jones rounded the corner. The other bodyguard had his weapon drawn and was about to realize his partner was engaging in combat with Jason. He'd be firing on Jason in another minute or less.

She didn't wait for Raul's response. She took aim, checked her visual cues for wind direction, and made her calculations in barely a moment. She didn't breathe, didn't shift her position, only focused on her target and squeezed her trigger.

The armed bodyguard jerked back as her bullet impacted his right shoulder. He dropped his firearm and fell to the ground. Mr. Jones surprised her by abandoning his bodyguard and diving behind the poolside bar, disappearing into the alcove. Raul and Taz came around the corner and began to secure the wounded bodyguard.

Not good. If Raul and Taz were addressing the downed bodyguard, then the area behind the bar was clear. The alcove was mostly protected from her line of sight. "Bravo, do you have eyes on our target?"

"Negative," Raul growled into the comm. "There's a door back here."

Shit.

"Charlie, this is Juliett. I did not end up taking a swim." Jason crouched next to his opponent. The man was on his belly with his arms secured behind his back. Jason was in the process of patting him down and divesting him of his weapons.

She refocused on him. "Is that your blood or his?"

Jason looked up at Raul and Taz. "A little of both. He got a good hit to my face. I think I've got a cut over one eye but I can see."

It could've been worse.

"Good." Raul rose from the wounded bodyguard and approached the door. "We're still in pursuit of our target."

"Copy that." Jason fell in with Raul and the two of them disappeared behind the bar.

Arin scanned the rooftop club one last time to be sure the team hadn't missed any other runners, then adjusted her position to continue her watch over her teammates, including Jason.

* * *

Jason let Raul and Taz take the lead. He'd spent enough time with Arin to know the working dog had a better sense of what was ahead of them than he did. They proceeded down the corridor, clearing one or two small storage rooms along the way. Yes, it was slower, but they had to be thorough or risk missing their quarry hiding somewhere. The Search and Protect team was thorough. Jason had to give them credit for that.

As they proceeded, Jason rode the wave of adrenaline, channeling it into careful focus. He resonated with this team, with Raul and Taz, and with Arin and King. They had a level of excellence he'd encountered here and there in his experience, but never in a concentrated group of professionals like this. Zu Ayanwu had put his team together carefully, and Jason was taking mental notes.

He allowed himself a fierce grin. He didn't want to join a team like this. He wanted to assemble one. The queries he'd put out there for new positions were all designed to take the next step, looking for the opportunity to step into a leadership position and create a new team. This was what he'd strive for.

The memory of Arin flashed across his vision and faded as he continued to follow Raul and Taz. He wasn't ever going to find someone like her again, not professionally to add to his team, and not personally. What she did to him...he didn't have any desire to match those memories of her in anyone else.

Raul came to a stop and Jason studied the split in the corridor ahead of them. Was the dog going to be able to tell them which way to go? No. Jason remembered Arin saying something about the dogs needing a scent to search on. Jones hadn't dropped any convenient hat or article of clothing.

"This is Bravo," Raul murmured into his comm. "We're splitting up. I'll go to the right, deeper into the building.

Juliett will proceed forward along the north side of the building."

Several voices responded with quiet affirmatives. Zu's was one. Arin's was another.

Jason moved forward without hesitation, walking quickly with the gun he'd acquired from the downed bodyguard drawn and pointed to the ground at low-ready. Running would've been stupid without his target in sight.

The hallway curved slightly, following the shape of the building. It was lined with tall windows. The light streaming in was a combination of moonlight and the glow from the signs lining the buildings across the street. As Jason approached the apex of the curve, he noticed an alcove built into the inner side of the hallway. Restrooms. Farther down, at the end of the hall, an exit sign shone over a door to the stairwell.

Jason slowed, caution overruling his impulse to rush to the staircase even though it was the likeliest escape route for Jones to choose. The alcove was dangerous, because it was a dead zone. He needed to clear the space first before proceeding.

A sliver of envy poked him. Arin always had King with her. Raul had Taz with him. Those dogs were incredible partners. Even when Jason had been part of other contract groups, he hadn't had the tight camaraderie the Search and Protect team shared. He definitely hadn't ever experienced the kind of bond they had with their canine partners. He'd always worked with a level of independence. Alone.

Arin's voice whispered into the comm. "Juliett, this is Charlie. I'm with you."

He grinned, despite the gravity of the situation, and gave the window his back, concentrating on approaching the alcove. These last few days working with her, being around her, had made him happier than all his years in this business. He wasn't sure how to express that to her. But she was everything he hadn't known he'd been missing. Friend. Teammate. Lover. She was amazing. And he had no idea how he could tempt her into staying a part of his life, not when she had a place here doing what she loved already.

As Jason got closer to the alcove, he saw Jones waiting as far back as possible, tucked into a corner. The man wasn't alone.

Jones had grabbed the pretty woman in the white dress Jason had met earlier. She must've gone to the restroom and had had the bad luck to run into Jones on the way out. Or Jones had ducked into the restroom and found her. Either way, the bastard had her in front of him, held in a rough headlock with a gun pointed at her head. Somewhere in the struggle, she'd lost her shoes. Jason hoped she'd managed to dig a heel into Jones's foot or leg before Jones had made her lose them.

"This doesn't end well, Jones." Jason tried to keep his voice even, gauging Jones's reaction. It was important not to push the man into hurting, or killing, his hostage. "Let her go and let's talk."

"I'm not stupid." Mr. Jones sounded so reasonable, the pleasant tone of his voice coming across as incredibly creepy. He tapped the muzzle of his gun against the woman's head. "I saw the dog. There's no way I can outrun the thing. So you are going to make sure all those cops step back and let me disappear. Otherwise, I'm going to ruin this pretty white dress my friend here is wearing."

Pressed against him, the woman's eyes widened even further with fear. She didn't beg for her life, though, or say anything at all. She didn't make any noise to further antagonize the man. Jason was thankful for that. It'd be worse if he had to manage a panicked hostage as well as Jones. Jason couldn't make eye contact with her or give her any other comfort, not when he had to watch Mr. Jones's face and posture for any hint as to when he was going to move next.

"No taking time to think. Put your gun down." Mr. Jones tightened his choke hold on the women, wrenching her neck at an awkward angle as she clutched at his arm, desperately trying to loosen his hold. "I will kill her."

"Okay." Jason crouched down slowly to place the gun on the floor, carefully kicked it far down the hallway, then straightened, holding his hands out slowly. "No more weapon, see?"

Mr. Jones smiled triumphantly. "Don't come any closer. I know all about that distance you people talk about, where you can get to me before I shoot you. You stay back where I can see you and shoot you if I have to."

"Get him to move down the hallway a little more, in front of one of the windows." Arin's voice was a purr in Jason's ear. "Keep him facing you, if you can."

Jason raised his arms, hands empty. "Sure."

He could've been addressing Jones or Arin. The former assumed and the latter knew exactly which of them Jason was responding to.

"Good." Mr. Jones jerked his head toward the stairwell. "We'll go over there. You stay as far away as possible coming past us and lead the way down the hallway."

As Jason complied, the captive woman's eyelids started to flutter. "Unless you want to carry her, you better give her some air."

Mr. Jones's face twisted into an ugly grimace, but the woman gasped as she took in a short breath. "You do what I tell you to and don't try to get smart about giving her a chance to get away from me. I'm not letting her go."

Jason kept moving past them at a steady speed until he

was a little over twenty feet ahead of them. "Okay. We're all going to keep calm."

"Of course we are." Mr. Jones started to follow but the woman was doing her best to drag her feet. Mr. Jones snarled and kicked her feet out from under her, then used his hold around her neck to drag her up until she got her footing again. "We're all going to do as we're fucking told or you are going to die, bitch. Remember that. You're the first to go if you don't listen to me."

"We're all listening to you, Jones." Jason wanted the man's attention on him.

Step by step, Jason backed farther down the hallway to the door. He kept his gaze on Jones's face, willing the other man to glare at him. They passed one window, then another.

The woman's head might be obscuring Arin's ability to get a clean shot. Was that why Arin hadn't fired yet? Snipers had to account for so many variables. There was wind between the buildings and this was different from the outdoor area. The shot would have to come through glass. Jason slowed. Maybe Arin needed more time.

"What are you slowing down for?" Jones's voice raised in pitch and volume. The tension was getting to him. He extended his arm fully, pointing the gun at Jason.

The window didn't shatter; there was only a small hole. The distinct sound of breaking glass was quieter than a person would expect, especially since it was overshadowed by the sound of Jones yelling in pain as Arin's bullet hit him in the forearm. He dropped his gun.

Jason closed the distance even as the woman bit down hard on Jones's other arm. Jones cursed and yanked his arm free as he staggered back a step, giving her the chance to get away. She took the opportunity and stumbled away from Jones, not into Jason's arms but past him.

Arin's voice came across the comm. "She's clear."

Jason had run into a number of smart women recently.

He grabbed Jones's injured forearm, digging his thumb into the gunshot wound. Jones screamed. Jason interrupted the sound by driving the palm of his other hand into Jones's face, fingers extended to stab the other man's eyes. Following up and through, Jason lifted his elbow high and brought it straight back down over Jones's nose.

Jones crumpled to the floor, one hand covering his crushed nose as he hugged his bleeding forearm to his chest.

Raul came around the corner and up the hallway with Taz, and the dog rushed forward, barking at Mr. Jones.

"Get down on the floor and the dog will not attack." Raul snapped out the warning.

Jason wondered wildly whether he should comply, too.

"Steady." Arin's voice whispered in Jason's ear. "Taz will focus on our target. Just don't make any sudden moves."

Jason was dubious but remained standing, resisting the urge to back away from the dog.

Taz did stay focused on Jones, barking viciously until the injured man got down on the floor as instructed.

Raul approached and gave Taz a sharp command. Taz stopped immediately and returned to Raul, coming to the man's left, legs stiff and fur standing up all around the big dog's shoulders and down his back.

Search and Protect had some damned intimidating dogs.

"Juliett, you can secure the target now." Arin's voice came across the comm, more formal.

Jason caught a few zip ties Raul tossed his way and began to bind Mr. Jones's wrists behind his back.

"Charlie here. No other hostiles in the area. Can we call it a win?"

Jason chuckled over the comm. "I would. Thanks for having my back, Charlie."

* * *

Jason sat at the back of the ambulance, watching the rest of the raid play out in relative safety. King sat next to him, possibly playing guard duty, but Jason preferred to think Raul had left King with him for company. The big dog sat calmly next to him, ears twitching as the noisy reading of rights and general confusion went on around them.

"I guess she's continuing surveillance from her vantage point." Jason decided talking to the dog wasn't out of line. No one else was listening to him at the moment and he'd handed his comm piece back to Raul so he couldn't hear the current communication between them.

King looked up at him and tilted his head to one side.

"Your lady is good, very good." He hadn't known where she was located and he had been scanning the surrounding buildings, looking for likely vantage points. He wasn't a sniper himself but he'd worked with a couple. He'd looked for any telltale signs, like shifted items or open windows, maybe light reflecting off her rifle or scope or even on her person. Nothing. She'd been completely hidden and even after she'd taken each shot, he hadn't seen any movement or had more than a vague impression of where the shot had come from. "She could make bank being a sniper for any of the private contract companies out there, or if she's really a loner like she thinks she is, she could go freelance and be a downright scary contract killer."

King still seemed to be studying him, listening.

"But then she's got you. I don't think she likes to be away from you for long." Jason casually kept an eye on the crowds around them and looked upward on the off chance he might see her out there. He was too keyed up to rest but it was easier to relax a fraction with King sitting next to him. Surely, the dog would see or hear anything out of place or potentially threatening before Jason did. "She could've left you crated at home or loose at the Search and Protect headquarters. But she didn't. She kept you close. You're a major part of her life, even if she doesn't express it as openly as other humans do."

The last part Jason pitched in a softer tone. King responded with an almost inaudible whine.

"You're lucky." Confiding in the dog was easy and Jason tried not to be jealous of King but damned if he didn't wish Arin wanted his company as much as she wanted King's. "You aren't going to be asked to work with another handler at the end of a tour. She's not going to leave you because her tour is over. The two of you have a steady place at Search and Protect. It's a good deal."

King snuffled Jason's pants leg and his forearm where he'd propped his elbow on his knee. Then the dog took Jason by surprise and rubbed his head against Jason's pants.

"Got an itch?" Jason reached down, hesitant to move too fast and startle the dog into biting him. King was well-socialized, but he was still a highly trained working dog. Fast hand movements toward the dog's face or neck could end badly if Jason made the dog feel the need to defend himself.

King watched him, studied the hand Jason extended, then ducked his head and pushed his muzzle up under Jason's palm.

Permission to pet, granted.

Jason rubbed the top of King's muzzle, then moved to scratch around the base of the dog's ears. The fur on the dog's face and skull was way softer than he'd anticipated. King issued a groan in response to the attention and leaned into Jason's fingertips.

"Excuse me." The feminine voice wasn't the one he wanted to hear, so Jason spent an extra second or two scratching King before looking up.

It was the lady in the form-fitting white cocktail dress. She had the gorgeous burnished gold skin tone and black hair characteristic of the Polynesian islands. She'd been a smart woman, too, astute in conversation and every part of her appearance carefully put together to hold the attention of the men in the club. She'd also gotten clear of Jones as soon as she'd had the chance, and stayed out of the way while Jason had disabled her attacker.

Her coral lipstick was still bright despite having been smeared earlier by Jones's hold on her. Even though she'd been through a harrowing encounter, her hair was back in the kind of loose ponytail that invited a man to tug slightly for all her hair to fall loose around her shoulders. He'd appreciated her skill in her profession earlier in the evening and he'd respected her immediate chill once he'd pretended to be looking to buy girls rather than bottles. Now, he was seriously impressed with the way she'd pulled herself together.

"Thank you for saving me." She sounded sincere and the huskiness in her voice was more from the strain of the night and not contrived for seduction.

He shrugged. He wasn't in the business of being a hero. Her thanks made him extremely uncomfortable.

She smiled, a real one, and held out a business card. "I hear there's a research group on the island working with the police, trying to place victims of the trafficking ring once they're free and assisting them in applying for visas or asylum to stay. If they need help finding work for those girls, busing tables or serving drinks, have them contact me. Nothing they don't want to do. I'll watch out for them."

Before he could take the card, King leaned forward and took the card gingerly in his teeth.

The woman looked startled and Jason just shrugged. "He'll get it where it needs to go."

She glanced to where Raul stood with Taz at his side, directing the task force and right in the middle of everything. "I guess so."

A moment later, she was gone. No good-bye. Well, Jason would make sure Raul or Arin got the business card to Mali. He looked at King and held out his hand. "Are you going to give it to me?"

King, card still carefully held in his front teeth, looked from Jason's face to his hand and lifted a paw, placing it into Jason's palm.

"Not what I meant." Jason tried not to growl at the dog. He figured King was better at it and this was definitely a mind game. Unfortunately, Jason didn't know the actual command to make King drop the card. Instead, he stared into King's eyes, then looked pointedly at the card and held out his hand again. Pitching his voice deeper and putting more punch behind it, he gave a more brief command. "Give it."

King hesitated. It wasn't the right command. Then the dog slowly extended his neck and placed the business card in Jason's hand. Win.

"He likes you."

Both Jason and King jerked back to attention at the sound of Arin's voice. She was dressed in muted solid colors, deeply dyed indigo jeans and a dark grey T-shirt with a medium grey jacket tied around her waist. The colors would've allowed her to fade into the shadows of the buildings, but the outfit was normal enough not to catch the eye as she walked down the street. Nothing about her said sniper or military to the normal onlooker. Even the duffel she wore as a backpack looked like any other duffel, but Jason was guessing the slightly longer length was to accommodate her rifle. She could blend into a crowd if she chose to, and most of the time she did. But now that he knew her, had the taste of her in his memory and the feel of her skin against his, she stood out against the background to him.

Arin was singular, captivating, and she was waiting for him to say something.

Jason cleared his throat. "That's a good thing, right? Him liking me?"

Arin approached and gave King a caress on the side of his face. Where the dog seemed to like Jason's attention, King melted into Arin's hand. Jason didn't blame him. "He's not an overly friendly dog. It's unusual for him to let other people pet him. I'd say he's very discerning."

She hadn't quite answered the question but Jason was going to take her partial response as a yes. He handed her the business card and explained from where it'd come. She nodded, her expression unreadable, and pocketed the card.

"Has anyone looked at you yet?" She studied his face.

Jason shook his head slowly. "It hasn't been long. There's a raid going on, you know."

"Uh huh. Feeling lightheaded?" she asked.

"Nope. The bleeding has mostly stopped." He was being careful, though. He'd had a concussion within the same week, so any hit to the head warranted extra caution.

Arin sighed and shrugged out of the straps on her duffel bag, pulling it off her back and laying it carefully under the back bumper of the ambulance. Then she climbed up into the back with him and started rummaging in the supplies. "It could be a while, then. We left a few of our targets bleeding so they get priority. We want them to live to see prosecution. Swing around."

Jason complied, shifting his position on the bench to face her as she sat opposite him. King sat on the outer edge of the ambulance, angled so he could watch both the outside activities and Arin with Jason.

"Let's get you cleaned up some. If it's stopped bleeding, maybe we can get away with just butterfly stitches." She ripped open a few sterile wipes and gently touched his face.

He held as still as he could under her ministrations, but he was extremely distracted by her close proximity. He wanted to lean into her and breathe in her lavender and mint scent, relax against her as he began to come down off his adrenaline rush. "You've got some? I didn't find them when I looked through the supplies in here."

She held up a few narrow adhesive strips for him to see. "I keep them handy."

"Ah. Yeah, I like the idea of those rather than actual stitches or sutures." He grunted as she began applying disinfectant to his cut.

Chuckling, Arin paused to make eye contact with him. "What, you don't like to use crazy glue and duct tape?"

"I'm not saying I've never used those but these come off easier." Jason smiled. He enjoyed the concentration in her expression as she tended to his cut. This was one of the unspoken ways she cared for people important to her. He soaked up the moment because she might never get around to expressing how she felt about him otherwise. He also wondered if he could settle for this much.

He wanted more. But then again, it'd been him wanting more from the start. He'd wanted to find her, get to know her. Then he'd wanted to spend more and more time at her side. What he wanted now—he wasn't even sure how to make it work without one of them giving up their career, and that wasn't fair to her. If he was going to take her as she was—and he definitely thought every aspect of her was amazing—then he couldn't ask her to feed his need for validation in this relationship they were developing. He was done being selfish, at least where it came to her.

Instead, he took this moment and savored it. The two of them, surrounded by chaos, and he had her undivided attention. It was enough for now.

CHAPTER TWENTY

Arin was wrung out by the time she, King, and Jason returned to her apartment. Their debrief had been mercifully short and Zu had sent them back to get as much rest as they could before their next operation: heading out to the container ship Pua had identified and intercepting the shipment of human captives. But she wasn't drained by the wrap-up activities. Those were standard and usually gave her time to come down off the hyper-awareness she had during an active part of a mission. No, she was churning inside and Jason was the reason for it.

He waited for her to clear her apartment and give him permission to enter her living space. Even having stayed and gained very intimate familiarity with her, he hadn't presumed. He was thoughtful and considerate, extremely helpful and exceedingly capable. In the short time she'd gotten to know him, he'd continued to go above and beyond her estimates of what his skill levels were, or what he might do.

Guilt nibbled at her. She'd done him a disservice in expecting the worst from him. But her restlessness was caused by more. She'd watched him from a distance and covered him in a way no one else could do better, but she'd still worried about him. When she'd seen him sitting in the back of the ambulance with no one but King at his side, her own anger had caught her by surprise. Why had no one cared for his wounds? He deserved better consideration.

"You should get some sleep." Jason stood in the kitchen, pouring two glasses of water, one for him and one for her. Then he refreshed the water in King's bowl.

She shook her head. "Still too keyed up to sleep yet."

He met her gaze and his eyes were full of an intensity she didn't quite understand but was drawn to nonetheless. Without consciously making the decision, she crossed the distance between them and pressed her lips to his. His lips burned against hers and before he could raise his hands to hold her, she pulled away, taking his hands in hers and tugging him back toward the front door. "King can stay here. It's too close for me in here right now."

Jason allowed her to lead him back to the door. He raised his eyebrows when she didn't bother with shoes. Instead, she just grabbed her keys and led him out of her apartment, locking the door behind them. Then she padded on silent feet down the hallway to the elevator and punched in the code for the topmost floor.

It was late, very late, and there was no one at this level. She brought Jason past the common lounge and game room, through the gym to the pool area. It was enclosed by glass and looked out over the beach and hotels, offering a spectacular view. In the corner, where the view was at its best, was a generously-sized hot tub.

"I like the way you think." Jason immediately began to strip down to his underwear.

She'd removed most of her clothes, too, but waited until

he looked up at her. Then she deliberately removed her bra in a slow tease. He stilled, watching, his eyes following her every movement as she dropped her bra on top of her pile of clothes, then moved to slide her panties down off her hips ever so slowly.

She stepped carefully into the steaming water of the hot tub. "Joining me?"

He ditched his boxer briefs and stepped to the edge of the tub, jabbing the button to turn on the jets before stepping in, too. Before he could get too far in or reach for her, she placed her palms on his chest and pushed him back to sit on the edge of the tub.

"I thought the point was to get into the hot water." He sounded puzzled but his statement held a note of anticipation.

Good. She had plans for him. So far, he'd been a generous lover. She wasn't much for words but if she made any kind of erotic request, she was betting he'd go out of his way to fulfill it and enjoy it as he did. This time, his needs were coming first and she'd have fun, too.

"Patience," she told him. The water level in the hot tub came up above her waist, the bubbles from the jets tickling the undersides of her breasts. His gaze dropped and her nipples tightened under his regard.

It was her turn to coax his knees apart. He was fully erect and damn, she wanted him in her mouth. But she didn't take him right away. The man had a mouth on him and he was good at using it to piss her off and give her pleasure. The least she could do was give him a little of his own back.

She ran her tongue along the length of him, looking up to lock eyes with him as she did. If anything, he grew harder and he swore a blue streak.

This time, she grinned at him. Then she returned her attention to his cock. Swirling her tongue around his tip, she caught the tiniest taste of salt before she opened wider and took him into her mouth. He cursed again and grabbed the edge of the hot tub on either side of them, like he was holding on for dear life.

Oh no, she didn't want him to keep control. He'd been exercising the self-control of a saint dealing with her and she appreciated it. Now, she wanted him to lose it. Besides, she enjoyed the texture of his soft skin in contrast to the hardness of his erection. She continued to use her mouth on him, alternately working her tongue along his length and sucking.

"Arin." He gasped her name in some impossible combination of a command and a plea.

She liked hearing him say her name because he'd listened and cared to say it correctly and not how others thought her name should sound.

Easing back, she flicked the tip of her tongue along the head of his penis. She wrapped one hand around his shaft and used her free hand to caress his balls. The delicate skin of his scrotum tightened at her touch and she used her fingertips to find the super soft spot just behind his balls, lightly brushing him until he lifted his hips off the ledge.

She took the head of his penis into her mouth and tightened her grip on his shaft.

He let out a strangled shout. He reached for her with one hand and gathered up her half-wet hair in his fist, not tight enough to hurt but just enough to prevent her from taking him deeper into her mouth. She refused to let him hold her back, pumping her hand and keeping her mouth on him in a slow, steady suck as she met his gaze again.

His eyes were burning with intensity and she could almost see her own reflection in them as he watched her in the water in front of him. He was devouring her with his gaze and their eye contact was enough to make her drown.

He'd loosened his hold on her hair, instead cradling the side of her head and she dropped her lids to half-mast for a moment to nuzzle his palm before she decided he was done holding on. She laved the length of him with her tongue, enjoying the taste of his skin and taking her time doing it before lowering her mouth over his tip and sucking on him again. Starting light, she sucked and licked and sucked again until he groaned. Yes, he'd lost hope of keeping control and he knew it. She wanted him to come apart for her the way she had for him. She wanted him to trust her enough to do it.

Because she'd opened herself completely to him.

*   *   *

The dawn woke Jason. He was surprised at how loose and limber he felt, until he remembered the very enjoyable time they'd spent in the hot tub upstairs before coming back down to bed. He grinned at the memory and dropped a kiss on Arin's hair. Waking up next to her was almost as good a feeling.

He seriously considered going back to sleep because they both needed the rest, but then he heard a low whine from the closed door to the living room.

Arin stirred. "Mmm. King needs to go out."

He pressed a kiss on the bridge of her nose. "Stay asleep. I'll take him."

"Yeah?" She struggled to open her eyes. He wondered if she'd slept at all the previous nights or if she'd spent them reviewing data Kenny or Pua had sent to her.

"When we find out how the next shipment is coming in, we'll need to act fast. Get the rest now so you don't end up dead later." He climbed out of bed and reached for his pants. "Look, I'll go commando and be right back to get some more sleep, too."

She snuggled into the pillows—all of them, including the ones he'd been using—and smiled. "Sleep is good."

He pulled the covers up and tucked them around her. Seriously, when it came to blankets and pillows, she was incredibly cute. "Pillow thief."

He stepped out of the bedroom and faced King. The GSD looked into the bedroom at his mistress, then back at Jason and tilted his head to the side.

Jason retrieved King's leash. "Let's come to an agreement. You and I are on good enough terms to get you to where you need to go and come back, right?"

King was trained to obey a specific set of commands and Jason didn't know them. He was fairly sure any of the ones he remembered Arin using weren't going to help him in this moment, so he was going to have to rely on King's intelligence. Fortunately, King really had to go because the big dog followed Jason to the apartment's entryway and allowed Jason to hook the leash to his collar.

They headed out and down to the ground level, took care of business, and came back with no issues. Okay, maybe Jason had been tempted to engage in an actual pissing contest because, really, he had the sense of humor of a kid and the dog could manage to take a long-ass piss in the morning. Only the possibility of someone human seeing them from the towering apartment complex stopped Jason from giving in to his inner twelve-year-old.

They re-entered her apartment and Jason unhooked King's leash. The big dog immediately headed for the bedroom.

"Not a good idea," he called after the dog. He was just

going to have to kick the dog out of the bedroom once he and Arin really decided to wake up because he fully intended to execute a morning ambush on her.

King stopped just inside the bedroom and turned back to look at Jason, then circled once and lay down in a heap next to the bed—Jason's side of the bed.

Dick.

Jason chuckled despite himself. Before he went in to settle this challenge from the GSD, he stopped to check his phone. It lay where he'd left it on the end of the kitchen counter alongside Arin's. He snagged hers, too, and brought them both in to the bedroom to charge. Her charger was on her nightstand so he figured she rarely slept with her phone out of reach. He was pleased and more than a little proud she'd been so caught up in their night that she'd left her phone out in the kitchen area.

As he checked his notifications, he stopped short and tapped the screen to open up his secure mail app. Reading, he woke fully, coming to full alertness.

"Mmmph." Arin stirred on the bed. "Both of you back with no issues."

"No issues," he answered absent-mindedly, still reading.

She sat up, pulling the sheets up with her to cover her chest. "What's up?"

"Nothing bad." At least he didn't think so, but the uneasiness in his chest made him hesitant to share further. He didn't want to let go of the comfortable mood they had going.

Arin didn't say anything. She didn't pry or behave as if she was entitled to know his business. He liked her way of respecting his privacy and tried to give her the same. But this—he'd need to share this sooner or later and it probably wouldn't get easier later.

"I got a job offer."

"Congrats." She waited, then her fingertips brushed across his back when he didn't turn toward her. "It's a good thing, right?"

He sat down on the edge of the bed, set his phone on the nightstand, and leaned back against the headboard. She shifted to make room for him and also so she could face him.

"I've been looking for exactly this kind of contract. It's head of private security for a candidate in a semi-democratic country in Asia. The candidate is facing the kind of opposition that might try to have him assassinated rather than await the outcome of the election. Should be a challenge." He met her steady gaze. "I had feelers out there for a new position. I said I was going to see this through here, and I will. But this opportunity won't wait long for me so I'm going to have to leave as soon as we complete the next objective. The election is in nine months and they're talking about keeping me on retainer for at least a year afterward. It'll be around-the-clock work, no vacation time but worth it."

"You think so?" Her tone was carefully steady, as if she was still waiting for his answer even as he was giving her information.

He didn't blame her because there was more to say. He didn't know what, though.

"This could make my name out there." He sat up, leaned toward her slightly. Maybe if he explained why he'd wanted this job, he'd see his way clear to what came next. He'd never shared his career aspirations with someone before, never worried about what someone else might think of his choices or what they might decide to do in turn. "You know how competitive our work can get. I'm not great at the networking shit. I don't plan to be anonymous thug number two forever, and I'm definitely getting older than the optimal age for the kind of action we see. I should be in more leadership positions soon. Eventually, it's going to be difficult to get new contracts. I need this kind of lead position on my resumé to plan for the long term."

He'd been trying to make progress in a career, but he was realizing he'd only been taking it one move at a time and some moves were to adjacent positions rather than advancing. He'd gone from job to job, always building but never making something of the cumulative experience. This next job had to be different. He was going to create a real future for himself.

"Are you leaving right away?" She gave him no hint to her thoughts. Neutral tone of voice, calm expression, but the spark he'd enjoyed in her gaze was gone.

When he looked into her eyes now, it was like hitting a wall.

"I need to get there by the end of the week."

CHAPTER TWENTY-ONE

A part of her tore out of her chest and hid, burrowing deep into some compartment where she tucked away the other things she couldn't deal with in the heat of the moment. She was going into defensive mode, combat ready. She recognized it and didn't even try to stop herself.

"So you never planned to stay." Arin put a choke hold on the emotions threatening to make her scream. Never. Never before had news hit her and made her want to rage like this. She didn't even know why his news hit her this way. She'd made a conscious decision not to ask him. She'd have thought she'd be happy for him. "Me and you, this, was just the interim before you left for the next thing."

Hadn't she known? She'd been the one to make it clear their first time was a one-time thing. She'd made herself a liar and a fool. He hadn't ever lied to her. Worse, he'd made her start to believe he'd be here each time she turned to look for him.

"Well," he hesitated, unsure. "I wasn't thinking about the next thing. I was thinking about you."

So they were both idiots, her for hoping and him for not

thinking ahead to the obvious fallout. She should've kept her head firmly grounded in reality. It would've been wiser than believing there might be a fairy-tale ending. It'd only been a few days, a week, and his leaving had only been a matter of time.

If she'd had it to do over again, would she have taken different actions?

No!

Then she better pull herself together. This didn't need to get any messier than it had to, and she'd prefer to shake this off and get back to what she was good at: her job.

"I'll see this next operation through." Jason sounded totally reasonable, echoing her intent on where to take this conversation. Maybe he'd thought this through previously. She wasn't sure. But every word out of his mouth only made her angrier. "The shipping container on Big Island was rigged, and your team doesn't have an explosives specialist. Someone in his organization, close to the shipping operations, made that bomb. I'll go to help you defuse any other IEDs you encounter. Once we intercept this shipment, Mr. Jones won't be able to recover even if he manages to survive prison. This human trafficking ring should be unrecoverable. I'll have done my part to make it up to the victims."

Ah, yes. The original reason he'd been out at Big Island. It was why he'd been with her every step of the way since, to assuage his guilt over being any part of the human trafficking. It was noble, really.

She hadn't realized she'd hoped so much that he'd been staying because of her. "That's it, wrapped up in a neat package. No strings left hanging?"

He watched her, not touching her. "You tell me."

What did he want to hear? It didn't make any sense to tell him what she felt because it was unreasonable. She wanted him to stay when the very nature of her job meant she was constantly off the island and traveling all over the mainland, sometimes overseas. She had what he wanted, a long-term position. What was he supposed to do, stay here playing house and waiting for her to come home? It wasn't him and she'd never ask him to give up who he was. She wasn't sure she could continue to respect him if he did. So much of what drew her to him was the way he was a match or a complement for her, in every way.

"I'm good." She didn't want to hold him back. "This thing was supposed to be a few nights, no attachments and no loose ends to worry about. Easy."

Liar, liar. She'd never liked herself for hiding behind what she was saying when the underlying truth was something completely different. She wasn't admitting to him what this would do to her. It'd hurt like hell, but she wasn't ever going to hang around lost, pining over someone.

His normally animated face went grim. "That's a relief."

Ouch. Her anger drained away. She'd started this. If she came clean, tried to explain what she wanted, maybe they wouldn't go their separate ways cold. But it would only make it harder. She'd already shared more with him than she'd ever expected to. They might try to give each other false promises or platitudes, but she didn't want that for them either. Those were too close to lies and she hated them almost as much. This was what they both handled better: harsh, brutal honesty and a clean break.

"Fine." She shut down, completely, withdrawing within herself and cutting him off emotionally. She'd deal with it after he was gone. "Can you go out in the living room while I get dressed, please?"

He opened his mouth to say something, thought better of it, and got off her bed without protest. He circled to the other side and grabbed the rest of his clothes. King scrambled to his feet, confused as Jason left, but Jason closed the door behind him, leaving her dog in the bedroom with her.

*   *   *

That could've gone better.

Jason sat on the sofa for a minute then rose, restless, and starting pacing. He snagged his duffel bag from where he'd tucked it between the sofa and the wall and started pulling out gear. He didn't have much, a shoulder harness for his primary firearm and a secondary ankle holster for a smaller backup weapon. He also had a utility knife and a few other handy items small enough to stow in the pockets of his cargo pants.

She'd kicked him out, dismissed him, really. And it'd been out of more than her bedroom. He hadn't been expecting to hear back from the potential employer so soon, and he hadn't thought through what would happen when he did. So yeah, he handled breaking the news to her badly. But hell, it wasn't as if they owed each other anything.

Actually, they did. They'd been watching each other's backs since Big Island. Thinking on it now, he wasn't sure he had many colleagues from past contracts who'd do the same for him.

So fine; he hadn't thought ahead. He was absolutely capable of acting on lessons learned. If he considered what might happen next, it'd mostly depend on her and what mindset she was in when she walked out of her bedroom. She had a mission to get to, so she'd be all business. It was a mission run by her team.

Even if they'd let him be a part of it for last night's operation, he wasn't an actual member.

Her face floated in his memory, those fiery eyes going dead flat and her expression hardening into a pleasantly polite mask.

Fine, she'd said.

Then she'd nicely asked for him to get the hell out of her room.

She was going to leave him here, or tell him to head to the airport. He had places to be, after all. She didn't need to include him on this mission regardless of his desire to make amends. She could shut him out and no one on her team would blink. Jason wasn't a part of her world, not really.

How much did being a part of this mission matter to him? He'd already helped those people on Big Island. He'd contributed to keeping her little sister safe. Hell, he'd played the dandy to get enough evidence to arrest and prosecute the reptilian Mr. Jones. It was enough, wasn't it?

Jason zipped up his duffel and dropped it near the door. Then he stared at his boots, sitting neat as you please next to hers. She had tiny feet, her boots dwarfed by his. She also delivered a kick with enough power to break most bones, depending where on the body she'd made contact. Agile, lethally fast, and stubborn enough not to budge even when she was inside a blast zone.

He dragged his hand through his hair. He couldn't let her kick him out of this operation. He was sure she'd run into more IEDs and Search and Protect didn't have the experts on hand to deal with them. He didn't know how to convince her to let him accompany her, but he wanted her vibrant life to continue.

Grabbing his bag, he headed out the door and started running toward Search and Protect headquarters. He had to beat her there. The only way he was going to make sure she didn't bar him from this mission was to go directly to Zu Anyanwu and offer his services for the duration of the mission.

Maybe by the time they got through this, he'd have figured out how to think ahead more than a couple of steps at a time.

CHAPTER TWENTY-TWO

Arin watched the helicopter lift off, having left them safely on the deck of the container ship.

"Your kennel master has some seriously unexpected connections." Jason leaned toward her so he could be heard without shouting for everyone to hear.

She shrugged. Todd Miller had been in the business a long time. Like any of them, he had history. She wasn't precisely sure how he'd pulled the favor, but she was not going to ever comment on the nature of the helicopter that'd transported three of the search and rescue handler and canine teams, plus one unwanted freelance contractor, out to this ship in international waters. Usually, the client arranged for their transport or paid for transport arranged by the Search and Protect team. Since this was a special circumstance, Miller had called in a favor rather than going through the usual channels.

Jason stood at her shoulder even if she was doing her best to freeze him out, and King seemed unperturbed by Jason's proximity. Raul and Taz were standing a few feet away with

Zu and Buck, watching the ship's crew scramble to meet them.

"Getting on this boat shouldn't have been this easy." Jason had his hand on her firearm. All of them, including the dogs, were wearing protective gear for this operation. Zu had given Jason a spare set and permission to join the team for this mission.

She was currently in a steady state of pissed off. She'd been extremely hurt when she'd emerged from her bedroom to realize Jason had gone, but finding him waiting for her at Search and Protect had reignited her temper. She had to give him grudging respect for anticipating her thought process, though. It'd been well-played, the jerk.

"Too easy. Agreed." Zu kept his gaze on the approaching ship's crew. "They didn't argue too much when we radioed to inform them we were boarding."

Zu had taken the lead on talking to the ship as they'd approached. He'd been vague as to who they were, but he'd given the impression they were investigating potentially dangerous cargo that posed a risk to the ship and crew. The captain had allowed them to board based on the possibility there were explosives on the ship.

"We say as little as possible while we conduct our search." Zu stepped forward. Arin and Raul fell in to flank him, leaving Jason to stand at Arin's left. "Mister Landon. I appreciate you adding your expertise to our effort. Stay with Charlie team. Your call sign will be the same as previous."

"Understood, sir." Jason was all business. He hadn't pushed Arin to speak to him once they'd left Search and Protect headquarters. The both of them had settled into work mode and there wasn't room for emotional upheaval.

Beside her, King was eager and ready to work. Fine tremors passed through his body as he looked back and forth to each of them as they spoke, sensing their tension and listening to the cadence of the conversation.

"Will being out on the water mess with their scent abilities?" Jason asked quietly.

Arin huffed. "We're not directly on the water and we're not trying to find something in the water. He's going to be searching for scents here on the container ship, and it is a big ship."

The container ship stretched out in front of them, not the biggest class in the world but definitely not a small interisland transport either. This one had forty and forty-five foot containers stacked neatly on deck, making maximum effective use of the space available, or it should have.

"Normally they'd fill every space, but there are gaps between the containers here and there." She didn't like it. If she could tell at a glance, the ship's captain would have noticed too. The gaps were at regular intervals, though. "It'll be worth asking the captain why the ship was loaded this way."

The hold probably held many times more containers. It was gearless, meaning it didn't have a shipboard crane for handling its cargo. It was designed to go to ports that had pier-side container cranes, as opposed to smaller ports, which might not be equipped with them. All of that meant a reduced chance of a person getting a close and personal look at each container.

"This is going to be like searching for the veritable needle in literal stacks." Jason's gaze swept across the ship's containers, out across the seas around them, and back to the crewmen who'd almost reached them.

"The dogs can do this, but we need to find them a scent to track." They were betting one or more of the crewmen were on Mr. Jones's payroll. It was doubtful the captain or the entire crew, but the possibility was there. Pua had run through the captain's finances and the ship's history, coming up with no red flags so far. So they were proceeding on the premise of one or two hostiles. They'd be ready in case it was worse.

The ship's captain finally arrived, accompanied by two crewmen. He approached them cautiously, a firearm obviously at his side. Piracy was a real possibility when it came to sudden boardings like this. Arin couldn't blame him. She and the rest of the team remained as passive as possible, their hands obviously empty and at their sides.

"This is very unusual." The ship's captain scowled. "You are sure my ship is in danger?"

"Yes, Captain." Zu spoke for all of them. "I'm Azubuike Anyanwu. I lead this team. We will start by searching crew quarters and expand to the rest of the ship. Anything you can do to facilitate our search will expedite this process and hopefully, we'll be off your ship as quickly as possible."

"What is it you're looking—?" One of the crewmen started but his companion cut him off.

The captain scowled at them both, then addressed Zu. "We have submitted to inspections willingly in the past, but I question your jurisdiction. I allowed you to board, but I am not fully convinced you are not associated with pirates."

"We're looking to make this quick and painless for all involved," Zu rumbled. He had a baritone voice that had a way of soothing jumpy people. "Pirates don't generally announce their arrival. We have been direct in our communication with you and are actively seeking your cooperation in this search."

The captain studied each of the dogs. "This is the first time I have seen dogs at sea like this. We do not have drugs on board this ship."

Lie. The captain was not the best of liars. His eyes tended to dart to his left and he had trouble making eye contact at all, much less when he was making his assertion. He was nervous. She was willing to bet the captain didn't allow illegal substances on his ship, but he was also aware some of his crew might be dealing. It was fairly commonplace. As long as he didn't catch them and their duties were completed, he was probably looking the other way. She watched his crewmen and caught the looks they traded between them. Now those two might be involved in drug deals or taking bribes to look the other way. It'd be interesting to know what other bribes they might be taking.

Zu patted Buck on the head. "Captain, we both know illicit substances may be on board this ship. I thank you for allowing us to fulfill our duty and I assure you these dogs are not drug detection dogs. There will be no issues in that regard."

"Fine." The captain was still torn. Arin guessed he didn't want them searching his ship, but he also feared the consequences if there really were explosives on board.

They hadn't lied to him. Considering what she and Jason had encountered on Big Island with the other shipping container, the probability was high.

"We will start with crew's quarters, as you say." The captain led them forward.

* * *

Jason stuck close to Arin as they made the long walk from mid-ship to the far end of the ship where the bridge and cabins were located. They climbed the tight stairs in single file and entered the cramped area. It was going to be seriously awkward for all of them to go into each cabin and perhaps the captain realized it. He motioned for them to go to the far end and work their way back to the front.

Zu hung back. "My partner and I will start here."

"Why?"

"We promised you we would work as quickly as possible. We'll halve the time it takes if we divide the cabins," Zu informed the captain. "My teammates will accompany you."

The captain looked as if he was going to protest but Arin gave him a disarming smile. "Perhaps we could start from the top? We'll leave Raul on the next deck up."

"Fine. This way." The captain strode forward, obviously eager for them to get this over with. Most likely, he was regretting letting them on this big-ass boat at all.

"Both Taz and King are scent-discriminating dogs. Each of them tracks a specific scent and gives an alert only if they find the source of the target scent," Arin said to Jason in a low, conversational way. The captain and his crewman probably heard her chatting but weren't likely to be able to make out what she was saying over the wind and the waves. It was damned loud on deck. "Buck is non-scent discriminating. He will look for any human scent and give an alert. None of the containers we passed as we came here caused an alert so we've reduced our search pattern by at least one set."

They climbed a spiraling set of stairs and Raul peeled off with Taz to search that deck as they continued upward.

"Here." The ship's captain had reached the landing. "This is the highest deck containing crew quarters."

"Thank you." Arin waited for him to proceed into the hallway and they entered the first cabin.

The cabins were better accommodations than Jason had thought they'd be. They each had bathroom and shower facilities, a bed, and a small desk. Some of the cabins had two twin beds with lockers for each of the occupants. All of them looked lived-in, but that was no surprise as this ship had been at sea for at least a week and probably longer.

Arin hadn't put King to work yet. Their goal was to find something out of place, a hint to tell them this crew member was checking on the shipping container containing the captives for which they were searching. Some of the rooms were neatly kept and they had to do some snooping in all the drawers and lockers. Other rooms looked like they'd been thoroughly tossed with articles of clothing and even food wrappers everywhere. They still searched as thoroughly in those cabins, but in those cases, most everything was lying out in the open for inspection.

They reached the last cabin on the upper deck and the crewman was actually inside, clothes in hand and apparently trying to clean up.

The captain scowled and ordered the crewman out so Arin, Jason, and King could enter. The quarters were comfortable for one or two people but calling them cozy would be kind. Two adults and a large dog was about the limit to fit in there and they were all bumping into each other.

"Sir, if you'll just let me finish folding—"

"It's not necessary to tidy up the cabin. We're honestly not interested in taking any of your belongings." Jason stood at the door, blocking the crewman from entering while Arin and King took a look—and a sniff—around the place.

The crewman was sweating and his eyes darted from side to side. He definitely had something to hide. Question was whether it was a drug stash or actually what they were looking for.

"Somehow, I don't think these belong to you." Arin came up behind Jason, holding up a pair of brightly dyed leather designer sneakers. Her hand was shoved inside a large ziplock bag to prevent her hand from transferring scent to the shoes. "These aren't practical footwear on ships like this and they're fairly expensive."

The crewman gaped. "Yes, they're mine. I wear them ashore."

"But why bring them on this voyage when you're only in port long enough to unload and load shipping containers?" Arin asked sweetly.

The captain, grim faced, didn't come to his crewman's rescue. "I, too, would like to know the answer."

The crewman paled. "No. I...no. I won't help. It's only fair for me to take those. They would die without me giving them food and water."

"Who?" The captain was alarmed now.

Jason moved out into the hallway to block the stairwell in case the crewman tried to bolt. He was well and truly caught now. There was no telling what crazy action he might take.

"You can tell us where they are, or we will find them without you." Arin's words were cold, hard. "Either way, you will be held accountable with the authorities once you reach port."

"Yes." The captain's face was darkening with anger. "Explain. What is this about?"

"Let's continue this questioning on deck," Jason suggested. "It would be helpful to know if there's anyone else involved."

Minutes later, they were back on deck and the captain looked ready to toss his crewman overboard. Thus far, the man seemed to be working alone. The captain was questioning the offender closely and Jason was convinced the captain, at least, wasn't part of the overall scam. Which was a good thing, since they'd all need to board the helo to return to Oahu ahead of the container ship. But the crewman was still refusing to admit there was even a container on board.

Arin still had the shoes and she held them for King to sniff thoroughly before bagging them and tucking them into her backpack. Then she let King off his leash. "*Such.*"

King searched forward, alternately sniffing at the ground

and lifting his nose to the air as he moved back and forth across the deck. Arin followed a few paces back, careful to stay down wind.

Jason shook his head. He'd seen King do some amazing things, but the deck of the container ship was buffeted by gusts and winds coming off the ocean. The dog wasn't going to catch a scent lingering on a breeze up here.

But King surprised him, sticking close to the containers and moving to check the air between them. Sheltered areas existed there, even if a person wouldn't fit, and the dog was checking for scents where the wind wouldn't steal them away. King was systematic, checking ground and container sides as well as the air around the containers thoroughly before moving on to the next. Jason hung back, trying to keep an eye on the captain and Arin at the same time.

Finally, Raul emerged with Taz. Jason motioned for Raul to keep eyes on the captain and the crewman, then followed Arin and King. The pair had gone around a container and he jogged a few steps to catch up to them. They were working their way down an aisle, containers stacked high around them. Suddenly, King paused and sat, looking up at Arin.

Jason rushed to catch up to her.

Arin was studying the side of the container. "This is the long end. I didn't expect him to catch a scent here because air tends to leak from the corners and edges."

She reached out and touched the metal wall. "Clever."

"Find something?" He leaned close to look where her fingertips ran down the painted surface.

A fine seam was almost hidden and as they explored more carefully, they found it was a rectangular trap door cut into the side of the shipping container.

Well, hello there.

CHAPTER TWENTY-THREE

Last door. Zu had searched every cabin on the floor thoroughly with Buck's help. He'd entered every cabin, even if Buck hadn't signaled the presence of a human on the other side of the door. Buck might be able to scent people in these small cabins from the hallway, but Zu hadn't wanted to chance missing a hidden person tucked into a bathroom or in a closet or footlocker. Each cabin had a different layout, so there was always the possibility they'd miss something if they didn't conduct their search thoroughly.

Zu insisted on thoroughness and attention to detail from his people. He held himself and Buck to the same standard.

Zu unlocked the door with the master key the ship's captain had given him earlier and turned the knob, shoving the door open quickly and bringing his gun up to be ready to fire on any perceived threat. As the door was opening, Buck sat and looked at Zu, issuing a short bark.

Talk about last-minute warning.

An object came flying and Zu tipped his head to the side to avoid it. He got a good look at his target, a woman standing at the far end of the cabin, and lifted his finger clear of the trigger. Zu could tell by her aggressive stance that she was someone who'd decided she had nothing left to lose.

He lowered his firearm and issued a barely audible command to Buck to quiet. The big dog had started growling as soon as she'd sent a projectile in their direction. To give them all time to take stock of the situation, Zu glanced at the object she'd thrown at him.

It was a shoe. Actually, this was an expensive shoe with a seriously high stiletto heel. The part of his brain constantly cataloging available items tagged it as a good thing to keep hold of in self-defense. A person could use that shoe to stab a potential attacker.

He took another good look at the woman in front of him. She might have self-defense skills because she had the other shoe in her right hand, ready to hit him with that sharp heel. Her bare feet were planted in a defensive stance with her weight forward on the balls of her toes. She was action ready, beautiful regardless of what she was wearing, and his blood heated at the sight of her. Her skin was pale and as luminescent as pearls in natural light and her dark hair was escaping in long wisps from a makeshift knot at the back of her head. She was dressed in a thin silken camisole and flowing linen pants. The fabric was as expensive as the shoes. This wasn't a runaway paying for passage to the US. This was a VIP or a relative of one.

He had about a hundred questions or more, but he decided on the most important one for now. "Can I help you?"

She blinked in surprise, the arm brandishing the shoe dropping a fraction before she lifted it again and maybe readied herself to throw it after all.

"The shoe won't do shit." He shook his head, eyeing the

heel. "The best chance you had was surprise and it's gone now. You should keep the shoes."

He turned and retrieved the first shoe, letting Buck watch her as he gave her his back. Once he had it in hand, and himself cooled down, he turned back and held it out to her. The shoes weren't appropriate for walking on the deck of a ship, but he didn't see any other alternative. If she didn't have to run—and he would do what he could to ensure she didn't—then having those on were more protection for her feet than going bare.

Her brows came together as confusion took over her expression. "Who are you?"

"Azubuike Anyanwu, Search and Protect Corporation." Easy enough to answer and maybe it would give her enough to trust him with the answer to his question. "We've boarded this vessel on a mission to help a group of people. You don't seem to be part of the crew. Do you need help?"

She didn't lower the second shoe. "Are you US Government?"

Not anymore. "Private contractor."

A hint of recognition and added suspicion entered her gaze and her thin lips pressed in a grim line. "Who paid you to board this ship?"

It'd be too complicated to explain, and he didn't know her connection yet to the human trafficking ring. "No one. This is an initiative in conjunction with a Hawaiian task force."

Her tension didn't ease. "What kind of task force?"

He was out of truth he was free to give, and he didn't lie unless he absolutely had to. "I can't tell you."

Her eyes widened. "But I'm supposed to trust you."

Her tone intrigued him. She didn't sound betrayed or disappointed. If anything, her response was warming up, maybe because he hadn't told her what she was most likely to want to hear. Intelligent and shrewd.

He shrugged. "I didn't tell you to trust anyone. I asked if you needed help."

She still hadn't answered him but she stood there, obviously weary, torn with indecision. He shouldn't continue to wear her out this way. She'd need enough energy to stay on her feet as they left this boat. If he needed to carry her, he wouldn't be anywhere as effective in defending them.

"I give you my word, I will not hurt you." Not a promise he gave often. He wasn't even sure why he was moved to do so. If he was patient, and he usually was, then she'd have come to the conclusion she had no better options. But he'd started, so he saw it through. "If you need help, I will help you. Or if I cannot, I will get you to someone who can."

She studied him for a long, searching moment. Her dark eyes glistened and a single tear spilled over the curve of her cheek, then she pulled herself together with a shake of her head. "Yes, please. Help me get off this ship and back in contact with my father."

He nodded.

"You don't want to know who my father is?" Her tone was incredulous this time.

"One thing at a time." He turned in the doorway to check both approaches in the hallway. "We're getting you off this ship. Put your shoes on, if you can walk in them. Then you can tell me your name as we go. We'll get to your father later."

" 'We'?"

He paused. "This is Buck. I have other teammates on board. Introductions might happen or they might not, depending on the situation."

"What kind of situation?" She had pulled on one shoe and come close enough to take the other from him.

"Gunfire. Maybe an explosion. Or both."

"Oh." Her voice trembled and her hands shook. She didn't try to hide it. But he watched her force herself to walk toward him anyway. She wasn't looking at him with fear, but at the door instead. It'd been one thing to fight when she'd been cornered inside the cabin with nowhere to run. It was taking her courage to walk out the door and into unknown danger.

"Buck and I are with you." He made the statement quietly.

Her gaze tore away from the door and settled on him. "I'm Ying Yue. My family name is Jiang."

"Ying Yue." He tasted her name and liked the sound of it as he tried to repeat the inflection she'd used when she'd given it to him. "Call me Zu. Let's go."

* * *

"They must've sealed this with epoxy or something and painted over it." Arin studied the trap door. "I'm not sure our crewman was supposed to have opened this at all. Otherwise, there wouldn't be as much residual scent on the outside, not after they painted."

There were lives at stake here—not only those they thought were captive inside the shipping container and their own, but possibly everyone's on board, depending on how powerful an IED might be hidden on this container. She preferred a straightforward course of action with a fast incursion and an equally fast extraction.

Next to her, Jason seemed to have a steady, infinite supply of patience as he continued to study every aspect of the exterior of the container. "Before you open it, let's look to see if there are any other ways to access this container. Our guy might have had his one way to access it to give them food and water, but there's got to be a reason the captives don't try to get out when he does."

Arin nodded. They'd been talking in whispers to avoid detection by the victims until they were ready. It was entirely possible the people theoretically inside couldn't hear them due to the wind and sounds of the ocean around them. Or if those people could hear, they might be too terrified of discovery to call out for help. Arin didn't like either possibility, but it was also not a good idea to call out to them yet, until she and Jason were ready to extract them. This container could be set up differently than the one they'd found on Big Island and the people inside might not react as well as the previous captives had. There were too many variables.

The other side of the container was too close to the next stack for anything but a rat to get between. The ends of the container were left and only one had a way of opening, by design.

"We've got a choice." Jason stood back with Arin as they both studied the real door. "We open it the way it was originally intended to be opened, or via secret hatch. Either one could be rigged with an IED. If our bomber was particularly industrious, both could be a problem."

They could go back and ask the man. Or they could bring him to the container and watch for signs of fear if they tried to go for the wrong door, but that would be assuming he knew about the risk of an IED. Better to study it themselves first to get an idea of what they were facing, before putting their trust in the reactions of the shady crewman.

"Side door would be less likely to be observed, but it wasn't meant for regular opening and closing. Sealing this makeshift exit with epoxy and painting over it was intended to give them a way to force their way out at the end of their journey if no one came for them, not come and go. This ship is still rocking with the waves so they know they're not on land yet. They know they haven't reached their destination." He was exploring all of the logical possibilities, trying to outthink their bomb maker. "I still have a bad feeling about this. The last bomb was a victim-operated improvised explosive device, a booby trap. The only reason it didn't go off when you triggered the trip wire was because he had a delay mechanism on it. I had time to defuse it. In this case, the maker could've shortened the delay or not used one at all. We need to do everything we can to reduce the risk and I don't trust that crewman to tell us anything about a potential bomb even if he actually knows."

"Fine, maybe he knows about it, maybe he doesn't, but he's still been getting in there without getting blown up." Dealing with the threat of the bomb was exactly the kind of psychological mind-fuck she hated the most because her opponent wasn't even here. Maybe. She stared at the container as well. "We need to make a decision before we leave international waters. We can't just leave people in there."

He nodded. "The way he's refusing to help, our friend might be stalling. As long as this ship is in international waters, the jurisdiction's ambiguous."

"He can't know that's why we risked intercepting this cargo." She was certain the crewman couldn't be that shrewd. But she hated second-guessing and this was wasting precious time. Once they left international waters, Search and Protect would be treading on someone else's jurisdiction, and none of them wanted to handle the legal mess.

"No," Jason said slowly. "But he might be sure there'll be help once the ship gets closer to their planned destination."

Enough. They'd gathered as much first-hand data as they could.

Arin returned to King and hooked the leash back to his collar, then she and her dog headed to where Raul and Taz stood with the ship's captain and the crewman. The crewman was still trying to explain his way out of the trouble he was in with his captain.

Arin strode right up to the crewman and he flattened his back against a shipping container as if she were an oncoming freight train, eyes so wide she could see the bloodshot whites of them. "We found it. Don't deny it exists."

The crewman quit his blubbering and snapped his mouth shut.

Beside her, King had picked up her aggressive attitude and reinforced her. The dog's fur around his neck and shoulders lifted, making him look huge. He leaned forward with his ears back, legs stiff as they stepped even closer, getting into the crewman's face. "You interacted with them, even stole shoes from one of them."

Tears and snot started running down the man's face. "Please. They have to sit in there with their own waste. I was only supposed to give them fresh drinking water, maybe some fresh food. I only get paid for the ones who make it to the delivery alive."

Well, there was impetus to check on them, then.

"Show me how you checked on them, exactly, step-by-step." Perhaps she wasn't cut out for prolonged interrogation, but she did intimidation and placing people under extreme duress just fine.

The crewman scrambled through the shipping containers, returning to the one King had found unerringly. It was a good thing because if there'd been more than one, Arin wasn't sure she could take the mental somersaults required to handle multiple containers possibly rigged with IEDs and the various ways each of them might blow them all up.

Jason had remained with the shipping container and moved to block the crewman's headlong rush to get to the container. As Arin gave a shake of her head, Jason stepped aside. "Slow down. Let me see exactly what you're doing."

The crewman complied after stumbling a few steps away from the growl in Jason's command. Jason did intimidating well, too. In an impressive, sort of distracting, definitely hot kind of way.

The crewman went to the side door. "Here, the paint was chipping away but I didn't open. They didn't tell me to open here, so I didn't."

Huh. Had it ever been opened at all then? Maybe the paint had come away and the epoxy hadn't completely sealed around the edges of the makeshift door. Maybe the people inside had tried to open it and stopped for some reason.

The crewman went around to the actual door of the shipping container. "I opened here. I never go inside. Never. Bosses made it real clear to me they'd kill me if I touched any of the cargo. Just made them throw me the shoes in exchange for the water. I never touched any of them, I swear."

Obviously, the crewman believed in the possible ramification if he'd touched only the "property."

"Do it slowly." Jason stood by the man with his firearm trained on his head, watching every move.

The man complied, visibly cowed by Jason's tone and the threat of the gun. The door opened on well-oiled hinges, making some noise but not enough to call the attention of anyone not in the immediate vicinity. As the door opened, light flooded in and the people inside lifted their hands to shield their eyes. All of them cowered. None of them moved to come to the door.

A horrific stench hit her, the combination of days of unwashed bodies and human waste mixed with spoiling food was enough to knock a person out. At the far end of the container, there were what looked to be waste receptacles. There were also small fans all along the sides, hooked up to...car batteries? There were empty water bottles everywhere and even empty cans of juice. But nothing, no litter or blankets or anything came close to the front of the container.

Arin stared at the door and then looked at Jason. "What kept the people inside from rushing him? Why didn't they try to get out, even for a breath of fresh air?"

Jason was grim. "They know. It's why they were testing the side door. They know about the front. The bosses probably warned them, too. Look at their faces. They're beyond terrified and they aren't trying to come to us. The front door means death to them. It's not likely he'll trip whatever it is going in. It's rigged to be a threat if they try to get out before they're supposed to."

He had motioned for the crewman to step away from the container and he leaned closer, studying the edges of the entryway. "No trip wires here, which means whatever sets off the bomb is inside, closer to them. What are the chances I can convince you to take this guy back to his captain and let me handle this by myself?"

"None." Arin grabbed the crewman, who was still babbling about how he hadn't damaged any of the goods. She shoved him face first into a different shipping container and pulled his arms behind his back, securing his wrists with multiple zip ties. She then walked him to a somewhat protected space between containers and ordered him to sit, zip-tying his ankles as well. All within line of sight of Jason. "I'm staying right here."

Jason's mouth was pressed in a grim line. "There's a

chance there's no bomb. The assholes who put these people in here might've scared them to death with a lie. But I have to proceed assuming there is at least one IED, maybe more. We can't afford to hope there's not. I need you to promise me you and King will not get into this container. It's not made to let anyone out before they reach their destination and someone who knows how to disarm this thing lets them out. We don't make another move until you promise me you will not enter this container."

She glared at him but his gaze was steady, his stance unyielding. This was his area of expertise and now wasn't the time for her stubborn streak. "I promise."

"Thank you." He flashed her his rakish, lopsided grin, the one that made her heart thump hard in her chest once before she could get herself together again. Then he stepped inside the container.

CHAPTER TWENTY-FOUR

Jason Landon, you had better come back out of there in one piece so I can tear into your hide."

Jason grinned wider as he heard Arin's calmly delivered statement, the tone making her sound way more threatening than if she'd shouted it at his back. She was prickly, with one hell of a temper, and she cared. He'd do his best to fulfill her request.

"In the meantime, it might be a good idea to talk our new friends through what's going to happen next and how they can best work with me."

He had no idea if these people spoke English. The intel they'd received indicated the shipping container originated from East Asia, but where the actual victims came from before they'd been loaded into the container and onto the boat was anyone's guess. They might be a family or people kept together for some time before being shipped or complete strangers. All of that would have to wait for interviews and gentler souls than either he or Arin. But Arin was shorter, less physically imposing, and as far as he was concerned, she had an amazing voice. He could listen to her for hours on any topic. She spoke in a mellow alto and it projected calm to the people around her, settling them and bringing them together.

"Talk to them." He stood just inside the container, surveying the situation from the interior. "We've got sixteen total, fourteen women and two boys. There's a ton of blankets piled in here, lots of plastic bottles and trash, and...a lot of shit in those containers."

He was doing his best not to gag. Hell, it was probably better in here than it had been before they opened the container. He wasn't surprised most of the captives were curled up and miserable. One or two were unresponsive, breathing but not looking at him. The rest were casting fearful glances at him and mostly trying to make themselves as small as possible.

"We are here to help." Arin began speaking as he'd asked. She kept her sentences short, her cadence slow but not insultingly so, and stuck to the key points. "Stay where you are for now. Let us look for danger. When we are sure you are safe, be ready to move when we tell you to."

Most of the captives understood. He saw the comprehension in their eyes, and more importantly, the hope. One or two started to tug at blankets, clearing them so he could see the walls and floors more clearly. One boy was all hands and feet. He might've been in a growth spurt before beginning this journey but now he was emaciated. He must've been the boy the crewman stole the shoes from because he had no footwear to speak of. The others were clothed, even if their clothes were a hodgepodge of items. "They're listening, Arin, keep going."

He made his way to the interior side of the improvised trap door first. They'd all tried to be sure not to be near it either. As he leaned to examine it more closely, one of the women made a croaking noise of dismay. He paused and looked at her. She looked frantically at the door and back at him and shook her head. He did his best to look reassuring and nodded his head, keeping his hands low and obviously away from the door.

He also kept as close an eye on all of them as possible. He couldn't risk any of them bolting before he'd managed to disarm the bomb.

The woman made another noise, coming to her knees but not fully rising to her feet. She placed her hands on her chest, fingertips at her collarbone.

Hell.

He took a closer look at every one of them. He hadn't noticed on his initial assessment because they'd all had scarves or shirts or whatever they could find covering their noses and mouths, the fabric falling to cover the lower half of the faces and necks. This woman had removed hers, and revealed the collar strapped snugly around her neck.

"I have good news and bad news," he called to Arin in as pleasant a voice as he could manage under the circumstances. He was gagging over the stench. "I now know why they didn't try to get out."

"I'm listening." Arin managed to be equally sweet. "Raul and Taz are here now, by the way. Zu is calling in the helo to carry us out."

No arguments there. By the time the helo arrived to retrieve them, either Jason would've resolved the currently volatile situation or they'd need a pick up to get away from the damaged ship.

"They are frightened out of their minds to move because the bomb is set based on proximity." He saw mostly exhausted terror on the faces around him. "They've all got collars around their necks. I'm betting they were told if any of them go near the doors, the bomb will go off. If any of them try to remove their collar or someone else's, the bomb will go off."

He studied each of them in turn. A few, including the woman who'd first gotten his attention, nodded.

"There's no trip wire around the entrances or any kind of similar trigger attached to them. Just the collars." He continued giving as much information as he could.

But the distance to the doors was different. It seemed above and beyond for the trigger to be set to the distance for each of the doors. During stormy seas, the captives would've been tossed around the container some and the chances one would roll close to the makeshift door were too high. Maybe the captives had been told they simply couldn't approach the doors, but based on their positions, it was more likely they couldn't get too far away from the bomb. The one thing they were all closer to than they would be if they could've huddled against the doors was probably exactly where the bomb was.

Oh, for fuck's sake.

"That was the good news." He really didn't like what he was going to have to do next.

"Fantastic." Arin sounded less than thrilled. "What's the bad news?"

"There's too much room for error trying to disarm and remove their collars one at a time. I need a direct look at the bomb."

There was a beat of silence, then she offered a hesitant, "That's not good."

He laughed. "Still working on your ability to put a positive spin on things, huh? Everyone needs to stay where they are, no matter what. I'm not going to want to talk more than I have to as I do this."

"Care to explain why?"

"Because I'm pretty sure the bomb is behind four 30-gallon containers of shit or in one of them." He'd done some awful things in his time. This was going to be one for his personal records.

"I'm guessing behind, for what it's worth." Arin managed to sound both sympathetic and encouraging. Then again, she wasn't the one trying to breathe inside a refuse-filled steel box. "They wouldn't put a bomb inside a container that people would be dumping things into. Refuse could be all sorts of caustic, especially if they were urinating in there, too."

"You have a point." Honestly, the practical thought cheered him a little.

He retrieved a small tactical flashlight from one of his pockets and approached the containers. Behind him, Arin continued to soothe the captives as she repeated instructions to them. They were holding still, tense, but not on the edge of bolting yet. He used the light to study the area around the containers first, then did his best to see behind them. Sure enough, he located the bomb.

Fortunately, the bomb had no connections to the tubs of stench so Jason was able to shift one out of the way to give him better access. The bomb was similar to the one he'd seen previously, with one or two key differences in the trigger mechanism. He could do this; it just wasn't as easy as it looked in the movies. Seconds turned to minutes and the calm cadence of Arin's voice helped tune out any distractions around him, though he was distantly aware of others arriving outside the container while he concentrated on his task.

Finally, he called out to Arin. "Tell them to exit the container. Slowly."

Arin did as he instructed. The captives scrambled out of

the container. Raul and the ship's captain himself entered to carry out those who couldn't leave on their own power. Once the container was empty, Arin stood at the entrance, waiting for him.

"I promised you I wouldn't step inside." She stared at him as he gently lifted the bomb mechanism and carried it toward her. "Nothing you say will make me leave without you."

* * *

Arin sat in her office, elbows on her desk, hands raised. She tended to press her lips lightly against her interlaced fingers when she was thinking and there'd been a lot to think about since they'd returned from their somewhat grey operation to intercept the container ship. Raul had his hands full handling the logistics after the fact with the task force. Mali was similarly busy working to get the rescued captives medical attention and places to stay.

And Jason. Jason was washing the muck off from his stint inside the container. Thankfully, he hadn't had to go searching through those waste buckets, but he'd definitely ended up with excrement smeared across his shoulder, arm, and back while he'd been disarming the bomb. He'd gone straight to the showers in the Search and Protect offices to wash off the stench.

Her heart had stopped the minute he'd walked into the container. She'd done everything she could to work with him, support him, do whatever was needed to keep the chances of him coming out alive as likely as possible. Now, she was shaken.

She wasn't sure when he'd become a part of her core. She'd always kept herself protected, compartmentalizing emotions and experiences. Her ability to compartmentalize and prioritize in fractions of a second were part of why she was good at her line of work. She could take action without being frozen or confused, afraid or horrified. There were few at the center of who she was, souls she couldn't set aside for the sake of any mission. Mali, King, and now, Jason.

She had no idea what to do with the realization. He'd achieved what he'd set out to do before he left Hawaii. There wasn't anything left here for him. He had a contract waiting, a career-making opportunity. It would take up every waking hour he might have for nine months and beyond.

He hadn't said he wanted to meet her again.

What did she even want? She had better figure it out quickly. Otherwise, she'd be wasting his time if she didn't actually have any ideas of what she hoped for from him, for them.

Zu appeared in the doorway of her office, lightly rapping his knuckles against the open door. The broad man filled the space and sometimes Arin wondered if he turned ever so slightly to clear the sides of the doorway when he walked through. Buck was at his side and King came around from his place next to her desk to sniff noses.

Of the dogs on the team, King and Buck were the two most dominant, and their greetings were always a little stiff-legged and wary. They got along because their handlers watched them carefully and because there weren't often reasons for them to test each other. In a lot of ways, the dogs reflected Arin and Zu.

"Any feedback on how I handled the situation?" She preferred to preempt discussions with leadership, and Zu was one of the few commanding officers she'd met who wasn't threatened by her tendency to manage up. He considered her efficient, valued her initiative.

Zu shook his head once. "Not what I would've done but your approach was effective."

It wasn't a criticism. It was more like an acknowledgment of their different methods for tackling a problem.

"Landon was helpful." Zu surprised her by adding the praise for Jason. It might not sound like much, but from Zu it was a freaking shining compliment.

She wasn't sure she wanted to make the suggestion, but Zu was looking to expand the team and Jason deserved every opportunity out there. She'd never mentioned it to Jason because she hadn't had the chance in the last several days to talk to Zu first. "He gets along well with the dogs. He doesn't let them push him around. He's got potential as a handler."

Okay, maybe she was fishing to give Jason a reason to stay. Something other than her feelings for him, which she was still unpacking mentally.

"His experience in EOD is valuable, too. I've seen more than one call for experts like him." Zu paused. "Usually people who want to work with dogs seek out the handler positions. Maybe he gets along fine, could even take over a working dog if something were to happen to a handler in a combat situation, but he'd have asked more about what we do if working with dogs was his calling."

Arin nodded. What else could she say? Zu was right and she'd been searching for a reason to keep Jason close. The Search and Protect team needed good people, yes, but those people also needed to embrace every aspect of what they did as a vocation. It couldn't just be a good idea and they couldn't take Jason just because he got along with the dogs.

Zu stood there, still and apparently tapped out for commentary. After a moment, he huffed out a breath. "You and I, we don't use words well when we talk about our feelings."

She stared up at him, startled. "We don't."

"The man doesn't know he has a reason to stay." Zu crossed his arms over his chest. "But he gets you. Try him. He'll hear you."

"I…"

Zu didn't wait for her to respond. He turned on his heel and left, message delivered. Buck followed. After a moment of staring after him, she chuckled quietly. He didn't want to hear what she was thinking because it was meant for Jason.

CHAPTER TWENTY-FIVE

Jason had his duffel bag and not much else in terms of tangible belongings. He stood in Arin's office and wondered what he should do next. She wasn't there and neither was King. At least if King had been waiting, Jason would know she'd be back before long. But no, she'd left without waiting to say good-bye.

He deserved it. He'd left her apartment and gone over her head to make sure he'd be able to accompany them on the mission to the container ship. He could imagine what she might've thought, the hurt she might've felt, when she'd realized he'd left. He could guess at her anger when she'd arrived at Search and Protect headquarters to find him there and ready to join the mission with Zu Anyanwu's blessing, regardless of what her thoughts were on the matter.

She'd been completely professional on the boat and more. Then she'd shut down again as soon as they'd gotten transport back to Oahu, and he didn't blame her for withdrawing. But he'd thought he'd at least have a chance to talk out what was between them once he'd gotten cleaned up.

He sighed. Maybe he should've taken the risk and tried to talk to her while he'd still been covered in crap. Standing in her office, waiting for her to come back, wasn't an option. Anyanwu had been tolerant so far, but Jason couldn't haunt the place.

"What are my options?" he muttered, not to anyone in particular. There wasn't even a dog to hear him. He was literally left talking to himself.

If one of the other Search and Protect people popped into Arin's office, they were going to ask what he was doing. Or maybe he should look for somebody. Arin might've left a message with one of them.

He stopped himself. It was an age of modern technology and Arin had his mobile number. She could've texted him and been more certain he'd get the message than leaving a verbal with someone who might or might not see him inside an office where he didn't belong. He could call her but he was looking for some kind of sign she actually wanted to talk to him.

Next possibility.

She could have gone home. He knew the way to her apartment and he didn't need a car to get there. But the building required a key or virtual access code to enter the lobby and the key to access the elevators, not to mention her apartment door. He could find his way through all of the security, sure, but she might not be there once he had gotten through. She was unpredictable at best, but the one thing he'd learned about her was that she didn't like to be any place where someone would look for her. Her apartment wasn't where she'd be at the moment.

Next option.

He could search the island for her, but she was every bit as wily as he was, and it'd be a waste of time to try to find her before his flight in the next couple of hours. Even if he had a few more days, he still probably couldn't catch up with her on the island if she didn't want to be found. Plus, she had the means to leave the island. Running around looking for her didn't make sense and asking her little sister could be perceived as an invasion into Arin's family life. Considering that he wasn't Arin's favorite person at the moment, her teammate Raul wasn't likely to welcome Jason anywhere near Mali. And Mali wasn't likely to give up any information about Arin without Arin's okay.

Fine. He had one real option, to go ahead and leave, which was what he'd been wanting to do. Really.

So why did he feel like shit?

He walked out of the Search and Protect headquarters, letting the glass doors slide closed behind him. He couldn't turn back and wait for her in her office now; he didn't have an access card to reenter. He kept walking, continuing to narrow down his options with every step. As he waited for the elevator, he considered his next action. He could call a cab or use an app to get a car service from the lobby of the building. The elevator arrived and he stepped inside, punching the button for the ground floor. Car, airport, new job; he had his immediate next steps and he was thinking further ahead just like he'd intended, taking a step closer to his dream of establishing his own company with his own team. He still felt like his future was about as boxed in as he was in the damned elevator. By the time it reached ground floor he'd revised his thought process.

He needed to see her again.

She'd told him she wasn't good with words and she'd probably made herself scarce so she didn't blurt out something she'd regret later. But he wanted her to tell him what was inside her head. He wanted her to know he'd listen. And when she was done, he hoped she'd let him tell her how much she meant to him.

She gave everything she had to her little sister and to her team and to King. Sure she was violent, in a beautiful way, and she might be always ready to dive into a fight. But she wasn't addicted to the fight itself. She wanted to clear the way for gentler people to thrive. Arin was hung up on people describing her as violent, but he saw the way she cooked and cared for people. He thought about rice balls and hot dogs shaped like cephalopods and the heart that shaped those things. Arin was a nurturing, loving person inside the prickly exterior she'd established to protect herself. She'd opened up to him and he'd told her he was leaving.

He was definitely an idiot.

All of that flashed through his head as the elevator door finally opened. Jason stopped cold.

King sat in the lobby.

Okay, it could've been another black and tan German Shepherd Dog who looked exactly like King, but Jason was pretty damned sure it was Arin's dog. He could tell King from Taz at this point. Besides, who else would be sitting in the lobby of the building where Search and Protect headquarters were located?

The elevator doors started to close with him still inside and Jason had to reach out to stop them. It took another full three seconds for his brain to reconnect with the rest of his body and get his feet moving to carry him forward. By the time he reached King, he saw Arin sitting curled up in a chair partially hidden by a giant potted plant.

A random part of his mind noted how horrible the decor in the lobby was from a security perspective. There were too many dead zones and big things chosen out of consideration for aesthetic rather than taking into account the way they blocked line of sight.

The part of his brain that interacted with people and made words sent up a red flag. He was staring at Arin and hadn't said anything to her yet. "I was looking for you."

Well, he hadn't started but he'd decided to, even if he had to miss his flight.

She flowed out of the chair and stepped forward until she was standing toe to toe with him. "I let you find me."

* * *

Arin hadn't meant to sound so arrogant. She'd rehearsed what she planned to say a bunch of times inside her head so she wouldn't be off-putting when he finally came downstairs. But he'd spoken first and she'd been thrown off by the need to answer him. She could get back on script but now she felt stupid and short-circuited.

"You said you had a flight to catch after you showered." She clung to an existing fact.

She'd been floored when he mentioned it on the way back from the container ship. He'd timed it so close. If they'd taken longer or had to go farther out to sea or had more follow-up responsibilities with the Hawaiian authorities, he'd have missed his flight. Okay, it was easy to reschedule a flight. What had gouged her was him booking the flight in the first place, as if he couldn't wait to be out of here once he'd completed his quest.

Jason stared at her and nodded, not saying anything.

His dark hair was slicked back a bit, still damp from his recent shower. He hadn't shaved, so he had a really sexy day's growth over his jaw. And how had she not ever teased him over the cleft in his chin or the severe expression he got when he drew his brows together. He was devastatingly handsome, she had to admit, and it was even more striking when she wasn't working hard to ignore his magnetism.

She wondered how many full nights of sleep it would take to heal the shadows under his eyes. Considering how tired she was, it'd be at least a long weekend for her to overcome her sleep deficit. They both needed to rest, take care of their bodies. Maybe he would, but she was going to dive into work as quickly as possible. She wasn't ready to process her memories of him, at least for now. As if she could forget what his touch did to her.

"You should sleep on the plane."

He scowled at her. "I doze but I don't get real sleep surrounded by strangers, trapped in a tin can."

Neither did she. If she was with her team, she could sleep deep despite the noise and lack of comfortable seating. But if she was on a commercial flight, there were too many strangers and never enough room to keep them all from jostling elbows.

He reached into one of his pants pockets and pulled out his phone, checking the display.

"You have to go."

He nodded. "Yeah."

"I was going to give you a ride, then I decided not to." Because it would've been the most awkward car ride in history and she wasn't going to be able to be completely forthcoming if she had to split part of her attention to keeping them safe on the ride.

It hit her belatedly just how spiteful her last comment could sound. He didn't wince or get angry at her statement, though. He just shook his head. "I called a car service. It's all good."

Except she'd been doing a lot of thinking trapped inside

her head and so far, tiny babble had come out of her mouth. As conversation went, she was making Zu seem like a freaking chatterbox.

"I've asked Zu to step up our contracts in Southeast and East Asia." There. She'd conveyed an important bit of information.

"Yeah?" Jason stopped looking at his phone display and met her gaze.

Their eyes locked and she felt herself falling hard for him all over again. What man had any right to have such amazing lashes framing his beautiful eyes? "Raul is on the Hawaiian task force and he should be able to cover activities here on the island on his own with Jones behind bars. It'll free up the rest of the Search and Protect resources to be staffed to other contracts. I asked Zu to focus mine in Southeast and East Asia."

Facts were easy. She needed to get to why.

Jason only nodded. "Why the preference?"

She could kiss him for the question. She could answer questions. "You."

"Say again?" He was startled. He might've squeaked.

"This job is the right thing for you. Take it." She swallowed, trying to wet her dry mouth and throat. But she was too nervous. "I want you to build the life you need. But I want you to know, I'll be around. You said you'd be working twenty-four seven, but people have to sleep sometime. I'll keep you up to date on when I'm in your area and if you can spare a few hours, we'll catch up on rest together."

She'd said it all in a rush. It was still only factual options, the how and not the why. She needed to give him the why.

Jason nodded slowly, his gaze darting over her shoulder and back to her. "My car is here."

She nodded and stepped to the side.

He walked forward until he was even with her, then his hand darted out and caught her by the nape of her neck, pulling her in for a kiss so hot, so raw, they both ended up breathless. "Call. I'll make time."

She shook her head. "You do your thing. I'll fit into your schedule. Or I won't. It'll depend on the way my contracts line up with your work. I'll adjust. Nine months, a year, doesn't matter. I've been on longer deployments."

"Same." He grinned, then, and she became aware of her heart beating as if it'd been stopped up until now.

She needed to tell him why. "I've spent every day since I found you on Big Island wondering when you were going to leave, sure you were going to. You're leaving. Fine. You matter to me, Jason, so I'm coming after you. You've gone from job to job and no one valued you enough to keep you. This is me, telling you I value you, I want you, I need you. So I'll keep coming to you until you come back to me or you tell me you don't want this."

His hand tightened on her neck and he pulled her in for another kiss. This one left her weak in the knees and he pulled her up against his hard body, encouraging her to wrap her legs around his waist.

"Your car is here," she gasped.

"I know." He bent and picked up his duffel bag, still carrying her, and started walking through the lobby to the car. "King, let's go."

"Let me down." She beat his shoulder with a fist, not hard. "You can't take us with you now."

He reached the car—which turned out to be an SUV—and opened the door, waving at King until her dog hopped in and landed in the trunk area. Then Jason cradled her head to his shoulder as he climbed inside. "We've got ten minutes to the airport and I'm about to make the most of it."

Straddling his lap, Arin glanced over her shoulder at the driver. The man had his eyes glued to the road. She turned back to Jason. "You are incorrigible."

He laughed. "You are amazing and I love you, Arin Siri. Don't forget I said it first because we're going to call each other often and I want to hear you say it back to me at the end of every phone call." ‑

I love you. His words cracked her chest wide open.

He settled his hands on her hips and leaned forward until their foreheads touched. "I mean it. You're everything. Even if you weren't coming out to find me, I'd come back to you. I love you."

She placed one hand on the side of his face and her other over his heart, feeling his accelerated heart rate. It was a match for hers.

"Tell me," he whispered. "It's okay. I'll catch you."

She closed her eyes, leaning in to his forehead and letting their breaths mingle. "I love you."

And she fell completely for him in that moment, no safety lines.

Raul's lucky to have the best partner a man could ask for: a highly trained, fiercely loyal German Shepherd Dog named Taz. But their first mission in Hawaii puts them to the test when a kidnapping ring sets its sights on the bravest woman Raul's ever met...

See the next page for an excerpt from *Total Bravery*.

How can I help you?" The man on the other end of the call didn't laugh or crack a joke in response to Mali's request for help. Honestly, it'd come out as a plea, and she'd been half expecting him to dismiss it. He didn't ridicule her or tell her he'd get her sister to call her back when she returned.

He was paying attention, and he was absolutely serious.

She swallowed against a fear-parched throat, relief and hope trickling in past the constriction in her chest. "There's someone—several people—chasing me. I think I lost them in the crowds at the big shopping center."

"Are you safe where you are?" His tone was calm but managed to convey urgency, too, and it helped her focus.

She glanced around her. "Maybe? Probably not. I walked fast, but I walked, didn't run. So they might not have seen me leave the mall area. I tried to blend in with the tourists."

The moment she'd seen her pursuers, a childhood memory of her sister's voice played through her head, telling her to never run from immortals—or predators in the real world—because running attracted their attention. So she hadn't. Random, maybe, but here she was with a chance to evade some very scary people. She'd take advice in whatever form it came.

"Can you get to the Search and Protect office building?"

She laughed, the sound harsh to her own hearing. "That's why I was near the Ala Moana Shopping Center. I was trying to get there."

God, had she even said the name of the place right? She was so not a local. This guy didn't sound like one either. Would he even know how to find her?

Taking a deep breath, she fought for calm. "I took a taxi there first, trying to get close to the office building. But then I spotted the people chasing me waiting nearby and left."

They hadn't been standing right out in the open, but they'd been dressed in suits. In the heat of the day, not even the office workers actually wore full suits as far as she knew. Not on Oahu or any of the other Hawaiian islands. It'd set off alarms in her head, and she'd veered off, falling into step with tourists headed from the mall to the other shopping areas.

"Okay." His calm acceptance helped her settle. "If you walked away from the mall and stayed with the crowds, are you near the beaches now?"

"Yes." *Hurry*. They both needed to communicate faster. "Around the big hotels. I figured there'd be more security near them."

"It's mid-morning, still cool out. Good time for shopping until people get hungry and start looking for places to eat lunch." His words were coming quicker, too. "There's always catamarans over there, launching from the beach for a sail out to deeper water. Vendors sell tickets to tourists all up and down the streets. They go out for an hour, maybe two. Do you see any signs for those? You can buy tickets right on the beach."

"Yes." Once he'd told her to look, she spotted one or two right away. "There's one right between two of the big hotels with boardwalks."

"Good. I know where that is." His tone took on a crisp quality, full of confidence. "Get on one of the catamarans. Don't drink much but do what you need to, to not stand out. That'll take you out of reach until I can get to you. I'm headed there now. When you get off the cruise, I'll be at the ticket booth waiting for you."

"How will I know it's you?" She'd never seen any of her sister's friends, not from the military or whatever Arin did now.

"Look for the guy with the service dog. I've got a GSD."

"A what?" Even as she asked, she hurried toward the ticket booth and fumbled for her tiny change purse where she kept her cash, one credit card, and ID. She struggled to juggle it and her phone while she tried to keep aware of her surroundings. The thing was cute but it was a pain in the ass to get what she needed out of and back into it.

There was a sigh on the other end. "German Shepherd Dog. He's big, black and tan, a lot like Arin's partner. We probably won't blend in with the crowd."

That was okay though, right? Once he came to get her, she'd be safe. No one was going to just grab her with some badass mercenary.

"It'll be okay. Get on the catamaran." His voice was soothing and sounded so good. She wanted to know what his lips looked like shaping those words.

"I'll get a ticket." And maybe she could take the time on the waves to reassemble her scattered mind.

"Go ahead, Mali. I'll be there as fast as I can." He ended the call.

She tucked the phone into the back pocket of her shorts.

When she reached the small booth, her heart plummeted. The catamarans went out at the top of the hour. She had at least a forty-minute wait. Buying a ticket and a floppy hat to protect her dark hair from the sun's heat, she tucked the ticket into her change purse and tried to maintain a casual attitude as she scanned the area around her.

Suddenly, being between the big hotels didn't seem like such a good idea. The streets between them were more like alleyways, shadowed by palm trees, with lots of random doors and archways to get pulled into. There was nowhere to run on the narrow boardwalks, and it wouldn't be easy to jump over the waist-high walls into the private pool areas. Maybe a hot action movie star could vault those retainer walls and sprint across the hotel grounds to lose his pursuers, but she was a skinny postdoc who could at best be described as vertically challenged.

She'd left the sidewalks along the street thinking it'd be harder to grab her and stuff her into a car, but was the beachfront area so close to the hotels much better?

Every man walking past her seemed to be staring at her through his sunglasses. Every woman seemed to be looking the other way. The women who did look in her direction could've just as easily been after her, too.

She rubbed her palms together. It was the beach, though. She'd spot suits a mile...

Cold fear washed through her, and her stomach twisted hard as the distinctive black fabric of men wearing ridiculously hot suits appeared at the far end of the boardwalk. They were so far away that they were barely more than dots but they stood out in stark contrast to the sane people wearing light colors and airy warm weather wear.

They were still trying to find her. They had to be. They couldn't know exactly where she was because they'd have made more of an effort to sneak up on her. Wouldn't they? If she could see them coming so easily, she still had a chance to fade away before they spotted her.

Time to walk in the opposite direction. Removing her light-colored hat so it wouldn't catch the eye as she moved, she held it close at her side. She forced herself to move at the pace of the people in front of her, only passing tourists on the narrow boardwalk when others were. There were the occasional picture takers halting to capture a memory here and there. She slipped around them and counted each as one more obstacle between her pursuers and her.

Her heart raced as she tried to catch sight of the people behind her in any reflective surface. Suddenly, every person wearing sunglasses was a rearview mirror. She didn't dare bring attention to herself by looking over her shoulder.

Her memory of her big sister's advice came back to her again, echoing in her ears over the harsh sound of her own breathing. She even remembered the childhood movie that'd inspired her sister. The lesson had been simple. There'd been two things to remember. Don't run. Don't look back. These weren't immortals and she wasn't a unicorn, but they were definitely predators, and she didn't want to attract their attention if they hadn't spotted her yet.

The boardwalk ended, and the beach spread out in front of her. Too many people stood idle on the path ahead. Her thoughts crystallized almost painfully as it occurred to her that the men behind her could be dressed so conspicuously to drive her into an ambush ahead of her. It'd been a miracle no one had grabbed her yet.

She couldn't keep walking. They might have others ready to meet her where the path led back to the street. Getting shoved into a car would end her chances of being rescued by Raul Sá and his GS— whatever.

He'd told her to do what was needed to keep from standing out.

Her gaze passed over the beach dotted in sunbathers. The awesome thing about Waikiki was the way some people came prepared with towels and beach bags, but others just showed up on a whim and lay out on the sand using nothing but their shirts.

She began unbuttoning hers.

In moments, she'd slipped up close to a scattered collection of local girls, all lying out. Some had shirts, some didn't. They were all gorgeous. The best Mali could do was be thankful she'd always tanned easily and had been on the island long enough to develop summer color. Her Southeast Asian heritage gave her dark brown skin with golden undertones, not quite the same but similar to the local islanders. She wouldn't stand out as tourist-pale among them.

Wearing a bikini under her clothes had been a regular thing for the last several days as she and her fellow postdocs took advantage of the locale to enjoy the beaches every bit as much as their research. She was leveraging the habit to hide in plain sight.

Dropping her shorts, she laid them out and spread her shirt over the sand. She stretched out on her belly quickly, hiding her dark hair under the floppy hat, and watched the feet of passersby. Hopefully, people couldn't see her trembling.

* * *

"Damn." Raul fumed at the delay as he and Taz threaded their way through the crowds on the sidewalks. Even in late morning, traffic headed into the Waikiki area—or "town," as locals called it—was insanely slow. On the island of Oahu, it seemed like it was tourist season year round, and Waikiki was overrun by them.

He headed down the side street he thought would bring him out at the beach closest to his destination. It was a risk because he was going by memory from a vacation years ago. He hadn't had time since he'd arrived to refresh his knowledge of the area.

Hopefully, Arin's little sister was going to see him coming and give him a sign or he was going to be screwed trying to spot her right away. Hawaii, especially Oahu, had a huge number of Asian visitors and locals with some Asian ancestry, so it wasn't as if the woman was going to stand out in the crowd just based on physical features. He could spot Arin in a heartbeat, even in a crowd, but Arin had told him that she and her sister didn't share a strong physical resemblance. It was a family joke. Beyond that, Arin didn't talk much about her family besides how incredibly smart her sister was. Intelligence didn't help when Raul was trying to recognize her on sight. And considering the places he and Arin had served in, neither of them had carried pictures of family or those close to them.

His best chance had been looking in the hallway closet. He'd traded instant messages with Arin the night before, the way they did a couple nights a week. Arin had told him how she'd met with her sister for dinner. How it was funny her sister was on the island for some sort of research thing and Arin hadn't known ahead of time. Mali had simply texted her out of the blue. Mali had forgotten her jacket at dinner, and Arin was holding onto it, expecting to meet with her again.

There'd been one jacket in the closet that looked like it belonged to a young woman. It was more of a lightweight hoodie in teal. Arin rarely wore anything outside of a monochromatic black and white color scheme so Raul had grabbed it, guessing it belonged to her sister. The rest of the core members of their team were male, and Miller's wife was of a completely different build. No way did the hoodie belong to her.

As he and Taz came out on the beach, Raul headed straight for the catamaran booth where tickets were sold. The catamarans came back up on the beach in right about the same place. To his left and right, big chain hotels rose up and towered over the beach.

No one else was waiting around the booth. The next sail wouldn't go out until just before sunset. A quick scan up and down the boardwalks extending in either direction revealed no suspicious characters. Of the people out and about, he and Taz were actually the most conspicuous. Then again, there weren't a lot of big dogs on the island, and Taz was wearing a service dog harness.

Stealth wasn't one of his objectives today. In fact, if his presence scared off whoever was after Mali, all the better.

There were a bunch of women wandering past. Several of them glanced at him with interest, but there was no flash of recognition. None of them approached him. Just about every female in the area was with a partner, friend, or group of friends. No lone woman anywhere, much less one looking nervous or waiting for someone.

"Taz."

His partner looked up at him immediately, ears forward and ready to work. If they'd been working alone, he wouldn't even need to use the dog's name. But here, in a crowded place, it was best to make it clear he was addressing Taz.

Raul retrieved the baggie containing her hoodie from the small backpack he'd slung over his shoulder. He held the plastic bag open for Taz, showing him the scent ar-

ticle inside and allowing his partner to sniff it liberally.
"*Zoek.*"

Track. Taz was trained to respond to Dutch commands,
one of the standard languages used to train working dogs,
and this was his primary skill set: finding people.

His partner went to work. The big dog ranged back and
forth in front of Raul, sniffing first the ground and then
lifting his nose to catch additional airborne scents on the
breeze. Taz proceeded forward once he'd systematically
checked everything within the current grid, from the sand to
the side of the booth to a nearby retention wall. In a few minutes, Taz froze, his stillness deliberate.

He'd found a trail.

"*Braaf.*" Even as he praised the dog, Raul's heart
pounded. Just because Taz had hit on the trail didn't mean
Mali was safe. It just gave them something to follow to her,
so long as the trail remained clear and wasn't disrupted farther ahead. Raul also didn't know if Mali had left the area of
her own free will. If she'd been taken or if she'd had to run,
there was no way to tell from the ground around the booth.
The loose sand and the passersby left no hints. All he knew
was that the woman he'd come to help wasn't where she was
supposed to be, and his partner had a trail that might be hers.
He needed to assume the worst and hurry as best he could.
"*Zoek.*"

Excited by the trail, Taz surged forward to the full length
of the six-foot lead. If this had been a sanctioned search
and rescue in coordination with local law enforcement, Raul
would've let Taz off leash. In this case, he kept the GSD
tethered. If they were stopped by police or other security,
he wanted to be with the dog when they approached so he
wasn't mistaken as lost or without a handler. But considering the urgency, Raul let Taz set the pace.

They moved at a fast walk. Taz followed the trail along the narrow boardwalk past the huge hotel. Despite the heavy foot traffic, the big dog proceeded with confidence. He was locked into working mode and wasn't allowing anything else to distract him. They paused once or twice as Taz sniffed the ground and the railing before continuing.

She must've paused in each of those places.

A few minutes later, they were moving out onto the broad expanse of Waikiki beach. It was getting to the hottest part of the day, and Taz was panting now between sniffing the air to catch scents. Heat rose up off the hot sand.

Raul called Taz to a halt and gave the big dog a quick drink, making sure his nose got good and wet. The water served two purposes. Taz's well-being was paramount. A handler always thought of his dog before anything else. The second reason was the impact of the harsh sun on the bare sand of the beach. As the area dried out from the morning, scent particles would be harder to catch unless the dog was well-hydrated. Taz's panting, the increased saliva, and a wet nose maximized Taz's ability to keep and follow the trail.

It took only moments and Taz was back on the trail. The dog veered away from the path. Mali must've decided not to go back toward the street. It was a smart choice, but where had she gone? Raul saw nothing but sunbathers and tourists lounging out on the beach.

His partner wasn't relying on sight, though. Taz weaved his way through tourists and locals.

"Don't touch the dog, please." Raul smiled to diffuse the disappointment as people sat up or leaned toward Taz. "He's working."

Even with a service harness on, there were a lot of people who tried to pet a working dog. Though a decent number of people scooted away when they caught sight of Taz, too.

At around eighty-five pounds of muscle, he was a good-size canine. His mostly black face, with only hints of tan, was intimidating.

Despite the reaching hands, Taz remained focused on his task, nose to the ground here and lifted to the air there. It was Raul's job as his handler to run interference so Taz could do his job.

They had a lady in distress to find.

In moments, Taz approached a group of girls. Raul hesitated, keeping his eyes on his dog, but Taz was all about the trail. The big dog sniffed right up to a petite sunbather with an amazingly shapely, tight behind and poked his nose right into her golden bronze hip, then sat, looking back at Raul expectantly.

"Taz." Raul was scandalized. Jesus, the hoodie must not have been Mali's. Instead, they'd ended up molesting some random girl...

The bikini-clad, dainty woman stirred and peered up at them from under a bright white, floppy hat. The face...

...was a ghost of Arin's, about five years younger, with a more delicate jaw and rounder cheeks. The biggest difference was in the eyes; the skin folds of the upper eyelids covering the inner angle of the eyes. Maybe most other people didn't see the resemblance, but he did.

Taz leaned toward the woman's face, sniffing, and then gave a soft bark.

No doubt about it, Taz had found his target. Raul pulled a well-chewed tennis ball from his pocket and tossed it to Taz as his reward, then turned his full attention to the woman. "Mali Siri?"

"My full last name." Her voice was hoarse. "You said you knew it."

Fair. Even if Taz was proof that Raul was the person she'd

spoken to on the phone, she was smart to get confirmation that he knew her older sister as well as he'd claimed.

"Srisawasdi." He fumbled over the pronunciation a little. The *r*, the last *s*, and the *i* were almost silent but he tended to miss the correct intonation. Intonation mattered in the Thai language, he'd learned, and could completely change the meaning of the word. So he spelled it out for her, too. "It was strongly implied that it would be better for your parents to shorten their surname to something easier to pronounce when they immigrated to the United States, so it was shortened. But Arin never forgot the full name and the meaning behind it."

Mali closed her eyes then opened them slowly, her expression weary. "Neither did I, but she's always been angrier about it. It's a long story. I'm just…tired."

Raul looked sharply at her face. Her lips were cracked, they were so dry. "How long have you been lying here?"

He kneeled immediately and handed over a spare water bottle. Now that he wasn't embarrassed out of his mind about his dog poking a strange girl's butt with a cold nose, he took a more serious look at Mali Siri. Her golden bronze skin had a red undertone to it. She'd been in the sun long enough to burn. "Sip that slow."

She did as he advised, her movement sluggish and her hands trembling. She spilled some water down her chin as she sipped.

Muttering a curse under his breath, he scanned the area to confirm no potential threats were nearby and then he draped her hoodie around her shoulders. "Take your time. You're safe now."

ABOUT THE AUTHOR

Piper J. Drake is an author of bestselling romantic suspense and edgy contemporary romance, a frequent flyer, and day job road warrior. She is often distracted by dogs, cupcakes, and random shenanigans.

Play Find the Piper online:
  PiperJDrake.com
  Facebook.com/AuthorPiperJDrake
  Twitter @PiperJDrake
  Instagram.com/PiperJDrake

Looking for more romantic suspense?

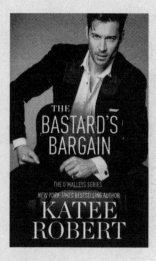

THE BASTARD'S BARGAIN
By Katee Robert

Dmitri Romanov knows Keira O'Malley only married him to keep peace between their families. Nevertheless, the desire that smolders between them is a dangerous addiction neither can resist. But with his enemies circling closer, Keira could just be his secret weapon—if she doesn't bring him to his knees first.

THE FEARLESS KING
By Katee Robert

When Journey King's long-lost father returns to make a play for the family company, Journey turns to the rugged and handsome Frank Evans for help, and finds much more than she was looking for.

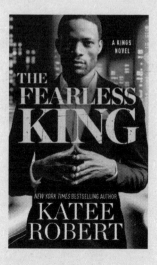

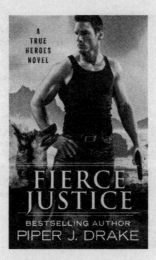

FIERCE JUSTICE
By Piper Drake

As a K9 handler on the Search and Protect team, Arin Siri needs to be where the action is—and right now that's investigating a trafficking operation in Hawaii. When an enemy from her past shows up bleeding, she's torn between the desire to patch Jason up or to put more holes in him. Then again, the hotshot mercenary could be the person she needs to bust open her case.

TWISTED TRUTHS
By Rebecca Zanetti

Noni Yuka is desperate. Her infant niece has been kidnapped, and the only person who can save her is the private detective who once broke her heart.

Follow @ReadForeverPub and join the conversation using #ReadForever.

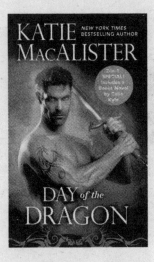

DAY OF THE DRAGON
By Katie MacAlister

Real scholars know that supernatural beings aren't real, but once Thaisa meets tall, dark, and mysterious Archer Andras of the Storm Dragons, all of her academic training goes out the window. Thaisa realizes that she really should worry about those things that go bump in the night.

TIGER'S CLAIM
By Celia Kyle

Cole Turner may act like a wealthy, gorgeous playboy, but he's also a tiger shifter determined to bring down the organization that's threatening his kind. Leopard shifter Stella Moore will do whatever it takes to destroy Unified Humanity, even if that means working with the undeniably annoying—and sexy—Cole.

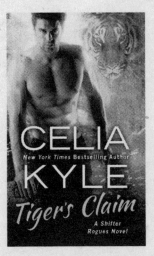

Visit
Facebook.com/ReadForeverPub